SEDUCED BY THE LAIRD

ELIZA KNIGHT

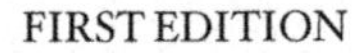

FIRST EDITION

December 2015

Edited by: Andrea Snider

Copy-Edited by: The Killion Group, Inc.

Cover Design: Kimberly Killion @ The Killion Group, Inc.

MORE BOOKS BY ELIZA KNIGHT

Scots of Honor

Return of the Scot
The Scot is Hers
Taming the Scot

Prince Charlie's Rebels

The Highlander Who Stole Christmas
Pretty in Plaid

Prince Charlie's Angels

The Rebel Wears Plaid
Truly Madly Plaid
You've Got Plaid

The Sutherland Legacy

The Highlander's Gift

The Highlander's Quest
The Highlander's Stolen Bride
The Highlander's Hellion
The Highlander's Secret Vow
The Highlander's Enchantment

The Stolen Bride Series

The Highlander's Temptation
The Highlander's Reward
The Highlander's Conquest
The Highlander's Lady
The Highlander's Warrior Bride
The Highlander's Triumph
The Highlander's Sin
Wild Highland Mistletoe (a Stolen Bride winter novella)
The Highlander's Charm (a Stolen Bride novella)
A Kilted Christmas Wish – a contemporary Holiday spin-off
The Highlander's Surrender
The Highlander's Dare

The Conquered Bride Series

Conquered by the Highlander
Seduced by the Laird
Taken by the Highlander (a Conquered bride novella)
Claimed by the Warrior
Stolen by the Laird
Protected by the Laird (a Conquered bride novella)
Guarded by the Warrior

The MacDougall Legacy Series

Laird of Shadows

Laird of Twilight
Laird of Darkness

Pirates of Britannia: Devils of the Deep

Savage of the Sea
The Sea Devil
A Pirate's Bounty

THE THISTLES AND ROSES SERIES

Promise of a Knight
Eternally Bound
Breath from the Sea

The Highland Bound Series (Erotic time-travel)

Behind the Plaid
Bared to the Laird
Dark Side of the Laird
Highlander's Touch
Highlander Undone
Highlander Unraveled

Touchstone Series

Highland Steam
Highland Brawn
Highland Tryst
Highland Heat

Wicked Women

Her Desperate Gamble
Seducing the Sheriff
Kiss Me, Cowboy

HISTORICAL FICTION

Releasing Early 2022
The Mayfair Bookshop

Releasing 2023
The Other Astaire

Tales From the Tudor Court

My Lady Viper
Prisoner of the Queen

Ancient Historical Fiction

A Day of Fire: a novel of Pompeii
A Year of Ravens: a novel of Boudica's Rebellion

French Revolution

Ribbons of Scarlet: a novel of the French Revolution

ABOUT THE BOOK

She vowed never to love again...

Lady Kirstin MacNeacail is determined to lead a life of piety in hopes of erasing a past filled with pain and transgressions. She takes vows at the abbey on the Isle of Skye that has sheltered her since she was a girl. But when Scotland erupts in turmoil, and she is sent as an envoy to Melrose, she runs straight into one of her past transgressions. Old feelings arise, never truly forgotten. Forced to face her past, she must choose between penance, and allowing herself to fall passionately in love all over again.

He's determined to change her mind...

Laird Gregor Buchanan receives devastating news for Scotland and must travel to Melrose where Robert the Bruce is laying low. With his country divided between those who are for Scottish Independence and those who have sided with the English, he must ferret out those who threaten their very freedom. On his way to meet his future king, Gregor intercepts a small party, coming face to face with the woman he's always loved and never forgotten. For the past ten years he'd searched for her, never coming close. Gregor does not want to let her go this time—and he's praying she'll give him a second chance.

For you, dear reader. Thank you for reading my stories!

I

Nèamh Abbey, Isle of Skye
August 15, 1305

"Sister Kirstin, ye must go to Melrose Abbey. Ye must leave Skye for a time."

Lady Kirstin MacNeacail carefully studied Mother Superior, her own flesh and blood. Her skin was still smooth, despite a few wrinkles at her eyes and the corners of her mouth. Her brows were still dark, and beneath her wimple, her hair was a beautiful, silky dark mass threaded with silver. The angles and lines of her face were so much like Kirstin's mother—they'd been twins like Kirstin and her own sister—that she sometimes had a hard time looking at her. She could only hope that she aged just as well.

They sat inside the chapel where Kirstin had been dusting pews. The sun streamed through the high stained-glass window creating rainbows of color on the altar table. Every place the sun touched was golden and brightly lit, but the shadows crept up onto the light giving the illusion and sense that many spirits resided within the chapel walls.

Without showing how much she truly did not want to leave the abbey, Kirstin brushed a rag over the top of the pew in front of her, disbanding of the dust and casually asking, "But Mother Superior, Aunt Aileen, why?"

A sigh that sounded a little too forced, stirred the air beside her. "A messenger arrived. We've been summoned, and I am too old and feeble to make the journey."

That was a jest if Kirstin had ever heard one. She bit the inside of her cheek to keep from snorting. Aunt Aileen would live to see them all in their graves. The woman was stocked full of energy and strength, while nearing sixty to boot. Kirstin hoped to have half her energy by the time she reached forty, let alone sixty.

"How long do ye think the journey will take?" Kirstin asked. She had not left the abbey in nearly a decade, nor her aunt's side for that matter.

The thought of doing so now sent a tremor of trepidation coursing through her.

She'd arrived at Nèamh fifteen years ago at the tender age of twelve. Until recently, she'd thought she was the only one to survive the siege on her family's castle, Scorrybreac, but just the year before, her twin sister, Brenna, was freed from her prison of a marriage and came to find her. The monster she'd been married too had literally kept her locked up like a brood mare for so long it was a wonder her sister came out of it sane.

Brenna was once more happily married to a handsome, protective warrior, Gabriel MacKinnon. Happiness Kirstin was never to have... again.

When Kirstin was eighteen she'd had a moment of weakness, escaping the abbey, only to return broken-hearted, her soul utterly defeated. And the pain had not stopped there. But, that was long ago, and she dared not think on it now.

"Two weeks," Aunt Aileen was saying.

"Two weeks to get there? I'll be gone for well over a month at that rate."

Aunt Aileen smiled winningly. "Aye."

That smile wasn't going to win Kirstin over so easily. She knew when her aunt was trying to persuade her, could feel it in her bones.

"But I've so much to do." Kirstin glanced around at all the dust coating the chapel. To her, spring and summer were always more dusty than usual. Everyone within the abbey had their part to play. One of the tasks she'd happily taken on at Nèamh was making certain the place sparkled. Since they took in sick people to help pray for their bodies and souls, the cleaner it was, the less illness they would spread.

Because of her penchant for cleaning and the other nuns having seen the benefits of it, they were quick to keep it that way, too.

Aunt Aileen shook her head. "That may be true, but ye are needed elsewhere. This can wait. Ye will not be gone long. I need ye to do this for me. I dinna want to beg ye, but I will."

Shifting nervously, Kirstin stood and went to re-light a few of the wicks on the candelabra. Beg? That was very unlike Aunt Aileen. She must want Kirstin to do this very badly to have stooped to begging.

"But—"

Her aunt followed her, taking the flint and forcing Kirstin to look at her. She subtly shook her head again, speaking softly. "There is a path ye must follow. This is your path."

Lower lip trembling, Kirstin wrung her fingers in front of her gray wool habit. How many times had she thought there was a path she was meant to follow and how many times had she ended up heartbroken? "What is it that I am meant to do?" She left off: *this time*.

"The abbot from Newbattle Abbey will meet ye at Melrose and relay to ye the reason."

"Please tell me what the summons is about?"

Aunt Aileen met Kirstin's gaze, graveness in their blue depths. "I do not know, but his missive was rushed. Ye must leave at dawn." Aunt Aileen scribbled something on a piece of parchment and then rolled it, sealing it with wax and her ring. "Give this to Mother Frances when ye meet with her."

Kirstin reached for the parchment, the wax seal still warm to the touch. There were so many more questions burbling up from her throat, but she kept her lips firmly sealed.

"I have arranged for an escort of six guards to attend ye, and one of our sisters, Donna, to accompany ye as your companion." She smiled warmly, sloughing the Mother Superior mask for something more maternal. "'Tis high time ye faced the world, child. Ye cannot remain hidden forever."

And why not? She wanted to ask. She'd spent the last nine years repenting for sins that still haunted her dreams. Besides that, she'd only just come back into contact with her twin sister, Brenna. And she'd yet to tell Brenna the truth of her past, even though Kirstin knew all of her sister's. Kirstin rather liked remaining hidden from the world. There was something safe in that.

"What about Brenna?" she asked, knowing the argument would do little good, but having to ask anyway.

"I will arrange a visit with her upon your return."

"There is no changing your mind?" Kirstin said, resolute.

Aileen pursed her lips and put her hands on Kirstin's shoulders gently. "What are ye afraid of, child?"

"I am afraid of nothing," Kirstin lied. Perhaps she feared herself most of all. Her proclivity for adventure and a life forbidden to her. One that had gotten her into trouble more than once. Mayhap that was where the safety of the abbey walls came into play. They kept her from herself.

"A strong conviction can help ye win battles, wage wars, but it cannot help ye if ye're lying to yourself."

Kirstin bit her lip and looked toward the worn wooden floor. "I am fearful of the world outside these walls." *Of what I will do with my freedom.*

Aileen nodded. "I can understand that. But will ye let your fear rule ye? Or will ye face it? Prove it wrong?"

"And what if it's proven right?" What if she fell again?

Aileen patted Kirstin's arm. "Many years have passed. 'Tis time to face it."

Face it.

It.

It was more like *them*. The nightmares. The sorrows. The many sins.

The reason she refused to ever take over her aunt's position as Mother Superior.

She'd been so strong when she'd seen her sister again. Been able to stand up for Brenna and fight for her. But... When it came down to it, perhaps that was all an act. She'd been shaking in her slippers and had spent many hours behind the door of her tiny chamber, heart pounding, and nausea making it impossible to eat.

There was no reliving one past without reliving it all.

Brenna's children... They were so beautiful. So full of life. All four of them. Pain tugged at her heart, contracted in her womb every time she looked on them.

Kirstin nodded, not wanting to say more, because saying more meant talking and talking meant thinking and reliving and she didn't want to do either.

"If there is no changing your mind, I shall go and pack a small bag."

"Good. Donna is overseeing the packing of the provisions already."

"And the men who will escort us?"

"Warriors of God. They are chaste and they are well-trained. The abbot sent them with the summons. Ye'll be in the safest of hands. They've already arrived. Ye shall dine with them tonight, so on the morrow they be not strangers to ye."

Kirstin swallowed hard, nodding.

When she returned to her chamber, lighting a candle against the waning light of the day, a little puff of smoke in the shape of a heart pulsed in the darkened room. A tiny pulse. A tiny remembrance.

She pulled her valise out from under her bed, one of the precious gifts she'd brought back nine years before. The bag had been sitting beneath her bed ever since. When Aunt Aileen tried to pull it out, tried to get her to go somewhere, Kirstin had prayed for an illness and her prayers were mostly answered, landing her in bed for over a week and nearly on death's door the last time. Conviction, indeed. Kirstin seemed to have a knack for making herself sick with worry.

Aunt Aileen had not asked her to leave again, and Kirstin had been praying for her own soul ever since.

As she swiped her hand across the bag, a cloud of dust rose in the air making her cough.

She needn't take much. The life of a nun was quite simple, really. She packed a chemise and a second habit. Her brush. A linen to wash her face. A stick of cinnamon for her teeth. An extra set of hose. Her prayer book.

Heaviness settled over her and she sat down on the bed, tucking her knees up.

"I'll be safe," she whispered to the empty room. "I am strong. I am pious."

A soft tapping sounded at the door and Donna inched it open, poking her face through the crack. She was pretty in a plain sort of way. Features that were pleasant to look at but not remarkable. Her sandy-colored hair was tucked under her hood and she smiled congenially. Innocent, but perhaps not naïve.

"Do ye need any help?" Donna asked.

Kirstin shook her head, assuming Mother Superior had sent the lass to her chamber to be sure she was packing and not under the covers feigning a fever.

"Thank ye, but I've not much to pack."

Donna stepped into the chamber, her excitement bursting out of her. "Aye, me either. Today was the first time in years I wished for something other than a nun's habit to wear. But I am very excited for the trip! I've not been off the Isle of Skye before."

"Neither have I." But that was a lie. She'd been off the Isle. She'd been far from the Isle. And it would seem, since she'd last been on the main land nine years before, that Aunt Aileen was truly determined to see her face her fears, for in order to get to Melrose, she would have to pass by the very places in which her life had been irrevocably changed.

"Then 'twill be a new adventure for us both."

Kirstin listened as Donna babbled on until it was time for them to head to the refectory for supper with the warriors who would escort them. The only thing in her mind was a constant begging to the heavens not to allow her to run into *him*.

Castle Buchanan
Stirlingshire
August 27

LAIRD GREGOR BUCHANAN STARED DOWN AT THE MISSIVE in his hands with a mixture of trepidation and foreboding. Not filled overly with words, it read simply:

Wallace has been captured by the English. Be wary of rebels rising and English raiding. Meet the council at Melrose Abbey.
-Robert de Brus

"Damn," Gregor muttered, blowing out a heavy sigh. The Bruce did not yet know the truth.

He walked toward the hearth and held the corner of the missive to a candle lit on the mantle. The parchment ignited, burning and changing the paper from creamy-yellow to black. He tossed it into the hearth and watched until the entire letter was nothing more than a pile of ash.

"What is it?"

Gregor's brother-by-marriage and second-in-command, Samuel de Mowbray, entered the Great Hall. Though the man was English, his two sisters were both married to well-respected Scots—the Sutherlands—and he was a double agent, pretending to work for the crown of England all the while spilling their secrets. The knight was lucky not to have been caught yet, and that he'd gained their trust else some of the Scots might have thought him a shady character. But Gregor knew the man well, knew he hated the way the English had invaded Scotland, and given who his sisters were married to, the man was an asset.

How Samuel had managed to get Gregor's sister, Catriona, to fall in love with him, was another question. Catriona was a right harridan, but she and her husband had proven their worth, allowing Gregor to concentrate on the War for Independence. Samuel had been instrumental to Scotland and at Castle Buchanan. And, Gregor rather liked it the way it was. At thirty-two summers, he'd yet to marry, though he'd come close once before. Having his sister act as mistress of the castle worked out perfectly given that he was still a bachelor.

Pouring himself a dram of whisky and another for Samuel, Gregor said, “Wallace has been captured.”

Samuel’s face hardened. “Damn.”

“Aye.”

They both swigged the burning liquid and refilled their cups.

“Can we rescue him?” Samuel asked.

“I’m not certain where he is of yet, but my guess is once they nabbed him they high-tailed it to the border. Likely headed to London where Longshanks can torture him.” Gregor ran his fingers through his hair. “I have to meet the council. ’Tis best if ye stay considering the increased rage toward the English at the current moment.”

“Are ye certain? I might be able to help given my connections.”

Gregor shook his head. “I dinna want to risk your safety.”

Samuel nodded. “I’ll keep Buchanan safe.”

“A shame really since ye’re likely to have information they could use.”

“I’d not heard anything of Wallace. But you’re right, if Longshanks has him, the chances of him still being in Scotland are slim to none. And I’ll warn you, the English king wants Wallace dead.”

Gregor nodded solemnly. “I know.”

With the loss of two important leaders in the War for Independence, first Murray and now Wallace, would Robert the Bruce be able to pick up where those two had left off, or would he simply fall to the whims of the earls who’d sided with the English years ago? Bribes of coin and lands had made the greedy bastards eager for Longshanks leavings. They’d amassed great wealth by betraying their countrymen. Greed was a powerful weapon, one Longshanks knew well how to wield.

“I am leaving within the hour. Hopefully I can get to the

abbey within two days at a maximum. There is likely nothing we can do for Wallace now, but we can secure our borders."

"Let us know if you need anything, and my offer to ride with you still stands."

Gregor clapped Samuel on the back. "Ye're a good man. I will. Give my love to Catriona when she wakes." His sister had given birth not too many days ago, and was still resting in her chamber—when she wasn't raising hell. Some things never changed.

"She'll be mad if you don't wish her farewell yourself," Samuel warned.

Gregor grinned. "What woman is not mad when she doesn't get her way?"

Samuel shrugged with a chuckle. "I know not the answer to that, but if it's all the same, I'd rather not have her railing at me... Well, maybe not railing at me any more than usual."

Gregor laughed. "Can ye not handle a wee Scottish lass, Sassenach?"

"She may be *wee,* but she's the temperament of a jackal of late." Samuel refilled his cup with more whisky. "God, I love her so damn much though."

That made Gregor laugh all the more. He climbed the stairs to his sister's chamber and tapped on the door. At first there was no answer, and then a soft bid to enter.

"Brother," Catriona said, sitting up in bed, her face flushed with the happiness of new motherhood. Beneath her eyes were shadowed with lack of sleep, but that didn't seem to make her less than cheerful.

"I've come to bid ye well. I must go away for a few days, but I will return."

Worry flickered over her features. Ever since their castle had been attacked some years before—and after a mighty fight, Gregor had been taken captive while Catriona, with Samuel as escort, had run away hoping to gain help for him—

she worried about anytime her brother or husband entered into a dangerous situation.

"Dinna fash, lass. I'll return shortly. 'Tis simply a meeting." Och, but he wished it *were* truly simple.

"There has been more than one meeting ye've taken where ye've ended up hurt." She frowned harshly, pushing her legs to the side of the bed.

"Aye." There was also that incident shortly before his abduction... Gregor rushed forward, and scooted her legs back under the covers. "But look at me." He held out his arms, showing he was still in one piece. "I'm here and well standing before ye."

Cat rolled her eyes and batted the air. "I'll pray for your soul, brother."

Gregor kissed her cheek. "Be well. Samuel is here to take care of things." He glanced around the room, wanting to get another look at his new nephew, but the cradle was empty. "Where's the bairn?"

"The nurse took him for a bit so I could rest."

"Ah, well, give him a kiss for me." Gregor bent and kissed his sister's forehead. "I'll see ye soon."

"Be well, Gregor."

"And ye, too, lass."

He left the chamber, heading toward his library to pick up the other missive along with the wooden box containing chilling contents he'd gotten the day before. It would seem he'd become the bearer of even worse news for his ruler.

2

Glasgow

Rain had them trapped.

A torrential downpour so heinous that all the roads had turned to rivers of mud and even the high points were slick enough to fell a horse.

Which was what had happened the night before, injuring one of the men who guarded Kirstin. As a result, they'd been forced to take refuge in a tavern that was less than reputable, and though she had five guards outside the door, they could do nothing about the buggy situation inside the room the innkeeper had rented her and Donna for an exorbitant fee.

The injured Warrior of God was housed in the room beside hers, and a local healer had been gathered to set his broken leg, but even still, he'd not be accompanying them the rest of the way, and Kirstin was not waiting here for the weeks it would take for him to be able to ride again.

As it was, it might be a century before her clothes and boots would dry.

"Put on this clean shift, Sister Kirstin. Might as well be

dry all over."

Kirstin groaned, the skin of her fingers and toes wrinkled and all her limbs waterlogged. She switched out the wet chemise for the one Donna handed her, noticing only a slight difference.

"Seems even our satchels were victims of this wretched rain," Kirstin grumbled.

Donna laughed, a singsong sound as she laid out their garments beside a small fire lit in an iron brazier. They'd cracked the shutter of the small window, but that didn't seem to help funnel the smoke out. The room was stifling and now the smoke made it even more difficult to breathe.

Kirstin waved the air in front of her face and coughed.

"Where are we anyway? Did ye hear anyone make mention of it?" Kirstin asked.

Donna cocked her head, thinking. "From what I've been able to gather, the horse fell somewhere outside of Edinburgh."

"What was the name of this wretched place again?"

"Gràinne's Tavern, I do believe."

Kirstin grunted. "Let us pray the rain ceases afore the sun shines so we can be on our way."

"If it will in fact shine again," Donna murmured peering out the window.

"It will. Dinna be a sourpuss, Sister Donna. Ye're the chipper one, remember?" Kirstin tossed herself onto the bed, and then hacked at the cloud of dust and other unpleasant things that invaded the space around her, fiercer than the clouds outside.

Donna twirled in her chemise and flopped onto the bed beside Kirstin. "Do ye think it always rains this much here?"

"I doubt it. Just a summer storm as we have on Skye."

"I'm hungry."

"Go ask one of the guards to fetch ye some supper."

Kirstin flopped an arm over her face. Would she have to mind Donna like a governess? That would prove most annoying. And even more annoying would be if her own sour mood continued.

"Good idea." Donna pushed off the bed, another cloud of dusts rising as she left.

Kirstin wished she could tell Donna to go and make the meal herself, better yet, to farm the food they would eat, then she'd not return for awhile and Kirstin could have a few moments of peace. At Nèamh, she did not have to share a chamber with anyone. She often spent much of her time in solitude and reflection. If she'd learned anything, the company of others frayed very easily on her nerves. Perhaps it was all that had happened in her past. An attack on your home as a child, the murder of your parents, and the loss of so many others, even as recently as a decade ago, well, it took a toll. She didn't want to get close to anyone, perhaps for fear of losing them all over again.

"He's to bring us something directly," Donna chirped, running her fingers along the table. "'Tis dusty."

Kirstin leapt from the bed, ready to say something quite rude, but steadied herself. "How about ye relax a bit and I'll try to make our arrangements a little more habitable."

Donna opened her mouth to protest, her position well below that of Kirstin's meaning she should be the one cleaning, but Kirstin held up a staying hand. "I insist."

Tuning out the sound of Donna's chatter, she went to work wiping down the table and chairs with the bucket of water they'd been given upon arrival to rinse the mud from their hands and feet. When that was finished, she moved to the floors. There was something calming in the repetitive movements. The lack of thinking it required. She could move round and round, and work while inside her mind always seemed to solve the problems she faced.

A knock at the door called her cleaning to cease, and Donna fairly flew from the bed to answer it, nearly tripping over Kirstin in the process.

The guard set a tray of food on the freshly cleaned table, then backed out without a word.

Kirstin expected to see moldy bread and half-rotting chicken on the table, but she was pleasantly surprised to see that the bread looked mostly fresh and the meat without a spot of decay. Donna separated the food and indicated for Kirstin to sit down. She poured them each a cup of ale and then went to eating as though she'd not done so in days.

When was the last time they'd had a decent meal?

They'd been traveling for well over two weeks, and Kirstin had barely eaten since they'd left the abbey. In fact, her clothes were starting to hang on her.

"Eat," Donna said around a hunk of bread. "Mother Superior will have me scrubbing the floors for a fortnight if ye come home half-wasted away."

Kirstin plucked at the chicken, putting a tiny piece in her mouth and chewing around the flavorless lump.

She'd been able to think of little else save for her last trip to the mainland years before. They'd made it through Glasgow without running into her past, and she thanked the Lord for that every moment. But that did not mean she was in the clear. Nay, she wouldn't be until she returned to Skye and the refuge Nèamh afforded her.

Not a refuge for any physically in danger, for she wasn't in any. Nay, it was far more than that. An emotional barrier she'd erected that wavered when she was outside of the walls. She needed the peace the divide of stone and mortar garnered her against the world.

"Can I ask ye a question?" Donna gulped at the ale.

"Ye just did."

"Another then?"

Kirstin sipped the ale, tasting sweat and old boots. Saints, but who made this? The image she conjured in her mind was of a half-bald, skin-slick man with a protruding belly, yesterday's supper in his beard, and that day's breakfast still greasy on his lips. She frowned and set down the cup. "If ye insist." She didn't want to answer any questions but she had a feeling she'd not get away with it. Donna hadn't stopped talking since the moment they'd met and if Kirstin didn't just answer the question, she was likely going to be tortured with more incessant chatter. "But after I answer, I would like some silence. To meditate."

Donna nodded. "Aye, that sounds fair." She flicked her gaze away.

Kirstin was immediately suspicious.

"There is a rumor," Donna started.

"Spreading gossip is a sin. And so is listening to it."

Donna swallowed. "Aye."

"Well, out with it then."

"Will ye tell Mother Superior on me?"

Kirstin rolled her eyes. "Just ask your question—" She cut herself off before she could threaten bodily harm.

"I've heard it said that ye *have* been away from Skye. Even so far as Glasgow. Is it true?"

Kirstin's mouth went dry, the small chunk of bread suddenly brittle on the inside of her cheek. She took a sip of ale, wetting her mouth enough to swallow the bread, then cleared her throat. "Where did ye hear such nonsense?"

Nonsense.

If only it were. If only she'd never run away from Nèamh, though it had been for a very good reason. She'd needed to find her cousin. Finn had saved her life all those years before when her family's castle was attacked. He'd taken her to the abbey, and then gone to search for her sister, never to be seen again, though there were rumors that he'd been spotted. That was when she'd escaped the abbey, needing to finally set eyes on him. See that she'd not been the cause of his death. Where her search led her, well... That was a path she wished she'd not taken, and those who'd witnessed it had been sworn to secrecy.

But it seemed someone *had* told Kirstin's story.

"Why would they spread such if it were not true?"

Kirstin eyed Donna, who had stopped stuffing her face long enough to study Kirstin.

"Sometimes people say things about other people because they want to hurt them." *Even if the words they mutter are true.*

One's own memories can often hurt the most.

Kirstin took another casual sip of her ale, and worked a smile on her face that she hoped looked disarming, even if it felt brittle. "Who did ye hear that from?"

Donna's eyes grew oversized. "Oh, nay, I couldn't share, Sister Kirstin. That would be participating in the gossip."

"Which ye've already done, might I point out?"

Tears brightened Donna's gooseberry eyes. "Can ye forgive me?"

As unpleasant as the memories were, Kirstin wasn't heartless. Donna was young and curious. She didn't mean any harm.

Swallowing away any ill feelings, Kirstin said, "I already have."

Donna let out an audible sigh, her hands clutching her neck. She shook her head, as though fighting a battle inside her mind and then she finally blurted out, "It was Anna."

"Anna?" Kirstin pressed her lips together to keep them from trembling.

Anna had been at the abbey when Kirstin arrived fifteen years before, and was there when Kirstin left to look for Finn. Anna was indeed, still there when Kirstin returned, heartbroken and unwell six months later.

Donna's head bobbed as she nodded, her mousy hair normally pulled back in a severe bun falling loose.

"How old are ye exactly, Donna?" Kirstin asked.

"Eighteen."

Kirstin dipped her head. "That is about the age I was when I left the abbey for the first time."

Donna bit her lip, holding her tongue for once.

"'Tis a sin to lie, so I will tell ye this once, and then ye must put it away and never ask me again."

"I swear it."

"When I was your age, I did leave Nèamh. I wanted to find my cousin. I had heard a rumor that he was serving the laird at Eilean Donan Castle." Kirstin tugged at the pins in her hair, running her fingers through her long, knotty, black locks. "I managed to climb inside a merchant's wagon, and stayed hidden for a day, but they soon found me and threatened to take me back to the abbey. So I escaped."

Donna looked ready to fall out of her chair, her face pale as she listened. Obviously, Anna's version of events were quite different.

"I stayed to the woods, running alongside the road, hiding when anyone came near. But two days without food and expending all of my energy left me hungry and exhausted. By the time I reached Loch Alsh, and the mainland was in sight, I had not the stamina to continue. A fisherman took pity on me when I told him I had family at Eilean Donan, and he gave me bread and water, then took me across the loch." There Kirstin paused, unable to move past the knot swelling in her throat, and the sudden emotional grip that burned her eyes.

"Did ye find your cousin?"

Kirstin shook her head. "Nay, I never did."

Though she had found something else.

3

"Tis late," Gregor said. "We'll not bother those within the abbey until morning. Let's set up camp here."

Gregor guessed it had to be nearing midnight. The rains had finally stopped, but the ground was still soggy. Nothing he hadn't dealt with before.

"Aye, my laird," Samuel said.

Though Gregor had wanted to leave Samuel at home for his own safety, as an afterthought, he'd decided it would be best to bring him along. The news was heavy, and Samuel, being English, and still considered a confidant of the King of England, could gain his orders from Robert the Bruce and most likely be on his way to England to find out who had been behind the capture of Wallace.

Not a decision that Gregor's sister would be too happy with, but that was a risk Catriona took by marrying an English spy.

Samuel issued the order to the men while Gregor dismounted and walked the perimeter of the abbey walls to be sure there were no others lurking.

'Twas unusual for an abbey to be attacked by outlaws seeking absolution for their sins, though there was the occasional desperate fool in need of money and food. As of late, the past seven years in fact, the abbeys had come under attack from the English.

Gregor had firsthand experience with the bastards. They'd broken through Castle Buchanan's defenses and taken him captive, threatened to rape his sister, and killed many of their people. Never again would he let them have an advantage over him. If he could help it, he'd make certain they never again had the upper hand on *anyone*.

The abbey was dark save for a few torches lit over the gate, a welcome to anyone who needed safe harbor. He admired their trust in absolutely everyone, even with all that was going on in the world. Melrose Abbey was so close to Glasgow, Stirling and Edinburgh. *Sassenach* hot spots. In fact, he was surprised they'd not come across a band of English bastards near the abbey to begin with. Perhaps they were all laying low given the recent change of events.

Just two weeks ago, William Wallace was snatched away by a Scottish defector and handed over to the English. And Gregor suspected the defector was someone Wallace had known, else how would he have been able to steal one of Scotland's fiercest warriors from his bed?

No one could be trusted.

Gregor's boots squished in the soggy ground around the stone walls of the abbey, his sword out and scraping in the trampled grass as he walked. He stilled at the sound of movement, a piercing cry of some creature caught, and then the shadow of it slinking away with its prize.

The laws of nature were not so much unlike the battles between the English and the Scots. There could only be one victor, and in the case of the fox and the soft creature he overpowered, the only way for the latter to win would have been by sheer mass alone. How would it be for him, his country?

Standing at the back of the abbey, nothing but darkness occupied the landscape beyond. He stood there admiring the silence, the peace of it. When dawn brushed the land, the gleaming green of the fields, and rainbow colors of wild flowers, the backs of white sheep and the sandy-brown of the cows would all be lit upon.

Gregor returned to the camp. A fire had been lit, and a few of the men warmed hunks of meat on sticks. Thick wool plaids were laid out to soak up the wetness on the ground. At least the temperature was not unpleasant. A balmy night.

"All's well around the abbey," Gregor told Samuel.

"Our scouts reported no one else making camp within the vicinity," Samuel replied. "I've placed Fingal and Connor on first patrol."

Gregor nodded and reached for the skin of ale in his satchel. He took a long drink, pressed his hand to his sporran where the missive he needed to give Robert the Bruce was safely tucked away.

The news he had to impart would be devastating. He needed more than ale to dull his senses. He pulled out a small flask filled with the heady whisky distilled by Big Abe, a member of his clan. Dark and thick, it burned a man's tongue on its way to his belly. Gregor never went anywhere without it, because the potent stuff was not only good for calming the brain, but for numbing and sterilizing a wound, too.

"Pass me some of that," Samuel said.

Gregor grinned and handed him the flask.

Samuel took a swig and passed it back. "You seem troubled."

Gregor grunted. He couldn't yet share the news with Samuel. Not until he'd had a chance to share it with the Bruce. A task he'd been sent to do, and one he wished he hadn't. In fact, when he'd received the Bruce's message to meet at the abbey, Gregor had already been planning to find his sovereign.

Gregor tightened the laces on his boots. The last thing he needed if woken in the night was to trip over the lines. "'Haps it's because I have missed confession."

"And you've much to confess?"

Gregor shrugged, taking another sip. "Does not every man?"

"Catriona prays for me morning and night," Samuel chuckled. "Says she wants to ensure I am accepted into Heaven. She fears for my soul."

"Well she should, ye are a Sassenach. Born to the devil's own country," Gregor goaded.

"Bah! No child can be born evil."

"A matter of opinion. I believe Longshanks has no good bone in his body. He is malicious all the way to his marrow. A man cannot be taught to be as mean as he is."

"I disagree."

"'Tis not unusual," Gregor drawled.

The two of them had become good friends, and Gregor always looked to Samuel for a different perspective. They always seemed to come to terms eventually, even if those terms were to agree to disagree. It was good to see another side of things. Made Gregor a better laird and chief to his clan.

Samuel leaned back, hands behind his head. "Your news must be grave, for you normally share things with me." Samuel cleared his throat. "And you'd never hide from the Bruce. Even if it was midnight."

Gregor ignored him, leaning back on his satchel and closing his eyes. "I'm not hiding. The man needs his rest."

Samuel grunted. "He's not a child." He cleared his throat

again. "I can guess what it is, brother, and I'd not want to be the one to relay it."

"Keep your thoughts to yourself," Gregor snapped, then thought better of it. He'd brought Samuel with him for a reason. "Though I appreciate your support, and if ye continue to please my sister, as ye seem to, I'll be forever in your debt." Gregor sighed. There was so much more to it than that, given Samuel had saved his life once. "Alas, ye best be prepared for the task ahead of ye, brother. For I've a feeling on the morrow ye'll be headed back to England."

"You're no more in my debt, than I am in yours for allowing us to marry. I'll do whatever I can to help your cause, that and Catriona's. Scotland is my home now. I am loyal to you and to your country. My children will be raised as Scots."

"Wish there were more Sassenachs with your intelligence. Too many of them have skulls filled with nothing but shite and rotting flesh."

Samuel sniggered. "And ballocks filled with Longshanks leavings."

Gregor snorted and rubbed at his eyes as though his flask had been upended into their sockets. "That's a foul image. Mighty foul."

Samuel laughed all the more, obviously proud of himself for having shocked Gregor, who never seemed to be shocked by anything.

"On that note, we'd best get some rest. Tomorrow I've a heavy task at hand, and the both of us I'm certain will be handed new orders." Gregor flopped his arm over his eyes, but couldn't get the disturbing images of the wooden chest or the letter's contents out of his mind.

He had to think on more pleasant things, else he'd not get any sleep and knowing there was likely to be none on the morrow, that only seemed to make his mind race all the more.

Sleep. Sleep. Sleep.

Elusive slumber.

Gregor rolled onto his side, gazing into the light of the slowly dying flames. All around him his men softly snored while two marched on patrol.

His breathing grew even and the bouncing orange fire took him into a trancelike state, just near sleep. He could here *her* voice, singing sweetly to him. Whispering how much she loved him. The subtle touch of her fingers sliding over his skin, threading in his hair.

Gregor had loved her, too, though he never told her.

Back then, he'd been young, reckless, the world just having opened up to him. He was a new laird. Plenty of women pulling back their sheets for him to slip between. A mug always in his hand, a sword in the other. His leather breeches and no shirt days, when all he wanted to do was impress and bed one lass after another.

What she offered him, a taste of paradise, a different life... 'Twas one he wasn't ready for.

Too cocky and bold.

Too afraid and immature.

He'd pushed her away. Said things he shouldn't have.

When he'd gone to apologize, she had vanished.

And he'd not seen her since. 'Twas as if she evaporated into thin air. A fairy come to play and love and then had faded into the realm of fantasy, where such spritely things existed.

Kay...

Sweet, lass.

There was many a night that Gregor wished he could take back those last few minutes together. Where instead of telling her she was wasting her time, that he didn't love her, he'd ask her to stay with him forever, and become his wife. Or that maybe instead of walking away from her and locking himself in his library with a barrel of Big Abe's whisky, he'd chase after her. Stop her from fading into the mist.

Alas, Gregor had not. He was a bastard of the first order. Forevermore, he'd regret his choices, and the loss of something so great, for Kay had left a hole the size of Scotland, nay, all the world, in his chest.

So on nights like these, he remembered the sweet moments. The first time he'd seen her, face smudged, clothes dirty, hair in disarray, but blue eyes filled with sparks of determination. She'd been climbing out of a fisherman's boat, tripping over the hem of her skirt.

Gregor had seen her brought in and fed. Not one normally taken to saving strays, though he liked to think himself chivalrous, he'd felt a connection to her. Wanted to help her. She was looking for her cousin, Finn, at the castle. A man they never did find, but they had found something else.

A bond, as though the fates wanted the two of them together.

Gregor had been working with Robert the Bruce at the castle, stayed there for several months in fact, and so did she.

Lingering, loving... Then she'd returned with him to Castle Buchanan.

"My laird," Connor woke him. "Someone approaches."

Gregor sat up, the nighttime sky having lightened to a purplish gray as dawn loomed.

"Who?"

"A middling party. Looks to be several guards and two nuns."

"Then why did ye wake me?" Gregor growled. "We're at an abbey. Did it not occur to ye they are simply returning home?"

Connor shook his head. "Nay, my laird. They could be. 'Tis only that the guards ride with their swords out as if expecting trouble."

Gregor wiped the sleep from his eyes and stood. Robert the Bruce had said they could expect trouble. What if the two women were not simply being escorted back to the abbey, but were in fact in trouble? Being held for ransom?

Arriving in the dead of night at Melrose Abbey and Gregor's unwillingness to step inside until dawn seemed to be a sign from above.

"Then, we'd best greet them to see if there is trouble coming—or if they themselves *are* the trouble." Gregor met the eyes of his men who had quickly woken, donning their weapons. "Pack up, we ride now."

Nothing like the threat of battle to wake a man in the morning. Exhilaration charged through Gregor's extremities, as though a wild horse had seized his blood.

4

"Melrose Abbey is in sight," one of the guards told Kirstin as he returned from scouting.

She nodded, trying to see through the gray haze of morning, and finding that the mist slowly lifting from the ground made it harder to see more than ten or twenty feet in front of her—hence the guards continued rounds ahead and back.

They rode their horses at a steady clip along a road through a wood.

"Tell me again why we had to leave in the middle of the night?" She stared hard at the guard, willing him to answer truthfully.

But all he said, once more, was, "We had overstayed our welcome."

That meant trouble. But what kind she couldn't be certain. She'd not heard any skirmish, nor had anyone banging down her door. The guards had ridden through the night with weapons drawn, which meant they expected whatever trouble it was, to follow.

"Our good coin should have paid for our stay through the

night, and very much been welcome," Donna grumbled, lack of sleep taking away from her normal chipper self.

Kirstin was also tired, but used to the lack of sleep. Years of waking throughout the night for prayers and from night terrors had caused her to become accustomed to exhaustion, not that it was a good thing.

Patting Donna's hand, Kirstin said, "As soon as we are within Melrose's walls, I will explain to the Abbess and the Abbot that ye need your rest. Ye're my companion, and dinna need to sit in on the meeting."

"Are ye certain?"

"Aye."

An eerie prickle crept over the back of Kirstin's neck just before the riderless horse of one of her guard's broke through the mist.

"Where is Owen?" the guard to her left, John, barked.

Mouth dry, heart scaling her throat, Kirstin grabbed hold of the dagger at her waist and advised Donna to do the same.

"What? Why?" Donna squeaked.

Kirstin looked her dead in the eye and said, "If ye dinna, then ye'll have no way to defend yourself. Owen was a capable rider. Something has happened to him, and..." Her voice trailed off as the hair on her forearms rose.

They were being watched.

She scanned the trees, waiting for whoever was stalking them to make themselves known. Wings flapped as a cluster of birds vacated a tree to the right. On the left, the sound of a branch cracking, and beyond that a vacant, soundless void.

Kirstin held her breath as the four guards she had left did their best to surround her and Donna.

Why hadn't she fought harder to stay at the abbey on Skye where she was safe?

"Show yourself," John shouted. "We can hear ye."

Men materialized from seemingly every direction, melting

from the trees, the mist, the air. Owen, too, appeared, a warrior's arm wrapped around his neck, a knife at his throat.

"Good morning," said their leader, his voice calm and familiar.

Eyes widening, a ghost sat his horse before her. Though he'd only ever been dead in her heart, in life he had in fact been very alive.

Gregor.

She ducked her head, hoping the fabric of her hood covered her features and that he'd not yet had a chance to recognize her. Her grip on the dagger tightened, knuckles turning white. The thing she'd feared the most about leaving Skye, was seeing him again. Reliving the broken heart he'd given her, the repercussions of their relationship he didn't even know about and that she'd sworn never to reveal.

The secret she'd never been able to share with him because the moment she'd planned to tell him, he'd pushed her away, said hurtful things. How alone she'd felt on her journey back to Skye. No cousin. No love. Oh, how she'd dreamed of introducing him to her aunt, to show her that she'd found happiness at last. That she'd been meant for more than what life had given her so far. She'd reached for the stars, grasped hold of one golden, sparkling nugget and it had been hers. Briefly. Before it was extinguished.

'Twas not meant to be.

And now fate was twisting the knife, carving her heart out one piece at a time, thrusting in her face how naïve and stupid she'd been.

"We seek no trouble," John said levelly. "We but need to get to the abbey. Let our man go and let us pass."

Gregor inched his horse forward, and Kirstin wished to sink inside her mount. Felt crushed by the emotions pummeling her chest. If he came closer, she would turn and gallop away. She couldn't face him. Not after how much he had hurt her. More than he would ever know.

"What is your business with the abbey?" Gregor demanded.

After nearly ten years passing, his voice was much the same, though perhaps finely aged, and a trace stonier. The sound of it sent a prickle along her limbs as though her body had been waiting all this time to hear him speak again. No matter how much her mind wanted to forget him, the rest of her refused. 'Twas as if she'd suddenly been sucked through some portal of time and landed right back where she was. With him. Barely unchanged.

But what did she know? The man had tricked her, used her, discarded her.

She'd fallen in love with someone who didn't exist, how could she possibly think to know who he was now, or recognize in him any little part of the past? He was a stranger. Always had been.

"That is none of your affair," John replied.

"As a matter of fact, it is my affair." Gregor drew even closer, his horse's muzzle only inches from John's own horse. "I've business there that does not include any outsiders."

Kirstin stiffened. What was he doing at the abbey? Robbing them?

He'd been a bit impulsive when she knew him, but nothing nefarious, only the things most young men with power and coin did. Drinking, flirting, gambling.

Och, there she went again pretending like she knew who he was. Perhaps he'd been a thieving murderer all along. He'd certainly stolen and then shredded her heart and soul.

"We are Warriors of God and these are two daughters of the Lord. The abbey is more our business than a shameless warrior who thinks he holds the power."

John's words were enough to send any man with an ounce

of pride into blows, but Gregor simply chuckled. The sound was menacing, and this time when a shiver raced over her it wasn't from the memories his voice elicited, but fear at what he would do to them now.

"I'll ask ye once more, what brings ye to the abbey?" Gregor's tone had chilled about thirty degrees, ice edged on every word. "Be careful in your answer, as ye can see your man here has a knife at his throat."

Kirstin discreetly glanced at Owen. He didn't look afraid at all, though a vein popped from his neck. His face had not lost any of its color, though 'twould be hard to tell with the new rusty-colored beard he'd grown over his cheeks and chin.

"None of your affair," John replied, deliberate and slow.

Gregor let out an audible sigh of irritation.

Donna whimpered, her horse skittering closer to Kirstin's so that the poor trembling lass was pressed up against her. Kirstin grabbed hold of her hand. Would Gregor kill Owen in front of them? Why didn't John try to save him?

"Keep your sense, sister," Kirstin urged in a low murmur. "Do not draw attention to yourself."

Or to me.

"I told ye I'd not ask again," Gregor said. "The fact that ye willna tell me leads me to believe ye've no business at the abbey."

The unmistakable sound of metal sliding from a scabbard had Kirstin's head jolting up and her gaze locking on Gregor. He still wasn't looking at her, but the deadly expression on his face spoke of his intent. He was going to kill all of them. He motioned to the warrior holding Owen who dragged him forward.

John held his sword out, a growl on his lips. The rest of the Warriors of God looked ready to take on the Highlanders before them.

A battle, death, was imminent if she didn't put a stop to it.

"Gregor, stop," she said calmly. More calm than she felt. She lifted her head, letting her hood fall back from her face.

There was an indrawn breath all around as the guards on both sides regarded both her and Gregor in shock.

"Kay?" Gregor sounded as though he were being strangled.

His eyes were as wide as the wooden bowls she ate porridge out of at the abbey, and his skin had paled five shades.

Kirstin inclined her head. "Please let us pass." She gulped in some air, trying to shore up her nerves, to steady her fiercely trembling hands. "I understand that perhaps ye are guarding the abbey, and I can appreciate that. Our houses of God need all the protection they can get these days. As a daughter of the Lord, avowed to live a life in service to God and the church, I assure ye, we mean no harm."

"A woman of God..." His voice trailed off. Not a question. Not really a statement. More like he was trying to wrap his mind around what she'd just relayed.

Perhaps, she, too, had misrepresented herself. She'd never told Gregor she was a nun. She'd never even told him her real name, instead calling herself Kay. At the time, she'd told herself it was for her own good, to keep her safe, in case the men who had captured her sister all those years ago and murdered her parents, were still looking for her.

Too quick to judge.

A sin.

Kirstin raised her eyes briefly to the heavens, begging forgiveness. She was in a perpetual state of penance, and she was certain she'd never be free of any of her sins.

"Please, Gregor. I'm certain my guards would not object if

ye wanted to escort us to the abbey." Even if she would object most emphatically.

Her heart hurt so much just looking at him. Talking was torture. If she had to be in his company a moment longer she was certain to break down in tears.

John made a guttural noise, about to argue, she guessed, but Kirstin stayed him with her hand on his arm.

"Gregor?"

The man was still speechless, his gaze on her, but she couldn't tell if he was truly seeing. A man beside him cleared his throat, and Gregor came to.

"Aye, Kay—"

"Sister Kirstin will do," she cut in. No sense in keeping that part a secret anymore.

Kay did not exist, and she wasn't going to dredge her up now.

"Kirstin."

Her name rolled off his tongue, and she could see in the way his eyes squinted before returning to normal that she'd hurt him, too. Even if it was only his pride.

"*Sister* Kirsten," she said once more, emphasizing her place in the world. "Then let us go. We are tired from traveling through the night, and my companion needs to rest."

Gregor nodded, and ordered his men to flank them, though his eyes never left her. She felt her cheeks begin to flame, her heart pounding so hard she was certain her ribs would crack.

Owen was returned to his empty horse, daggers shooting from his eyes. John and the other men shifted uncomfortably on their horses, but Kirstin didn't care. Gregor wouldn't hurt her, at least she knew that much. For as much as he'd broken her heart, he'd only ever protected her in the past. She trusted him.

Maybe that was enough.

Nay! What was she thinking?

Never again.

When she'd returned to Skye nine years before, and gone through the pains of washing herself clean of him, of their sin. And when she'd mourned the loss of her heart, her soul, a life, she'd once more given herself fully to God. Vowed to love Him and him alone.

There could be no place in her heart, or in her world, for Gregor.

Donna still whimpered beside her, and Kirstin startled, having forgotten all about the lass for a moment. She squeezed her hand and whispered, "Come now, all is well. Soon ye can seek solace in the chapel and a bed."

"I could sleep for a week," Donna said, her lower lip trembling.

Why had Mother Superior sent Donna with Kirstin? The lass was naïve and fragile as glass.

"I'm certain one night will do the trick," Kirstin said. "And then ye can explore Melrose's gardens. I've heard they are beautiful. Ye dabble in our gardens, do ye not?"

"Aye, I think I should like that." A smile touched her lips.

They talked a little more on gardening, anything to keep Donna distracted, though Kirstin couldn't keep her eyes off Gregor's back.

Thank goodness Donna was cheering up, no longer as frightened. Kirstin could really only deal with her own fears and worries at the moment, as uncharitable as that was. She'd just run smack into a nightmare from her past. Aye, losing her parents and sister in the attack had been harsh, but she and her sister had since been reunited. The guilt at being the cause of her cousin's disappearance, too, weighed heavily on her.

But, Gregor had taken so much more from her.

For a brief moment, Kirstin's hand came to her belly,

rubbing where a life could have been before she jerked it away.

They trotted down the road, two nuns surrounded by five Warriors of God and a dozen additional Highland warriors. Within the next few minutes, they'd be at Melrose Abbey, safe behind the stone walls.

Why then, did Kirstin feel so rattled? So *unsafe*?

'Twas nothing physical. Nay, she feared not for harm to her body, but what her mind was already doing, twisting and winding its way around her fortifications, like a snake trying to squeeze the breath from her, or her senses. Trying to erase the pain she felt, she grabbed hold of the good feelings of the past, the ones she wanted to repeat, but ultimately could not.

Gregor's fault.

If she'd not come upon him now, she would never have considered...

Considered what?

Returning to a life of sin? She couldn't. Not now. Not ever.

It wouldn't be a sin if they had married... Exactly what she'd thought would have happened. But he never asked. He used her and then discarded her.

And how dare he look so keen to see her? So full of emotion she could barely breathe at the look of him?

Oh, for the love of all that was holy! Why, oh why, did her mind play such games with her?

Gregor had only ever cared about one thing, and it hadn't been to make a life with her. That was not a life she wanted to lead.

When they reached the abbey, before she spoke with the Abbot about his summons, Kirstin would go straight to confession. She would pray. She would accept her penance. Ask for guidance. Beg for direction. Plead for strength. For she needed it, because in just the few precious moments of their reconciliation, she'd been willing to forgo the past in search of a future.

She would shore up her firm decision to never, ever, ever, let her heart be deceived again. Not by any man, and especially not by Gregor Buchanan.

5

Though he sat on his horse tall, his face void of emotion, Gregor was solidly shaken.

Kay—nay, *Kirstin*—was alive, well and sitting a horse just behind him.

In a nun's habit.

If someone had told him that the feisty, sensual woman he'd loved more than life itself had been a nun, he'd have laughed them all the way to hell. Was he damned for loving her? For the things they did together? Beautiful, sinful things.

Had he somehow entered an alternate universe? Where the hell had she been? She'd not been at Melrose this whole time. He'd have found her. He'd searched months for her. Still looked for her when he traveled to Eilean Donan, crossed a loch or passed a fairy glen.

She'd simply vanished, and yet, here she was.

Right behind him.

Not six feet away. Alive. Full of life. Just as feisty even covered in her gray wool nun's gown.

The blood running through his veins grew cold. He didn't know whether to be relieved, grateful, to leap from his horse and kiss the ground then raise his hands to the sky and thank the divine she was still alive, or to rage at her for simply walking out of his life, no matter what untruths he'd spewed the night he pushed her away.

Samuel cleared his throat expectantly beside Gregor, obviously wanting an explanation that Gregor wasn't ready or willing to give.

Samuel had not been with them when Kay had been at the castle. He wasn't even certain Catriona would remember. She'd been a young girl then, spending most of her days with her tutors and the other young girls of the clan, practicing how to run a castle, and not keeping tabs on him as she did now.

They cleared the trees, the heath opening out before them and the bell tower of Melrose within full view. The sun had fully risen, not a cloud in sight. The mist had melted away leaving a dew that glistened on the grass like diamonds. Like the sparks of light that would shine in Kirstin's eyes when candle flames lit a room.

Behind them he could hear Kirstin and her companion draw in a breath. Was this her first time seeing it? The abbey was something beautiful to behold. Bigger than most and the windows elegantly carved. He'd seen it many times before, but never had he tried to look at it through the eyes of another.

Doing so made him angry.

And there was the kicker, he *was* angry.

He might have pushed her away, but she didn't have to disappear like that, simply vanish, making him fear for her life.

How many nights of sleep had he lost over the past nine years? Last night included?

By the time they reached the wooden gates, Gregor was ready to rip her from her horse and demand answers. His muscles were clenched, veins at his temples throbbing. Unable to speak, he simply nodded to Samuel, asking him to take the lead.

Without question, though his eyes were filled with plenty, Samuel dismounted, disarmed and knocked on the doors. A moment later a small square opening was pulled back and the slim, aged face of an elder nun appeared.

"Sister," Samuel started. "I am Sir Samuel de Mowbray, loyal to the Scottish crown, brother-by-marriage to three of your countrymen, Laird Gregor Buchanan, the Earl of Sutherland and Lord Blane Sutherland. We have been summoned by the Bruce. Along our way, we found two of your sisters accompanied by Warriors of God."

The woman's eyes shifted, taking in each member of the group.

"Where is the laird?" she asked, her voice brittle with age.

The abbey was certainly trusting to have such a frail creature manning the gate.

Gregor dismounted and approached, finally able to move without fear of pulling Kirstin from her horse, though the urge was still strong. "Sister, I am Laird Gregor Buchanan. The Bruce is expecting us."

She nodded. "Ye know the rules. Leave your weapons."

Gregor disarmed, adding his weapons to the pile Samuel had already created. "My men will wait outside, save for Sir Samuel. He comes with me."

"Them, too," the nun nodded in the direction of the warriors flanking Kirstin and her companion.

The one who seemed to be in charge, who'd argued with Gregor before, quickly dismounted and joined him at the gate.

The warrior looked the nun right in the eyes and said, "Sister, I am Sir John of Dunkeld. Our weapons come with us. We have vowed to protect those who protect our souls. Our vows were given and blessed in the name of the Lord in the Lord's house. To be without them is to not be able to honor our vows."

The older nun frowned, pursing her wrinkled lips. "I need to check with the abbess."

"We know the abbot is here. Check with him," the warrior said.

Gregor raised a brow in Samuel's direction finding his appalled expression mirrored in his brother's.

"Wait here." The nun shut the tiny wooden door.

Gregor crossed his arms over his chest and stared hard at the man. "Now there's the possibility of none of us gaining entrance. What game are ye playing?"

"No games." The man looked ready to tear into Gregor. "We have our orders just as ye have yours."

"Who gives your orders?" Gregor asked.

"The Pope."

Gregor grunted. "And here in Scotland? Who receives the Pope's orders?"

"The Bishop of Dunkeld."

"Quite a ways you have come, then, given Dunkeld is at least four days ride."

"Longer, my laird," the warrior said, his face so empty Gregor couldn't help but wonder if all the warriors were simply vessels for the bishops and cardinals to wield. "We first went to Skye when summoned."

The Isle of Skye. Was that where Kirstin was from? He'd not checked there. Though perhaps that should have been the first place given she'd come from across the loch to Eilean Donan. Was it possible his mind had purposefully forgotten that place? Didn't want him to check there, afraid of what he'd truly find? That his love for her could have been a lie?

"By who?" Gregor demanded.

The man simply grinned, the first Gregor had seen. It

sent a foreboding chill up his spine. Before the day was out, Gregor was pretty certain that he and this man would come to blows.

The little door reopened and the nun appeared. She looked haggard, and her gaze wearily touched on Gregor.

She addressed the warrior, John. "The Abbot says ye are approved to bring in your daggers only." Her gaze roved back to Gregor. "All of ye. Leave your swords, maces, bows, and any other tools of your trade outside."

The holy warrior grumbled, but acquiesced, tugging a pile of sharpened steel from nearly every inch of his body.

"My men will stay with yours, Buchanan." John wasn't asking.

And Gregor didn't care. He shrugged. "So be it."

Gregor's gaze finally met Kirstin's—how could he avoid her?—and his chest tightened. His heart still beat for her and her alone. She skillfully masked her emotions, perhaps what a nun—*a nun*!—was trained to do. But even still, he could see the way her chest rose and fell at a rapid pace, the way she tried to hide her quickened breaths by slouching her shoulders. Was she nervous about the warriors, the weapons, the abbey, or because they had unfinished business?

Gregor had to get her alone, had to talk to her, at least to find out why in the world she had vanished. Had he been the reason she took vows? Had he pushed her so hard she never wanted to find love again? Wanted to be forever unavailable to him or any man?

"K—Sister Kirstin," he corrected. "May I escort ye—"

John stepped in front of Gregor, blocking his view, his face close enough that Gregor could smell the spiced jerky he'd eaten to break his fast.

"She goes *no where* with ye."

The warrior was too possessive of Kirstin. Did John care for her? Did she care for him? Was this all a ruse?

Fury, molten hot boiled in Gregor's belly. Restraining his fisted hands at his side instead of pummeling the man in the face, he stepped even closer. "Who the hell are ye to say where she goes and with whom? There can be no claim to the lass, as she's taken vows from the church. Ye're nothing but a bishop's errand boy."

That was enough to give Gregor exactly what he wanted —a fight. John wrenched back his arm and swung. Gregor ducked, punching John in the stomach. On the periphery somewhere, he heard the ladies scream, but the sound seemed to fade somewhere with the pounding rage inside his head. He bounced back when John got a solid hit to his ribs, pain radiating through his side. Gregor charged, his shoulder slamming into John's stomach, and he pushed forward, slamming the man to the ground with John's fists bouncing off Gregor's back.

The two men tussled on the ground, growling, punching, deflecting.

The other warriors allowed it to go on for a few minutes, before Samuel and a warrior of God, Owen perhaps, stepped forward and wrenched the men apart. Samuel held Gregor's arms behind his back to keep him from lashing out, so blind was he by his need to see John's blood spilled. John was similarly held, the both of them foaming like rabid animals.

Gregor was still flailing to get free of Samuel's tight grip, rage fueling him, when Kirstin's pretty face, screwed up in anger flashed before his. She stood between them, hands on her hips, lips thinned. Blue eyes, filled with diamond sparkles and fury. He couldn't help but grin, the corner of his lip stinging from where it was probably cut.

"That's quite enough," she said, her voice not raised, but the tone demanding obedience. "What in heaven's name did ye think ye were doing provoking him?" She whipped around to face John. "And ye? Ye know better than to start a fight. Ye are to live your life in peace, acting out in violence only when it serves the purpose of saving a life or keeping someone from desecrating holy grounds."

Gregor yanked free and straightened his shirt. 'Twas a good thing they'd disarmed themselves, else what had started as a punching match would have most likely ended in someone's death. The rush of the fight still pumped wildly in his veins, his breathing was hard. He barely felt the ache in the places John had hit him, but the hurt in his heart had only grown.

"Who is he to ye?" Gregor demanded.

Kirstin jerked back, looking confused, then understanding dawned and she scoffed. "He is my guard, tasked with keeping me safe, and if ye take issue with him, then ye take issue with me."

Gregor shook his head while John smirked.

"I dinna trust him."

"Ye dinna know him," she countered.

"'Tis a warrior's job to understand his enemy."

"He is no more your enemy than I." She glanced toward the gate, where the tiny little peep door had once more been opened, the old nun's face peering out. "Ye'll both be lucky if our kind Sister lets ye inside."

As the rush of fury started to slowly ebb, Gregor felt remorse for his actions. Aye, he'd egged the bastard on, but he'd felt the need to prove a point. John wasn't superior to him. Plus, he'd needed to release his anger and frustration. Fighting always helped.

Since seeing Kirstin perfectly well before him, he'd had the need to pummel something. Nearly a decade's worth of worry, regret and fear for her life had come to the surface with no outlet. Pounding John's face, a man who he suspected held feelings for *his* Kay, had seemed the perfect solution, however primal.

"Apologies to ye, Sister. I let personal feelings—my intense dislike of this man"—John hooked his finger in Gregor's direction—"get in the way of my duties."

Facing Gregor, Kirstin rolled her eyes discreetly, perhaps not meant for him even to see, but see he did. John might have harbored feelings for her, but those sentiments were thankfully not reciprocated, at least not on the surface. And the way she glowered at Gregor, they were likely not given to him either. But what more did he expect? She'd disappeared nine years ago without a word.

The gates slowly opened, and where Gregor expected to see the little old nun, their liege, Robert the Bruce, stepped forward, an abbot by his side.

"Well, gentleman, if ye are quite done trying to prove whose fist is bigger, we've business to attend to."

Gregor dropped to his knee, hand over his heart, his men doing the same. The warriors of God bowed their heads, as did Kirstin and her female companion.

"My lord, Father," Gregor said, addressing the Bruce and the abbot. "My sincere apologies for the way we have arrived."

The Bruce chuckled. "Nothing I haven't seen before. Now if ye can restrain yourselves, rise and let us speak."

Gregor motioned for his men to stay behind with the exception of Samuel.

"Sisters, we've been expecting ye," the abbot said. "Please, come inside."

Kirstin glanced at him one last time, her expression once more guarded.

"I'll behave," Gregor murmured.

Was that a laugh? That slight exhale of breath he heard? Or was it his imagination? Wishful thinking?

She walked, head held high, hands folded demurely in front of her.

Gregor followed with Samuel, and was cut off at the last second by John, who slipped behind Kirstin and her companion.

Grinding his teeth, Gregor kept his anger at bay. However long they were all within the abbey walls was going to be a true test to his willpower and his capacity for mental anguish. For he wanted to pound John's head into the ground, and he wanted to wrap Kirstin up in his arms.

Come hell or high water, he was going to get her alone, and he was going to get the answers to his questions. The past needed to be laid to rest, else he beg her to rescind her vows and continue a life with him. The one they'd started all those years ago.

Because the truth of the matter was, even if he hadn't been able to admit it to her before, he loved her greatly. Madly. Deeply.

6

Was this a test?

A test to see if she was worthy of the church? Why else would her aunt have insisted that Kirstin be the representative from Nèamh?

There could be no coincidence that Gregor happened to be called to Melrose at the same time. And yet, what purpose could there be for him to be here, other than as a distraction?

For certes, she was distracted.

Every emotion she could name had pummeled her insides since the moment she'd laid eyes on him.

So much left unsaid, unheard.

Crescent shaped dents were no doubt etched in her palms from the way she'd been digging her nails. When Gregor and John had been fighting, she'd actually feared one of them would end up dead. The Warriors of God were not men to be trifled with. They were trained to kill and had been absolved of all doings by the church. That made them deadly. No regrets, no remorse.

Yet, she'd seen Gregor play in tournaments and he'd bested most men, some days all. With so many years passing, he was certain to have grown stronger. As evidenced in the way he fought, the way his body had increased in muscle since she'd last seen him. He'd grown stronger. Maybe even a little taller.

Kirstin chewed her lip as she passed under the gates and entered the courtyard. Donna clung to her side, shaking.

"Calm yourself," Kirstin whispered. "We must be strong, and have faith. We are safe, no harm shall come to us."

Donna nodded uneasily.

Gregor and his man veered off with the king, while the abbot led Kirstin, Donna and John in the opposite direction. Kirstin couldn't help the way her eyes followed Gregor's back. The lines of his body hadn't changed much, only filling in from what she remembered. Broader shoulders. Muscles that seemed to have doubled in places. Thicker arms and legs. And his rear... When her gaze landed there, imagining the way his tight buttocks had looked nude, she quickly raised her gaze to his head. He glanced behind at her, startling her, making her face grow hot with unwanted emotion. His jaw was stronger looking, too. His face, more distinguished. A decade had made him more striking.

Staring at his body brought back memories of what it felt like to be in his arms. To have him hold her, kiss her, wrap her up in his warmth. And more. The way it felt to lie with him, to have him over her, beside her, under her... A twinge of longing in her belly gave her pause. She wanted to relish it, because it had been so long since she'd felt anything like that.

And yet it was a sin to have such impure thoughts. To have felt the touch of a man and given herself to him when she'd vowed a life of celibacy. But it had been worth it.

Sadness swept over her. She was sad for what she'd lost. All she'd lost.

The weight of it rested on her shoulders, nearly crushing her.

Gregor turned just before they disappeared from view, dark eyes penetrating hers. The look on his face was enough to make her knees buckle. Thank the saints she was held up by Donna.

"What is it? Are ye ill?" Donna asked, her gaze concerned, the back of her hand touching Kirstin's head.

Kirstin shook her head, offering a smile to Donna. "Nay, I am fine. Just a little nervous after that fight."

That explanation seemed to be enough for Donna who nodded. "Aye, 'twas fearsome. Thought I was going to faint and fall right off my horse."

"I hope the two of them have gotten it out of their systems so we need not witness such again."

"Aye," Donna mused. "I wonder why they did it?"

Kirstin kept her mouth shut. She knew why. Over the past two weeks John had taken a liking to her, one that they both knew could never go anywhere, as they'd both taken vows of celibacy for life in order to serve the church, but still, he'd flirted with her, and she had flirted back on occasion, having missed the back and forth banter she'd had at Eilean Donan and Castle Buchanan. Those six months had been the most carefree indulgences of her life.

In so many ways.

The memories were bittersweet.

"Men have a penchant for proving their strength over one another." Kirstin steadied herself enough to keep following the abbot through the cloister. The high arched ceilings and grounds were easily twice as large as Nèamh.

"I'm glad to be a woman then, can ye imagine if the nuns at Nèamh were always tussling?"

Kirstin grinned. "Women tussle, too, but more with their mouths and their minds."

"That's true."

The abbot had stopped walking, seeming impatient as he

waited on them to catch up. "I know your journey has been long, sisters, so I will simply introduce ye to the abbess, we will break bread together, and then I will have someone show ye to your rooms."

'Twas on the verge of Kirstin's tongue to argue. She hadn't traveled all this way to simply wait to find out the reason for her journey, but all the sudden she was extremely exhausted. Drained, both physically and mentally.

"Aye, Reverend Father," she said.

The abbot entered through a door, taking them into what looked to be a library. Books and scrolls were stacked on shelves from floor to ceiling. Tapestries depicting the Holy Mother and her baby, angels, and the heavens lined the spaces between shelves. Candles lit the space by the dozen. Mother Superior, looking just a few years younger perhaps, than Aunt Aileen, sat behind a desk and rose when they entered.

"Sisters Kirstin and Donna from Nèamh," the abbot introduced. "Mother Frances."

The two of them inclined their heads toward the abbess.

"Please have a seat." She indicated the chairs before her desk. "I have heard much about ye Sister Kirstin, from Mother Aileen."

Kirstin took a seat on the hard wooden chair, the muscles in her rear crying out as a reminder of how sore she was from their travels.

"Mother Aileen is too kind," Kirstin mumbled.

Mother Frances looked like a hard woman. There were lines around her eyes and not many around her lips. She was a woman who frowned much, and hardly smiled. She might have been younger than Aunt Aileen, but she was most certainly not as happy.

"We are pleased that a representative from Skye was able to join us. Much has changed within the realm and the church, but we will get to that tomorrow. For now, please make yourselves at home. Ye will join the rest of the sisters for meals, prayers and our various charitable activities."

"How long do ye anticipate us staying?" Kirstin asked.

"At least a fortnight, perhaps a month."

Kirstin nodded, wondering if Gregor, too, would be here that long. How could she face him? Or the memories he dredged up? From the expression on his face, she'd be naïve to believe he wasn't going to search her out.

What right did he have anyway? He'd pushed her away, not the other way around.

Though she had run off without leaving word or an explanation, she didn't really feel like she owed him that. At all.

"Sister Kirstin? Are ye well?"

Kirstin blinked, having been staring blankly at the abbess for who knew how long. Before she could answer, Donna interjected.

"We traveled through the night. She's not slept in quite some time. Perhaps I should get her to a chamber now?"

"Aye, of course." Mother Superior rang a bell and moments later two nuns entered who looked to be about Donna's age. "Please take Sister Kirstin and Sister Donna to our guest nun quarters."

The nuns bowed their heads and beckoned them forward.

Kirstin mumbled her thanks, her skin prickling. She needed to get out of here. And she didn't want to wait a month.

The two nuns before them, did not talk much. They smiled then faced forward as they led them down a darkened corridor, past several other nuns walking with their heads bowed, and a few scrubbing floors. She shivered despite the temperature not being cool. The virginals were being played somewhere, echoed by singing. The sounds would normally calm her, make her want to sing too, but now they only acted as an ominous backdrop for what the next several weeks held.

"Here we are," one of the nuns said, unlocking a door and pushing it open.

The door creaked, thudding softly against the wall.

"'Tis dark," Donna mumbled.

"There's a candle and flint on the table. With it being warmer at night, we dinna light any fires in order to conserve. If ye get cold, there are extra blankets in the wooden chest below the window."

And then the two were gone, drifting soundlessly toward the music.

"Hold the door open to let in some of the light from the corridor." Kirstin shuffled inside, her eyes adjusting to the light and making out large, black lumps of furniture.

She found the table with the candle and flint, and set sparks to flame on the wick, illuminating the room. The guest quarters were somber and sparse, not much unlike her room at Nèamh, except that she'd been able to add small touches over the years that made it hers.

The chamber had four cots in a row, headboards against the wall, a foot or two of space between each where a small side table sat. Each cot looked to have a pillow and a blanket. There was a chest beneath a shuttered window, which Kirstin pushed open to let in some air.

The rush of air caused the candle to flicker, and dust motes danced in the shafts of light filtering in. She wouldn't be surprised to hear they were the first guests to stay in this chamber for some time. The best rooms would of course go to the king and his council.

Gregor would have a room.

Where would it be?

"Suppose not many guest nuns come to Melrose," Donna murmured.

"Oh, aye, I'd forgotten she mentioned these were the

guest nun's quarters. Well, we'd best set to cleaning afore we rest, else either of us wakes up with an ague."

Too much dust often left Kirstin sneezing, stuffy and bleary eyed if she let it get to her. 'Twas one of the reasons she cleaned so much, besides the fact that it was one thing she could control. With a lifetime of events where power had been taken from her, and her destiny outside the grasp of her own control, she was glad for one thing in which she could calculate the outcome.

"All right," Donna agreed, knowing it would do no good to argue with Kirstin when she was in a cleaning mood.

They dragged their pillows and thin mattresses out into the courtyard, beating them with a broom she found, until not a speck of dust flew when they were hit. Next, they shook out the blankets on the beds as well as the ones in the chest.

Kirstin sent Donna to procure a bucket and some rags and if possible lye soap in order to scrub their floor. When she returned, the two of them got to work on their knees. Possibly two hours had passed, and at last the room was livable.

They dumped their wash buckets outside, fingertips wrinkled, then blew out the candle and sank into bed. But the rest was short lived.

A knocked sounded at the door, startling Kirstin from her sleep. She scrambled to stand in the dark, momentarily lost. Where was she? Why was she here? What time was it? Who was she again?

She answered the door, seeing one of the small nuns who'd led them there before.

"Time for supper," the lass said. "Come to the refectory."

Kirstin squinted to see Donna climbing from her bed. The two of them no doubt looked affright. Her face felt heavy, body even worse. She could have easily slept through the night, and she would have loved nothing more than to request their food be brought to their chamber, but though she was born a lady, she was also a nun, and she'd already agreed to eating with the abbess and abbot when they mentioned it earlier.

"We will be there."

"Five minutes," the nun said, then turned on her heel and walked briskly away.

Kirstin and Donna brushed out their hair and readjusted their nun's habits.

"I feel as though my head is swollen," Donna said.

"Mine, too." They'd barely had enough sleep, let alone enough during their two weeks of travel. "We shall eat and then sleep some more."

As soon as they were out in the corridor, Kirstin's nerves leapt a hundred octaves, causing all of her skin to tingle. The sun had set, but torches were lit to guide their way. They headed in the same direction they'd seen the nun scurry off toward, but still Kirstin felt there was someone watching. She turned catching a glimpse of a shadow at the opposite end of the corridor.

"Who's there?" she called.

Gregor moved out of the shadows. Tall, broad, deadly. Handsome.

Was he, too, coming to the refectory?

She couldn't talk to him. Kirstin whirled around. "Let us hurry."

Donna didn't comment, though she did frown.

"Kay," he called. "Sister Kirstin, please wait."

Please? Wait?

Kirstin sped up. From the sounds of his boot heels clicking, he was also increasing his pace. The man was not going to let her go.

With a sigh of resignation, she said, "Go ahead of me, Donna. I will meet ye there shortly."

"But—"

"Go. Please."

Donna's frown deepened, but she did as Kirstin asked.

Watching her companion leave, she found it hard to turn around. Her hands trembled. Knees threatened to turn as weak as mud. She didn't want to face Gregor. Not now. Not alone. Not when there was every possibility she'd break down in sobs and tell him everything.

Sharing with him would solve nothing.

And yet, then she wouldn't have to bear the pain alone.

7

"Why did ye leave me, Kay?"

"Dinna call me that. My name is Kirstin. That lass does not exist." She avoided his gaze, but what he could see from the lights of the torches shining on her face was regret, and pain etched around the corners of her eyes.

Even all these years later, she'd not lost any of her beauty. Not a strand of hair was visible beneath her nun's hood. His fingers itched to wrench it free, to see the cascade of her raven hair, soft as silk and scented sweet.

He drew in a deep breath, stepped a little closer. "She may have changed her name, but that lass was real to me. I'd wager she's still somewhere inside ye."

A bitter laugh escaped Kirstin and her gaze flicked to his. "I assure ye, she's long since buried along with any memories that could have been sweet."

Her words speared him, tearing into his chest with such agony he wondered if her statements were tipped with poison.

"Tell me why ye left," he asked again. "Please."

For the briefest of seconds her lower lip trembled. "I did not simply leave, Gregor. I was told to go."

"By who?" He'd kill the man who tossed her out.

Kirstin's lips twisted in outrage, something he'd not witnessed from her before. "Ye canna be serious."

"I am."

She shook her head, her features distorted in exasperation. "Ye are the most dense man I've ever met. Either ye are simply too stupid to function—which I doubt considering ye've managed to stay alive so long—or ye are purposefully attempting to anger me."

Gregor held up his hands and took a step back. "Please, my lov—" Old habits were hard to kill off. Gregor cleared his throat. "Please, Sister Kirstin, I meant no harm. I simply wanted an answer to a question I've been trying to figure out the answer to for nearly a decade."

"So ye are serious." She shook her head, her disappointment palpable. "If ye were not able to figure it out in nearly a decade than clearly me telling ye straight to your face is not going to do either of us any good. Good night, sir."

She started to turn, and instinctively he reached out, grasped her arm. Thinner than he remembered, and not as warm. What had happened to her to steal all the light from within? "Wait," he requested.

She shuddered, glowered up at him and tugged free. "Dinna touch me."

He let her go, feeling her revulsion all the way to the very core of him. Did she truly despise him so much? She crossed her arms protectively over her chest.

"I'm sorry." Guilt speared his chest.

The tip of her pink tongue was visible between her teeth as she bit it, then disappeared as she spoke. "As far as I'm concerned whatever life, whatever *lies*, we shared, they are nothing to me but a lapse of my memory, my sanity. I dinna wish to speak of it, and I wish that ye would simply consider me a stranger."

Gregor let out a low growl and ran his hands through his hair with frustration, wanting to throttle her. "Kirstin, what happened between us? Why do ye hate me so?"

"Why do ye not remember?"

"I remember everything. I remember every night. Thousands of nights have passed with me wishing ye were by my side and praying ye were not dead."

"Ye're a fool and ye've wasted your time." Her words were so cold, and contradicted the sadness in her eyes.

"I dinna consider ye a waste of time, nor myself a fool for having loved ye." *For loving ye still.*

"Then ye are even more of a fool."

Maybe he was a fool. Mayhap he was a complete and utter jackhole, but that didn't really matter to him. What mattered to him was...

"I'm sorry, Kay." He reached for her, his hands suspended in mid-air and her backing up. "For whatever I've done to make ye despise me so much, I beg your forgiveness." He needed it. Couldn't move forward without it.

She shook her head. "Not even a thousand nights lying awake is enough."

"What is enough? What can I do?"

Her eyes cast to the ground, and a single tear rolled down her cheek. "Ye can let me be."

He shook his head, his own eyes burning. "I canna. I willna."

"Ye have to." She glanced up at him, pleading in her gaze that tore at his heart.

"Nay."

"Gregor..."

"I've been waiting for ye to say my name again. To hear it on your lips." Gregor reached out and this time he didn't stop, he slipped his arms around her shoulders, and she didn't resist.

His Kay sank against him, sweet smells of sugar and soap. Her cheek rested against his shirt, growing wet from her silent tears. Slim fingers curled into his shirt, her elbows tucked against his chest. Gregor wrapped her up tight, cocooning her in his embrace. He could have stood there like that forever, holding her. His own breaths were shuddering, and he was so close to breaking down, from losing his masculinity in a puddle of tears of relief, of sadness.

Gregor had not considered before how much of a broken heart he had from losing her.

"Gregor, I must go," she whispered, pushing away from him. "If I do not I will miss my only chance for supper."

The place where she'd laid her head was suddenly cold, all of him feeling the loss of her touch. "I will make the kitchen give ye something. Please, there is much we need to say."

She shook her head. "That is not how it works for me. I cannot ask them to give me special treatment or the other nuns will resent me."

Saints, but he couldn't cause her more hurt. "I dinna want to be the cause of ye missing your dinner."

Gradually, she started to back away. "Then let me go."

Her request was not simply to let her go to dinner though. He could read between the lines and knew what she really wanted was to be let go forever. How could he go through losing her again?

He couldn't.

Gregor braced himself, wanting the exact opposite—never to have her out of his sight again. To tug her back in for a hug, but he had to be satisfied with what he'd gotten, which was progress. Wasn't it?

"I will wait for ye outside of the refectory."

"Nay, ye canna. 'Tis not appropriate. If anyone had seen us

just now... I would be punished."

"Then when can I see ye again?"

She shook her head. "Never. We must say goodbye. Again."

"I dinna want to."

A sad, forlorn smile crossed her lips. Lips he'd dreamed of kissing for so long. "We dinna always get what we want. Some of us even less than others."

And then she was fleeing, the fabric of her skirts and hood flapping in the gentle breeze and he was left alone.

Gregor leaned back against the wall, his head tilted up, and let out a deep, painful sigh. She was so close, yet so far away. He could still smell her sweet scent on his shirt.

Footsteps, booted and heavy, sounded down the corridor. "My laird."

'Twas Samuel.

Gregor rolled his head in his brother-by-marriage's direction. Perhaps it was a good thing to be interrupted, lest he chase Kay into the refectory and cause a scene. "What is it?"

"The Bruce requests your presence."

Gregor nodded. Earlier in the day when they'd arrived, Robert the Bruce had shown him to the temporary room he was using as a war office, though they called it a library as they were within abbey walls and didn't want to offend those inhabiting the place or make them fearful.

He'd not been able to share the missive as the Bruce had been called away by the abbot. When Gregor insisted he remain to hear the news, the Bruce had assured him he'd get his chance.

"'Tis about time," Gregor grumbled.

"Aye, I agree. I think he knows what ye have to share and he does not want to hear it."

"I wish it weren't true."

Samuel grunted. "What are ye doing over here anyway?"

"Meditating," Gregor said sarcastically.

"Outside the nun's eating hall?"

This time it was Gregor who grunted.

"I dinna know what the past holds between ye and the nun, brother, but 'tis dangerous and an offense to the church to seduce its daughters."

"I know it."

"Be careful."

Gregor shouldered Samuel none too softly. "I dinna need a nursemaid."

"That remains to be seen. If ye were to get into trouble, hurt, or saints preserve us, arrested, Catriona would kill me. And it would not be quick and painless. So believe me when I say, I'm simply protecting myself."

Gregor laughed. "I assure ye, ye're head, and your ballocks, will remain firmly intact."

The two guards outside of the war office nodded at their approach and indicated that they were allowed to enter.

The Bruce stood by the window, hands clasped behind his back, staring outside and looking very disturbed.

There were no informal or formal greetings, simply their leader turning, nodding and say, "Tell me your news, Buchanan."

"Of course, my lord." Gregor paused.

"What is it?"

"The council?"

"They dinna arrive until tomorrow or the next day. I would hear it now."

Gregor opened his sporran and pulled out the missive. He opened it slowly, the words he'd read a dozen times before etched into his memory.

He cleared his throat and began to read. "Here ye, here ye, lo to the man who reads this news. William Wallace, traitor to the crown, has been executed on this day, the twenty-third of August, the year of our lord 1305. As befitting his crimes, Wallace was dragged naked through the city of London. He was then drawn, hanged, but released while still alive. He was disemboweled, beheaded and then quartered. Find ye, the piece, a warning to thee and thou countrymen, to remain loyal to your good and rightful King Edward I of England." Gregor took a deep breath. "I have..." Lord, how did he tell his king he had Wallace's arm? "Samuel, can ye...?"

"Aye, my laird." Samuel retreated from the room to gather the carefully guarded chest in which their general's limb rested.

"I also have a part of him," Robert the Bruce said. "They dispatched his quarters to Scotland. I have his left leg, which they sent to Berwick. It arrived yesterday morning."

"I'm so sorry."

The king slowly turned, his face full of regret and sadness. "We've lost both our guardians now. Both of the men who rallied our country into rebellion, who stood behind me. I will fight for them. Every battle from now on will be in their honor, and I will not stop until this country sees its independence."

Gregor knelt, and so did Samuel. "Ye have my allegiance, my loyalty and the use of my body and my men for as long as ye need it."

"This country needs ye," Robert said. "More now than ever. The people will grieve deeply for Wallace, as do I. There will be many who question if we can go further."

"We can and we will. And..." Gregor hated this part of his duties, the bearer of such news. "There is more, my lord."

"Tell me."

"'Twas a Scotsman, in league with the English, who took him. Someone Wallace trusted."

"Do ye know who it is? I want his head."

"The man is ensconced in London right now, but I have

spies set out. We are working to find out his identity. The moment he steps foot back in Scotland, we will bring ye his head. And I believe, Samuel here, can get answers."

"Good." The Bruce nodded. "It smells of Comyn."

"Aye."

"I canna wait to crush that man."

"And we will. While ye have the council gathered, we should plan our next attack."

The Bruce nodded. "I agree. For now, keep this news to yourselves. And Samuel, gather what ye need to depart, sooner than later."

"Aye, my lord," Samuel agreed.

Gregor handed the Bruce the missive. "May I beg a question, my lord?"

The Bruce nodded, tucking the missive into a locked chest.

"What are the Warriors of God doing here?"

The Bruce laughed. "I wondered when ye were going to ask. Wallace's other arm was sent to Perth. They have delivered it to me."

"And the nuns?"

"They were called by the abbot. 'Tis a fact the English have been ramming down abbey walls and raping the nuns within. The sisters who've come have a very powerful Abbess as their Mother Superior. While they live simply, their wealth is greater than most abbeys in Scotland. She also has the same privileges and rights as an abbot which is unheard of. That is all I know. But I suppose, he wants to see them protected, as a loss of Nèamh Abbey would be devastating to the churches within all of Scotland."

Gregor nodded.

"Tell me why ye care, Buchanan. Why get into a fray with one of the church's warriors?"

"Pride. Nothing more."

8

The door to the refectory opened with a loud creak that made Kirstin's heart race, but it did not cease the mumbled prayers of those within. A low rumbling sounded from their throats. The air smelled of ointments, herbs and something more she couldn't quite put her finger on. The scent of a place that was generations old. As though the spirits of those who'd walked these grounds hundreds of years before had left behind a piece of themselves.

The nuns sat at rows of long oak trestle tables, hands folded on the worn tabletops, heads bent, eyes closed, lips moving.

The walls of the refectory were bare, save for a few sconces lit with tallow candles—perhaps giving the large hall some of its odd smell. There were no relics or other ornaments, only a marble statue of the Virgin Mary and her bairn Jesus that sat commandingly above a large barren hearth. Down the center of the trestle tables were lit candles, and placed before each nun was a wooden bowl, spoon and cup.

A quick glance around the stark room showed that the

abbess and abbot were not in attendance, most likely eating in her private dining area. Aunt Aileen often did that when she had a visiting member of the church. Kirstin had been asked to serve them on several occasions when the matters being discussed were super sensitive.

Tiptoeing so as not to disturb those at prayer before the meal, Kirstin scanned the room, walking between tables, a sea of hooded heads, in search of Donna. She finally found her and slipped onto the bench where a spot had been saved, and started her prayers.

"That took too long, many have asked about ye," Donna whispered, without moving, nor ceasing her prayer stance, which afforded her with a loud "Shhh" from one of the nuns on her other side.

"I am here now."

"I told them ye were having a stomach issue."

"Thank ye."

Another loud, "Shh," this time from Kirstin's side.

A moment later, a bell rang and the murmurs stopped as everyone looked toward the kitchen. Several nuns stood and exited the refectory, returning a few beats later with large, steaming pots and ladles.

A jug was being passed from one nun to the other, so Kirstin took it, then poured the thinned, light red, watered-down wine into her cup, wiggling her nose at the vinegary scent before filling Donna's and passing it down. *Vile.* It would sit in her stomach and burn for hours.

Kirstin watched the gruel, gray-tinged—most likely mutton—being plopped into bowls, the scent of garlic and onion overpowering. Loaves of brown bread were passed and Kirstin tore off a soft, warm hunk. She *hated* mutton. With a passion. The taste of it was foul. The very idea of eating a cute, fluffy sheep. She shook her head. Her aversion had started as a child when her father gave her a lamb on her sixth birthday. She'd raised that sweet thing and he'd followed her everywhere, her little cute pet.

Bandit she'd called him, because he was often stealing treats from the tables, slips of fabric left out within his reach, bones from the dogs. Anything he could get his little teeth on, he snatched. And when they'd try to get it from him, he'd lead them on a merry chase. Kirstin's maid, Meg, had called Bandit's tricks their daily exercise both physically and in patience.

When Kirstin's castle had been attacked by the MacLeod Clan, she'd lost Bandit forever. They'd had no time to do anything other than run for their lives, and even that had not worked out. Meg had been brutally murdered, her sister lost to her until recently, and her cousin Finn, still gone. Bandit had likely suffered the same fate as the other MacNeacail animals. A fate she didn't want to think on, and prayed that like his name, he'd stolen out into the wilderness where he lived a fruitful and delightful life.

So, nay, she'd not be eating any mutton gruel.

Luckily, her aunt and the other nuns at Nèamh had been sympathetic to her aversion. On mutton nights—which was several times a week—they allowed her to eat simply the bread and drink the wine. To some, missing supper might have seemed a punishment, but for her, it was a reprieve. And occasionally, an apple or pear would be placed on her pillow. Or, if Cook was in a pleasing mood, Kirstin could come and make a tart for dessert.

As the ladle-wielding nuns grew closer, she could tell by the scent of the gruel that it was indeed mutton. She resigned herself, no matter how hungry she was, that she was not going to be eating more than bread this night.

'Twouldn't be so bad, her stomach was already twisted up into knots from seeing Gregor, and eating was the last thing on her mind. The way she'd felt in his arms... Och, but if she'd not been afraid someone would come upon them, or that she'd be punished for being late to supper, she wouldn't have raced off to the refectory. It had been like finding home after being lost for so many years. His warmth, his scent, the look in his eyes, the sound of his voice, all of it had been so welcoming and she'd wanted to grasp onto it forever, to hold tight and not let go. And yet, seeing him again brought back a host of painful memories she'd rather not traverse.

What brief glimpse of happiness she'd had, disappeared from her life the moment she walked away from Castle Buchanan, and Gregor. What she'd come to have, and settle for, was a measure of quite peace and solitude. Devotion. A chance to rekindle her relationship with her sister, and to work on forgiving herself for her past transgressions.

All of that was now being disrupted.

By Gregor.

This place. This mission.

Why did Aunt Aileen have to send her here?

Kirstin swallowed away her complaints and tried to find the good in it, tried to accept that she had a duty to the church, and that perhaps this was a test to her fortitude.

The vat of mutton grew closer. Kirstin's lower lip trembled—the kind of wobbling that happened right before the contents of one's stomach reappeared.

She put her hand over her bowl when the kitchen aid reached her part of the table, but received a hiss and an elbow from the nun beside her, "Remove your hand. We all eat the same thing here."

"She does not eat mutton," Donna offered, trying to help.

"We all eat what the good Lord has seen to feed us. We are his sheep, and he has provided for us."

Sheep... Did the woman mock her on purpose?

"Nay—" Donna started, but Kirstin stilled her with a glance, and a soft touch to her forearm.

"'Tis all right." Kirstin obediently removed her hand and watched the grayish slop plop into her bowl, the smell, and sight, enough to make her throat constrict. She took a drink of her wine to keep from gagging aloud.

Donna leaned close. "Ye dinna have to eat it, Kirstin."

Kirstin nodded. She didn't plan on it.

The meal was eaten in silence. She moved the mutton around her bowl, like men moved chess pieces on a board. The bread was dull, the wine duller, but her belly was full and her mind fuller.

As the nuns finished eating in silence, each cleared their place, taking their bowls into the kitchen, and Kirstin followed suit with Donna beside her.

"What does that warrior want with ye?" Donna whispered as they walked.

"Nothing," Kirstin said with a subtle shrug, hoping her nonchalance would bore Donna enough that she'd cease her questions.

A hope that was misplaced given Donna's extreme curiosity. "Ye know him. From the time ye came to the mainland?"

Kirstin did not answer as memories assaulted her. Bonfires, laughter, dancing. Being in his arms.

"Is he a relative?"

"No relation." Her voice had gotten hoarse. As much as she wanted to hide her emotion, Donna was tugging them free.

"Hmm. He seems so familiar though, to call ye Kay. Surely only a relation—"

"Stop reaching, Donna," Kirstin snapped.

Donna giggled. "But it's the most intriguing thing I've encountered all year."

Her irritation evaporated. Donna meant no harm. She was young, inquisitive, and Kirstin couldn't hold that against her. For certes, she wished she could be just as carefree. Kirstin rolled her eyes toward Donna, a slight smile on her lips. "I can live without intrigue."

Donna bumped her slightly on the shoulder. "That is because ye are old, and ye've lived a life. I am but eighteen."

Kirstin settled her bowl in the bucket of soapy water, slipping quickly from the kitchen before anyone could notice it was full.

"I am only twenty and seven," she answered when Donna caught up.

"Aye, but that is past the age of child-bearing is it not? And, did not your aunt become abbess around that age?" Donna's voice had turned serious. She might have been young, but she was perceptive, though completely wrong about child-bearing.

Kirstin kept it to herself that her twin sister, who had borne four children with her first husband, once more found herself with child with her new husband—a man one-thousand times better than her previous mate. Seven and twenty wasn't too old. Or too late.

She touched her belly, sensing her womb contract at the thought. There was still time.

Then she shook her head, refusing to let her mind go there. Refusing to let herself think like that. There was no time. Not for her. And she was a nun. Forever in the arms of God and no mortal man.

"I think Mother Aileen was close to that age, aye, perhaps thirty," she answered instead, avoiding the child-bearing remark altogether.

"Ye see? Old." Donna giggled, knowing her comment would only get a rise out of Kirstin.

"Oh, do hush," Kirstin said, playfully, though she meant it.

Donna giggled again. So bubbly. What was in the sour wine?

"There is an orchard here." She pointed down one of the

covered walkways. "Over there I think. One I've heard rivals our own. The apples should be coming into bloom. Do ye want to walk with me before compline prayers?"

"Aye." Anything to get her mind off their current topic of conversation, and the lines in which her mind kept trying to cross.

Nuns headed in all directions, some also going toward the orchard to walk through the pathways. The aroma of the sweet apples filled the dimming sky. Kirstin took a deep breath, filling her lungs with the fragrance of the orchard.

"I wonder if we'll still be here when they harvest the apples, and if their cook would be willing to make anything special. Ye always make the best apple cakes and tarts. Oh, and your breads." Donna licked her lips, perhaps also finding the mutton gruel a bit lacking. "Maybe she'll let ye help her."

Kirstin smiled. She did love to bake, especially with apples. "Aye, I would be willing to ask, though I'm not certain any help on my part will be accepted."

At Nèamh there were certainly factions among the nuns, but even with those, for the most part their arms were open wide with acceptation. The reception they'd received here at Melrose was not so. There seemed to be an air of resentment toward them from the other nuns. As though they were the spoiled children of nobles come to mix with those of the common folk, but she knew it wasn't the case.

Kirstin rarely listened to gossip, but one of the things she did know was that abbeys were often judged on their productivity and their ability to be self-sufficient in addition to funding the church as a whole.

Nèamh far outweighed all of the other abbeys in Scotland as far as production and income, partly because of its location and reputation, they often received more daughters from wealthy households than other abbeys—which came with large dowries—but also because their abbess—Aunt Aileen—

was one of the most intelligent and cunning women Kirstin had ever had the pleasure of meeting.

Kirstin weaved between the trees, lush with green leaves and the perfectly shaped round globes of apples, yellow streaked with red. Her mouth fairly watered. Even if cook didn't want Kirstin's help with making a treat for the entire abbey, maybe she'd be willing to let Kristin into the kitchen for an hour or two to make a small batch to share with Mother Frances, as a thank you for her hospitality.

"Do ye know why we are here?" Donna asked, plucking a ripened apple from the tree and casually munching it.

"I dinna think ye were supposed to do that."

Donna grinned and shrugged with the carelessness of youth.

Kirstin sighed and ignored her own desire to pluck an apple, and when a trio of nuns walked by talking, turned Donna so they wouldn't see what she was doing, though the crunching noise was certain to be noticed.

"I'm not certain," Kirstin answered when they were once again alone. "I suspect that Mother Frances will pull me into her solar tomorrow to speak with me about it."

"I was listening in on a few conversations before dinner, and I think it has to do with money."

"Money?" Kirstin was immediately on alert. "Melrose is beautiful. Just look at all they have." Kirstin shook her head, though she wondered if that was indeed what this could be about. It would make sense, but how in the world could she be of use? "That canna be right."

"Aye, but they've been robbed before. By the English. They are honor bound by the rules of the church to let the enemy inside. Letting them in gets them looted. But, I dinna think it's about them being robbed. They want to fund something bigger."

"Like what?"

Donna shrugged, tossing her finished apple to the ground where a few birds not yet in their nests for the evening swooped down to peck at the sticky white flesh.

"They didn't gossip about the uses for the money?"

Donna rolled her eyes. "I know, ye wish me to now seek a penance for listening in."

Kirstin tugged Donna along the path until they found a bench. "That is not the case at all. I just feel so out of place. I dinna understand the reason for us being here either, and I feel like everyone but us knows."

They sat on the bench, and Kirstin kept her eye out for any nuns that might be slinking close to listen. Sneaky old biddies.

"As your elder, I absolve ye of any sin."

"What?" Donna giggled. "Ye canna do that."

Kirstin frowned. Theologically, nay, she couldn't, but that didn't mean she wasn't going to go with it. "Ye need to be our ears. I'll pay any penance on your behalf. I need ye to do this, Donna. Everyone ceases speaking when I pass. They are extra careful with me as I'm Mother Aileen's representative, but they are freer with their speech when ye are around. Use that to our advantage. I dinna like being in the dark."

"Me either." Donna picked a piece of apple skin from her teeth. "I will do it. As long as ye promise I'll not get in trouble, or on the day of reckoning be outside the pearly white gates with God pointing in the other direction."

Kirstin laughed. "I promise that willna happen from this incident, but I canna make promises from other areas of your life. In this, ye are helping me, your abbess and your abbey—your home."

Donna gazed around the orchard, nodding. "Aye. I'll keep my eyes and ears open then."

"Good." Kirstin stood, and smoothed her gray skirts. "Let us go and get our prayer books for compline then, and since the nuns will not speak with me nearby, dinna sit near me. I know at Nèamh many a rumor was spread through whispers at prayers."

A few torches already lit to illuminate their way to the guest wing of the abbey. Outside their door was a woven basket covered by a white linen. Odd.

Kirstin bent, pulling back the linen to find a dozen ripe apples and a rolled parchment tied with red ribbon.

"Who is it from?" Donna asked, clapping her hands. "So exciting."

Kirstin had an idea who it was before she tugged off the ribbon. She'd gotten little gifts like this before. A lifetime ago.

Once more memories assaulted her. Clinks of glasses, soft murmurs of love, running up the stairs, her blood charged with excitement.

She read and reread the scrawled words.

Dearest Kay,
There is an apple in the basket for every reason in which I'm sorry.
I'm sorry for being a cad. For not finding you sooner.
I'm sorry for not holding onto you when I had the chance. For letting you slip away.
I'm sorry for not telling you how much I wanted you, for taking you for granted.
I'm sorry for not saying the right things, for not being the man you needed.
I'm sorry for not protecting you, for not realizing sooner how wrong I was.
I'm sorry for not listening to you, for not letting you go now.
~G

"What does it say?"

Donna leaned over her shoulder to see, but Kirstin rolled up the parchment before she had the chance to see its contents.

Kirstin cleared her throat, swallowing down her heart, which had somehow clawed its way up her neck, lodging somewhere in the back of her mouth. Her eyes stung as tears threatened to spill. How could he do this? How could he write to her? Make her feel everything in a rush all at once. It was overwhelming. Her heart surged, her fingers trembled, arms prickled. She was cold. She was hot.

She was delighted and devastated at the same time.

Kirstin cleared her throat. "Run along to compline, Donna. I'm suddenly not feeling well at all."

"What about the apples?" Donna picked up the basket, sniffing the fruit with pleasure.

"They are yours."

For she couldn't eat his apology. Wasn't even certain how to accept it. He wasn't letting go this time.

This time.

Why, oh why, did her heart sing? Why did hope fill her at his persistence? There could be nothing between them. Not again.

And yet... She longed for it.

9

She was dizzy. Vision blurred and the wood beneath her hip where she lay on her side bit painfully into her bones. Water lapped all around her, and a slow breeze whistled on the wind. Blinking open her eyes, she saw she lay on the bottom of small fishing boat.

The boat rocked gently. Behind her an old man sat telling her a story about the loch and a sea monster that lived within its depths. His oar dipped into the water, the soft sound of a splash as he pushed them forward, slow and methodical.

"Coming to shore now, lass."

They gently hit the shore, the wood creaking as it slid against the bank. Kirstin tried to push herself upright, but she felt so weak, as though her limbs had been filled with steel instead of bone. She managed to lean up on her elbow, taking a break before she would try to sit the remainder of the way up.

The man stood, wobbly, stabbing his oar into the water and the shallow earth beneath the glittering depths, black with streaks of white from the moon.

"There's the castle. I'd best be heading back across the loch afore

that 'ole monster comes up to get me. Go on now. Ye said your kin's inside?"

Kirstin nodded, despite the water he'd given her, her tongue still felt too swollen to speak. She gazed up at the tall tower of Eilean Donan. Torches were lit along the wall, lighting up the massive and imposing structure. She'd made it. Now if only she could find her cousin. If she could even get out of this boat.

"Ye'll have to stand to get out," the old fisherman said. He reached a feeble hand forward, callused from decades of working oars and tackle.

"What's going on here?" A deep baritone voice echoed somewhere from onshore. Not the old man's, Kirstin was certain.

"Bringing this lass back to the castle. She was on the other side of the loch. Said she belongs here."

The soft crunch of boots on the grass, a swipe of reeds. A dark figure looming above her.

"I've not seen her here before," he said, his voice like a beacon. She reached instinctively out to him.

"Well, are ye calling me a liar?" the old man asked.

The younger man chuckled. "Not ye, sir."

"Her?"

"Maybe."

Kirstin managed to push up, catching sight of the man through her bleary eyes. He was large. Tall, broad. Steel glinted at his hip. A warrior. His hair was light against the night sky. Golden almost as the moon shone on it, and bound in a queue at the nape of his neck. His eyes, they studied her with curiosity and interest. Something within their depths told her she could trust him. Should trust him. And she did. For some reason, though she knew better than to trust a stranger, this man made her feel safe.

She tried to speak, only a croak coming out, and then again, "I belong here," she said, though it wasn't entirely true.

The castle had been her destination. She had to find her cousin, Finn, and rumors had spread across Loch Alsh that he'd been spotted at Eilean Donan. She intended to find out. After all, he'd been missing for the better part of six years, and he'd saved her life when the MacLeods had attacked her castle. She could have suffered the fate of her maid—death. Or the fate of her sister—abduction, possibly death. At the very least, she owed him her thanks.

"I'll take her," the man said, reaching out his hand.

Kirstin lifted a heavy arm, slipping her small hand against his larger, warm palm.

The old man straightened, somehow managing to put his wooden oar between the two of them. "Now, see here, ye'll not be ill using her."

"Never." The warrior stuck out his hand. "I am Laird Buchanan. I will see to it that she is returned to wherever she belongs. Ye have my word."

The older man gripped Laird Buchanan's forearm. "Aye, then."

Strong arms slipped beneath her weakened body. Why hadn't she planned better? She should have packed a satchel full of food, a water skin. A blanket. But instead, she'd rushed away from the abbey with nothing but the gown on her back. If not for the old man finding her across the loch and offering her passage, she might have laid there until she was dead.

She was lifted into the air, her chilled body sinking against the warmth of her savior's muscled form. Kirstin wrapped her arms around his neck and rested her head on his shoulder. He smelled good. Like leather and pine. Smelling him only reminded her how much she must reek, and if she wasn't so exhausted and weak she might have been embarrassed.

"Thank ye," she whispered to the old man, and to this new strong laird.

The old man muttered something, and then she felt herself floating, weightless in this warrior's arms. "Where should I take ye?" he asked.

"My cousin. Is he here? Finn MacNeacail."

"I've not heard of your cousin. But I will look. In the meantime, I will take ye back to the castle."

"Is it your castle?"

"Nay, lass. A friend's. But ye'll be safe there."

When she woke some time later, she was tucked beneath a thick blanket in the middle of a massive bed. Light streamed through a window. And dying embers lined the hearth. She sat straight up, unsure of where she was. The room was empty, but looked to be a man's room if the set of boots and various weapons were any indication.

Oh, dear, heavens. What had she done?

She yanked back the covers. She was only in her chemise.

Kirstin's hands flew to her face and she gasped.

She'd never been with a man before. She wasn't even married! Oh, now her reputation was sullied. She must have... the warrior from the night before...

Had she been so exhausted that she'd slept through it?

Tears sprung to her eyes and she tugged up her chemise expecting to see blood on her thighs. But there was nothing. She wasn't sore either.

From the stories she'd heard from the nuns at Nèamh, she would have suffered both, nay?

The door handle jiggled, and she quickly shoved down her chemise and tugged the blankets up. Limbs trembled. Teeth chattered.

A servant entered, a warm smile on her wrinkled face. Her arisaid was worn, her belly plump. She looked happy and well-cared for. "His lairdship said ye'd be sleeping. We brought ye a bath and some food to break your fast."

"His lairdship?" Kirstin asked.

"Laird Buchanan. He serves Robert the Bruce."

"Whose castle is this?"

"Eilean Donan?" The woman chuckled as servants filed into the chamber. "My where did ye come from, lass? The Bruce is holding the castle."

Kirstin tucked her knees up to her chest. "I am from Skye."

"A fairy, then."

That made her smile. As a child she'd often run through the fields of heather pretending to be a fairy. "My name is K—Kay."

"Well, Laird Buchanan says we are to see to your comfort. I'm Anne if ye need anything." The maid put her hands on her hips and started ordering the servants about.

"Thank ye."

"Ye're a lady. I can tell by your speech."

'Twas on the tip of her tongue to tell the servant she was a lady born who'd taken sanctuary in an abbey for the last six years, but she kept that part to herself. "Aye. I got lost. Your laird was kind enough to give me shelter for the night."

Anne nodded. "He's a kind man."

The crew of servants finished setting up a bath and filled the table with what looked like a feast for a dozen men, not simply her.

"Shall I help ye with your bath, Lady Kay?"

Kirstin shook her head. "I can manage." When Anne started to leave, Kirstin called out to her, "Can I have a cinnamon stick?"

"Aye. I'll bring ye some up."

As soon as she was alone, Kirstin stuffed a fruit tart into her mouth, crumbs spilling, she was so hungry. She gulped down a glass of goat's milk, then shrugged out of her chemise, sinking into the warm depths of the bath.

Dried lavender and rosemary floated on top of the water, their scent calming.

Kirstin washed with the ball of soap and linen cloth, and when Anne returned with the cinnamon stick, Kirstin scrubbed her teeth, then stood from the tub, reaching for the thick linen left to dry herself. A fire in the hearth warmed the room so she didn't freeze from the water on her skin. She climbed from the milk-soapy bath, feeling clean.

But there was a problem. The only clothes she had were the dirty chemise and dark woolen gown—both were nowhere to be seen.

Oh, no...

Was this when the 'nice' Laid Buchanan would return, holding her hostage, naked? If he'd not used her body the night before, would he now?

A knock sounded at the door, and she tossed the towel aside and sank quickly back into the tub, unsure of how else to hide herself so that her skin was no longer exposed.

"My lady?" That voice, his, stroked over her skin in such a delicious way, she might have questioned whether or not she'd initiated what could have happened the night before.

"I am not presentable. Do not enter," she called.

"I will not look. I promise."

"Nay!"

But he was opening the door. Backing into the room. Facing away from her. Not looking.

She narrowed her eyes, waiting for him to turn around. To grab her out of the tub and—

Why did that thought send a shiver over her skin? Wanton, wicked woman!

He carried something that he laid down on the bed. Kirstin's eyes widened when she realized what it was. A new chemise. A new gown.

"The other ones looked as though they'd seen better days. Our tailor was able to discern your size and had these taken in for ye. I'll leave ye to your bath."

"Wait!" She sat straighter in the tub, then sunk quickly back in when she realized sitting up exposed the tops of her breasts. She had to know what exactly had happened between them. "Did we... Did I..."

He chuckled softly, still facing away. "Nothing happened, lass. I'd not take advantage of ye. As I said, ye're safe with me."

"Why are ye being so kind?" She was confused, and yet she felt drawn to him.

"Because. I have a sister. If she were to wash up on shore, I'd want someone to do the same for her."

Kirstin smiled, feeling suddenly warm. And safe. Safer than she'd felt in years. "Thank ye. I dinna know how I can ever repay ye."

"My kindness needs no payment, lass. Enjoy your bath." And then in two long strides, he was out the door.

❦

KIRSTIN WOKE WITH A START, THE MEMORIES OF HER PAST, of Gregor so fresh she could have been reliving them. Sweat slicked over her skin. Skin that felt alive with memory. With want.

She curled up, rolling onto her side, hugging her pillow, recalling how she used to lay in bed beside Gregor, holding onto him just the same way. The sound of his breathing as he slept, the little groan of pleasure he made when he woke and pulled her into his arms.

The moon shone through her single window, lighting on the basket of apples. The basket of apologies.

She couldn't deny that the gesture was sweet. Thoughtful. Gregor had always been that way. Until the end, when he'd railed about the future they couldn't have together.

A piece of her had died that night.

Well, at least, she'd thought a piece of her had died. But whatever part of her heart had hidden itself the last decade awakened the moment she saw him on the road. The moment his eyes met hers and she felt struck. Like an invisible force had grabbed hold of her heart, and yanked it from its tightly locked box back out into the open.

There was no denying what was in her heart.

But could she trust it?

She'd done that once before and look what had happened.

Oh, how she wished her sister, Brenna, was here with her now. She could ask her what to do. Brenna had been miserable in her first marriage. Forced to marry a monster at age twelve, she'd been tormented until his death the previous year. Despite years and years of anguish, she'd managed to open her heart again. And had fallen deeply in love with her new husband, Gabriel. She was blessed with a beautiful family. Brenna was happy, ecstatic even. At peace.

Was that a possibility for Kirstin?

With Gregor?

They'd had happiness once. And it would seem he wanted to find it again with her. If the basket full of apologies meant anything.

Kirstin rolled over onto her back, arm flung over her face and stared up at the darkened ceiling.

Donna's soft snores filled the room, but Kirstin's thoughts and worries were louder.

"What should I do?" she whispered to no one.

She was torn between what her heart yearned for and what her mind told her was a mistake. If she opened up to Gregor again, there was every possibility he would shun her when she least expected it. But that was a risk one took when in love, wasn't it? Was it worth the risk? Again?

And then there was the backlash from her abbey, from the church. What would Aunt Aileen think? She could hear her aunt's voice clearly in her mind: *There is a path ye must follow. This is your path.*

Is this what her aunt had in mind? She doubted it. Aunt Aileen had once wanted Kirstin to study to become an abbess. By sending her off as emissary, wasn't her aunt in fact saying that Kirstin had a powerful position at the abbey?

Why didn't it feel like that was the path for her?

But, Kirstin had already followed her heart once.

Perhaps it wasn't such a good idea to follow it again. Especially since she wasn't certain she could come back from any pain that doing so might cause. The last time she'd been with Gregor, the disappointment and hurt had nearly broken her.

Her hands slipped to the small of her abdomen as they often did when she thought back. The slight swell of extra skin there the only evidence that she'd once carried a life. Phantom kicks of a child that had grown inside her. A child created in love. A child birthed in pain. A child whose heart stopped beating only a moment after he took his first breath.

Gregor's child.

Hot tears streamed from her eyes, falling into her ears.

Kirstin wasn't naïve enough to not to admit that now, after nearly a decade, if she had told him the truth, that their lovemaking had created a life inside her womb, maybe he wouldn't have turned her away. That he would have changed his mind. But then where would she have been? Trapped in a marriage with a man who only wed her out of obligation? Would she have her child in her arms now?

She couldn't go through that loss again. She had to be strong, no matter how hard her heart was shoving her toward Gregor. No matter if she dreamed of him every night.

That was a life she could never have back.

10

How low could a man sink?

Gregor stood in the center of the open cloister, the darkened sky twinkling with stars and a sliver of moon, when the bells rang for lauds at midnight just so he could catch a glimpse of Kirstin. He wasn't ashamed, but Gregor was certain if his men knew the reason he stalked the abbey this night, they'd rib him until his skin chafed.

There was an easy solution to that dilemma—he just wouldn't tell them.

He was their leader. Their chief. Their laird. Their general when at war.

But being in love with a woman, the heart-pounding, ache in the pit of his stomach, couldn't get her out of his mind type of love, was not something a man of his stature or power succumbed to or admitted to. Was it?

Well, Samuel certainly loved Catriona that way, and if he were to really think on it, there were plenty of men with his same status that loved their wives. So he wasn't completely alone in being in love.

But did any of them love a nun who may not love them back?

Did any of them love a woman who could never be theirs?

Gregor growled under his breath in frustration.

The fates were certainly putting him through a trial.

All was still quiet, no one had yet to appear since the bells had rung. Gregor leaned against a column, and crossed his arms over his chest. Would they ever come out? He didn't know how much longer his patience would last. Maybe a few minutes more.

Earlier, he'd watched from the shadows, as she'd read his note, and then passed the apples—his apology—off to her companion. Would she not accept his apology? Or did she no longer like apples?

The lass made the best apple cakes he'd ever had in his life. There would not be a sudden change in her palette, except for when it came to him.

Let me go... We must say goodbye, again... We dinna always get what we want.

The words she'd spoken earlier that evening haunted him. She was letting him go. Saying goodbye, and telling him to get over whatever feelings he might have. But he couldn't pass off his feelings as easily as she'd passed off the apples.

Maybe he needed to get out of the abbey for the night. Take a visit to the town, find the local tavern, pick a light-skirt to spend the night with and then all thoughts of Kirstin would disappear. There was a chance that his feelings weren't as strong for her as he thought they were. It could just be a trick of his mind, his memory wishing for the past to come back to him. They had good times. Great times. Magical times.

Anyone would want that back. Not just him.

Gregor straightened as a line of nuns emerged from a covered passage, their lanterns held out to light their path.

He sank into the shadows so as not to be seen. The sisters' robes swished in the night, their slippered feet whispering over the flagstone. From across the way, he spied another line, the visiting monks and abbot, the tops of their shaved heads shiny in the moonlight. Still more came as the Warriors of God who'd been camping outside the walls reentered to attend. They were a fearsome group, and he wasn't yet sure if he could trust them. John, despite having taken vows, seemed a little too interested in Kirstin.

And then hurried footsteps came from yet another passage—the guest quarters where Kirstin and her companion stayed. Gregor strained to see her beautiful, angelic face.

But, disappointingly, the steps were single. And not Kirstin's. 'Twas her companion, looking flustered as she hurried to join the others.

Disappointment pinched his insides, and Gregor knew it was time for a reprieve. Time to give his other plan a chance. The plan where he forgot about Kirstin. And lay all his memories to rest. She didn't want to be his. Couldn't be. She was different. Damaged. And he knew he was probably the cause of it, but he didn't know how to make it better, other than to leave her alone. As much as it pained him, and as much as his heart warred for him to change his mind, he knew what he had to do.

Her companion met his gaze as she passed, and a subtle shake of her head told him Kirstin wasn't coming. He resisted the urge to grab Donna's arm to pelt her with questions. Resisted the urge to traverse that corridor and knock on Kirstin's door.

And so what if she did happen to change her mind and come strolling toward the nave? What was he going to do, beg her to abandon the service so she could stay out in the cloister, at midnight, alone, to talk to him?

Lord, he was an idiot.

Gregor grunted and turned, heading toward the stable where his charger was housed. To the village, then.

He saddled his horse, and roused the stable boy to shut the gates behind him.

Gregor flipped the lad a coin, who caught it, eyes gleaming, then quickly stuffed it into small pouch at his hip. "Only tell Sir Samuel that I've gone."

Nodding his head emphatically, the lad said, "Aye, my laird."

As soon as the gates closed behind him, Gregor's men surged toward him to find out what he was up to.

"I need to think," he said. "I'm going to search the perimeter."

None of them questioned their laird, as it was not unusual for him to do just that. He urged his mount into a gallop toward the village, where a few lights still shone—the taverns most likely.

The short wooden wall, more like a fence, that surrounded the village was manned by a young lad, not yet twenty years, but close. He was asleep, a flagon of something clutched against his chest, his snores loud enough to let any outlaw within a mile know the place was not under guard. Gregor shook his head, and still sitting atop his mount, nudged the boy's shoulder with his boot.

"Wake, ye lazy maggot."

The lad startled. "Aye, sir, sorry sir."

"If the town is attacked, then any life lost would be on your head for not warning anyone."

The lad leapt to his feet, clutching his mug like a sword until he realized what he was doing. "Are ye here to attack the town?"

Gregor rolled his eyes. "If I was the one attacking, think I'd wake ye and tell ye to do your job?"

He shook his head, eyes bleary. "Nay, sir."

"Sober up, else I am compelled to tell your master to relieve ye of your position." Gregor rode through the gate and up the main road, past dark houses, shops and toward the lights of the tavern.

Another young lad, half-asleep, sat outside the tavern.

"Shall I take your horse to the stables, sir?" he asked.

"Aye. Feed him the best oats if they are available." Another coin flipped and caught, the same gleam of eyes. Did no one reward the lads of late? They'd both seemed surprised.

Gregor entered the tavern. Drunken men sat around tables, slurping ale and shooting whisky, tearing into roasted birds and crumbling bread on their chins as they stuffed it into their mouths. The talk was bawdy, the laughter grating. 'Haps this was a bad idea after all. He'd likely start a fight with one of the bastards before he had a chance to find a wench.

Gregor took a deep breath, summoning the strength to step further into the tavern. He had to do this. His mind—and body—burned for Kirstin. If he didn't expel some of it now, he was likely to go mad.

There were a few wenches serving ale, and one of them would have to do, so he nodded to the proprietor and found a table in the corner. Gregor watched as the lassies leaned over the men, giving them, and him, an unobscured view of all their assets before giggling and plopping down in their laps. One of the wenches, a pretty lass, if not a bit used looking, with chestnut hair and squinty brown eyes, caught his gaze and sidled over.

"What can I get ye, big fella?"

"Whisky."

She leaned closer, showing off her ample breasts. "Is that... all?" A clear invitation.

Gregor grinned and winked. "Maybe I'll have a bit of that

bird." He nodded toward what looked to be the kitchen, serving up capons like they were water.

She slid her finger along his shoulder toward the collar of his shirt and tugged. Not even an ounce of his blood stirred. "A tease, ye are. Name's Molly, and I'm happy to give ye *whatever* ye want."

Molly sauntered toward the kitchen, and Gregor sank back in his chair. This was going to be harder than he thought. Molly was willing—but was he?

For now, he settled down and listened in on the conversations around him. One in particular piqued his interest. Looked to be four locals, but their sizes and weapons indicated they were likely mercenaries, warriors for hire. None of their plaids matched in color, and their boots were worn. Scars on their arms and faces. Definitely mercenaries.

"But, where *is* he?" one of them was saying, a fist slammed onto the table.

"Rumor is he was taken by one of his own, to England." The largest of the four, a man with ginger hair and a long braided beard to match, leaned forward, talking conspiratorially.

"And he's probably dead," the third man, a scar where his eyebrow should have been, said. "Killed off by the bloody *Sassenachs*."

They had to be talking about William Wallace. Gregor sank further into the shadows, so as not to draw attention, though he intently listened to their conversation. 'Haps it was a good idea after all to get away from the abbey to assess what people knew about their current political situation. The Bruce would not be pleased to know how quickly the rumors were flying. They needed to get a handle on it soon, before it was too late for him to speak out on the matter publicly. One could only hope it would be before everyone made up their minds as to what they believed had happened.

"Aye, they'd not keep him alive," Ginger-Beard said.

"They'd not keep him in one piece either. Fucking savages. They've torn our country, men and women apart. The devil's spawn they are," said Eyebrow.

"Ye think Longshanks and all the bloody Sassenachs fornicated with his remains, cavorting with the devil?" Ginger-Beard laughed.

Gregor gritted his teeth, restraining himself from getting up and pummeling the bastards into the ground for even suggesting such a thing. The man, their legendary guardian, should be revered. Respected. And remembered for who he was and what he did for the country, not for what the Sassenachs would do with his body. There had been no one like Wallace before and Gregor doubted there'd be anyone with as much conviction, fearlessness, and intelligence after.

Eyebrow punched the vile gossiper in the shoulder. "Shut the fuck up, ye disgusting arse. That's Wallace ye're talking about."

At least one of the four seemed disturbed by their conversation. The fourth was silent, staring, and either listening intently or about to pass out from too much liquor.

A man from another table leaned back, the legs of his chair wobbling as he addressed the foursome. "What ye saying about Wallace?" he slurred.

"Nothing mate," spoke the silent one, his voice scratchy.

"Bring another whisky for my friend!" Ginger-Beard shouted to a raven-haired wench, pointing to the table where the man leaned back in his chair.

Molly came back to Gregor with whisky, a mug of ale and a plate full of meat on her tray. She settled the items in front of him and smiled.

"Got what ye asked for. What else can I get for ye?" Her gaze roved over his body, settling on the spot where table covered his cock.

Gregor grinned, shot the whisky down his throat, then scooted his chair back and pulled her onto his lap. He knew what she wanted. What he should do to get Kirstin off his mind, but every look Molly gave him, even the feel of her too-bony arse on his thighs made him uneasy.

She stroked his face, pushed her breasts against his chest and leaned in close to kiss his neck. Her breath was fetid, her body odor not much better. She made him feel sick to his stomach.

Poor lass.

He couldn't do this. Couldn't have another woman. And it wasn't just because she didn't smell good.

'Twas because she wasn't Kirstin.

Nobody could replace her. He closed his eyes, trying to imagine Kirstin as he wrapped his arm around Molly's back and nuzzled her neck.

Dammit it to hell!

This wasn't going to work.

He'd left the abbey intent on finding peace inside another woman. Intent on forgetting his past and his feelings for Kirstin, but all he'd succeeded in doing was thoroughly disgusting himself. Gregor lifted Molly and set her on her feet. He reached into his sporran and gave her a handful of coins—twice what he would have paid for her services.

"Another whisky, lass."

Her eyes shimmered at the coin, not at all offended. He paid her more than any of the other bastards in the tavern.

"Why, aren't ye a right gentleman? Ye can have all the whisky ye want."

She skipped away to do his bidding, and Gregor peeled off a piece of meat, listening to the conversations going on around him. The drunkard at the other table had been satisfied with his free drink, and the other four men huddled closer, lowering their voices to keep anyone else from overhearing their conversation.

Gregor had to listen intently.

Ginger-Beard, licked his lips, and rubbed his hands together. "There's a reward for anyone willing to capture and bring Wallace's enemies to Berwick. A trade—coin for Wallace supporters. And not a little bit of coin either. A whole sack of it. Enough to live like a baron for a year at least."

"Really?"

"Aye."

"And ye'd be willing to switch sides for coin?" Eyebrow said, while the other two remained silent. At least two of the men seemed incredulous.

Gregor's blood boiled, his hand moving to the sword at his hip. If the tavern emptied just a little more, he'd take all four of these bastard's heads, maybe give Eyebrow a chance to redeem himself and then present them to the Bruce in the morning.

"Did ye not hear me, ye bloody fool? I said a man could live like a baron for a year. I, however, dinna need to live like a noble. The coin could help me live the life of a drifter, give me a good bed and a willing wench to suck my cock for five years. I'd not have to lift my blade, only the one between my thighs."

One of the men grunted, and while the other man was nodding his agreement, Eyebrow looked on the verge of toppling the table and murdering the fool.

"Do ye truly think the English will give ye a reward? They probably want ye to do their dirty work. Then, they'll kill ye, too." Eyebrow shook his head. "Ye're a Scot, they dinna want ye to live."

Ginger-Beard shook his head. "I heard the Scot who

turned in Wallace was rewarded with enough coin to make him live like a king for the rest of his days."

"Who did ye hear that from?"

"Doesna matter." The man sat back, arms crossed over his chest.

Gregor's stomach soured. Clearly, he needed to have a more intimate conversation with that fellow. The cur knew too much. Even more than Gregor had been privy to.

Gregor nodded to Molly, and she rushed forward pouring whisky into his glass, simpering at him and wiggling her hips.

"Do me a favor, lass?" Gregor asked, using his most persuasive tone and slipping another coin into her hand.

"Anything." She licked her lips, still clearly not catching the hint that he wasn't going to bed her.

"See that man? The one with the braided beard?"

She glanced discreetly behind her. "Aye."

"Entice him out back for me. Tell him ye've been watching him all night, and this tupping is for free."

Molly's eyes widened, and she looked at him oddly, biting her lip.

"Ye'll not be tupping him, lass, and the coin I gave ye is for the task of luring him out, aye?"

She nodded emphatically, took a shot of whisky from his table, then sauntered over to the man with the braid and whispered in his ear. Ginger-Beard let out a whoop of excitement and slapped Molly on the arse. He downed his beer, then stood, picking her up and tossing her over his shoulder, before heading to the back door of the tavern.

The mongrel was bigger than he'd looked, but that only made the challenge all the sweeter. Slowly standing, he kept his eyes on the three friends as he slipped from the tavern, no one the wiser.

11

'Twas dark out back of the tavern. The buildings were close together, hiding the light of the moon. Gregor waited a moment to let his eyes adjust to the darkness then glanced up and down the alleyway.

He could hear the grunts of the man, soft, pretend whimpers from the tavern wench and the sounds of sloppy kissing. Gregor ground his teeth in disgust. The lout worked fast. Hopefully, not too fast.

Rounding the corner, Gregor spied their writhing shapes against the wall. The man, so intent on his purpose, did not hear Gregor approach. He had his mouth all over Molly's breasts. She, however, did hear him, and looked at him wide-eyed as she was molested. Thank goodness, the man was so interested in her breasts that it kept him from tupping her just yet as Gregor had promised.

Pulling his sword from his scabbard, Gregor tiptoed forward and held the tip at the man's neck.

"What the—" Ginger-Beard rounded on him, tossing the wench aside, who caught herself against the wall before falling.

"Back inside, lass," Gregor said with a grin. "Dinna let his friends see ye."

Even in the dim light coming from the windows of the tavern he could make out the fear on her face. She nodded and rushed around the building, disappearing from view.

"Who are ye?" Ginger-Beard asked, indignation ripe in his tone, and not an ounce of fear. He'd reached for the sword at his side, but Gregor had already disarmed him.

"Looking for this?" He tossed the sword aside, ignoring his question. "I need to ask ye a few questions."

"I got no answers for ye, only the tip of my sword." He stared past Gregor where his sword lay on the ground.

"Only the tip?" Gregor goaded. "My, that is a sad thing to hear from a warrior. Ye, see, if ye dinna answer my questions, I'm going to run ye through with the entire length of my blade. And little good your *tip* is going to do way over there."

"I'd like to see ye try, ye bloody fucking fool."

Gregor laughed. The man's bluster truly was entertaining. The lout could barely stand, and he grappled with swollen fingers toward his lifted leg and the *sgian dubh* tucked into his hose. Gregor let him try to grab it, but only to give the man some hope before he jabbed the point of his sword against the knot at Ginger-Beard's throat, nicking the skin at his neck when he resisted.

Gregor tsked. "Afraid that's not going to work for ye, mate." Gregor forced the man to back up against the wall.

Ginger-Beard frantically swiped at the small trickle of blood. "Ye cut me! Ye'll pay for this."

Gregor rolled his eyes. "Answer my questions, and ye might walk away from this."

"I'm not answering a damn thing!" Spittle flew from Ginger's mouth, landing in the thick hairs of his beard.

"What is your name?" Gregor asked.

"None of your damned business!"

"What clan is embarrassed to call ye their own?"

"Fuck ye."

"I see we are making progress," Gregor said sarcastically. "Let me try something else."

Gregor slammed his knees into the man's ballocks, feeling the crush of the man's precious jewels.

Ginger doubled over, his eyes bulging, veins in his neck pulsing, a groan that could wake the dead on his lips.

Taking a deep breath, Gregor tried once more, "Again, your name and clan?"

"Fuc—"

Gregor didn't let him finish his insult, but instead slammed his forearm against the man's neck, pressing him back against the wall, cutting off his air.

"While ye were in there wetting your throat with whisky after whisky, I remained sober. A fight between the two of us will only end up one way—me winning. So ye'd better answer my fucking questions, else I drain the life from ye."

Ginger nodded, making gurgling noises. "Name's... Alan."

"Clan?"

"Was MacLeod."

"And now?"

"I'm without one."

"Why?"

Alan shrugged. "Laird died, and his bitch wife remarried a man who kicked me and my friends out."

"Interesting." Gregor pursed his lips in thought. "Takes a lot for a laird to displace a member of his clan."

"What would ye know of it?"

Gregor shrugged, not seeing any sense in telling this man his business. "What do ye know of Wallace?"

"Nothing."

Gregor chuckled menacingly, then pressed hard on the man's neck again, coming within an inch of the bastard's face.

"I dinna want to play any more games with ye, Alan. I need my answers now."

"I've never met Wallace."

"But ye've heard rumors."

Alan's eyes frantically searched the back alley, perhaps thinking his friends would soon come to his aid.

"Ah, do ye think your friends are coming? They aren't. They watched ye leave with a willing wench over your shoulder. Doubt they'll come looking for ye until dawn. And if ye think they'll come when they see the wench return to work, they might, but I doubt it given they are just as drunk as ye are. They'd not know one wench from another."

Alan grunted, his hands wrestling with Gregor's arm, but realizing that he wasn't going to break free of Gregor's grip, or be saved by his friends, he stilled.

"What do ye want to know?" he asked reluctantly.

Gregor stared the man in the eye, not showing any signs of wavering. "Tell me what ye know of Wallace."

"Just what ye heard me tell my friends."

"Repeat it." Gregor loosened his hold on the man's neck.

Alan repeated what he'd said about Wallace being taken by one of their own. *Betrayed.* For coin! That the Scotsman guilty of treason had accepted a hefty reward from the English for his service to them, and that a new bounty was on the head of every one of Wallace's allies.

"Have ye told anyone other than your friends?"

Alan shook his head, but his eyes told a different story. He wasn't telling Gregor the truth.

He was definitely hiding something.

"Ye lie. Who did ye tell?"

"No one..." He coughed as Gregor's arm tightened on his neck. "I swear."

Gregor punched him in the ribs, satisfied with the man's pain-filled grunt. "Wrong answer, Alan, and ye're wasting my time. What good are ye to me alive if ye canna tell me what I need to know?"

"Please, dinna kill me. I'll tell ye. I've only told one other."

"Who?"

His words came quick now, filled with fear. "There was a man, he was standing near me when I heard it for the first time. He overheard and questioned me about it."

"Do ye know the man's identity?"

Alan shook his head, and this time, Gregor believed him.

"Who did ye hear the rumors from? Where were ye?"

"From a mercenary last week. We'd just finished a stint with a laird near the border."

"What laird?"

"MacLellan."

Gregor didn't know much about MacLellan other than he held a small holding that bordered the southern lines of the Maxwell, Gordon and McGie clans, and the north of England. "What did he need a bunch of wastrels like ye for?"

"There'd been a lot of raids by the English, and since they are right on the border, he needed help securing his lands. We fought off raiders and guarded the entry points while laborers built a high fence."

"Where is the man who told ye the rumors about Wallace?"

"Dead." Something dark came into Alan's eyes.

Gregor's stomach soured. He'd caught himself a real devil. "Ye killed him."

Alan didn't answer.

"Ye killed him, and the man who witnessed ye murdering the bastard is the one who ye told about the reward. Payment for keeping your secret. Ye should be hanged."

Hatred flared in the man's eyes, and he bared his teeth. Pushing his neck against Gregor's arm, he growled, "What business is it of yours?"

Gregor laughed and shook his head. "If only I could tell ye. We'd get a good chuckle out of your reaction. But I canna. So I'll just have to laugh to myself. But, bad news, jackhole, ye're coming with me."

Gregor rammed the hilt of his sword against Alan's head, knocking him out. Thankful for the dark, he tied the man up easy enough, and then carried the heavy burden to his horse, making apologies to the animal for the extra weight.

Alan never stirred on the ride back to the abbey. When his men and the Warriors of God who were on sentry, saw him return, they headed toward him, brows raised in question.

"This can't be good," Owen, John's second-in-command of the Warriors of God said.

"A prisoner, my laird?" Fingall asked, lifting the flop of hair to see Alan's face.

"Aye. A traitor to Scotland."

"Shall we watch him for ye?" Collin asked, grinning. "Be happy to question him if ye like?" Collin was always looking for a fight, and happened to be one of the best at interrogating prisoners.

"Sacrifice him?" Owen asked.

Did the Warriors of God sacrifice people? Gregor looked at the man, studying him, only to see there was a slight twinge of humor in his gaze. "Nay. I need him inside. But I'll be returning in a few minutes, and I'll need the two of ye to come with me," he said to Fingall and Collin. "We've got a few more to round up."

True to his word, the young stable hand was waiting for him, opening the gates. His eyes turned as wide as a full moon upon spying the unconscious man draped over the horse.

"Does the abbey have..." Gregor started, then thought

better of it. They wouldn't have a dungeon. "Where does the abbess keep those who need to be quarantined?"

The stable lad glanced at the knocked out mercenary then back at Gregor, eyes wide.

"There is a room, but only the abbess has the keys."

Lauds would have ended long before now, and the abbess was likely sleeping already. "I'll keep him contained in my chamber then until dawn."

The stable hand nodded, gripping onto the horse's reins. "Do ye need me to help, sir?"

Gregor dismounted, and hauled the large mercenary off the horse, bearing his weight over his shoulder.

"Nay, lad, ye've helped me much already." Momentarily balancing the man on his shoulder with only one hand to steady him, Gregor gave the lad another coin.

"Thank ye, my laird."

"On second thought, I need ye to guard my chamber."

"Aye, my laird."

"After ye tend my horse, and give him an apple, come to my chamber."

"Aye, my laird." The lad led his horse toward the stable, a spring in his young step.

Gregor headed toward his chamber with his prisoner. The Bruce would not be pleased to know men were already spreading word of Wallace's demise, nor would he be happy that they were conspiring to round up Wallace's allies.

He deposited Alan on his chamber floor, and checked the man's unconscious form for any hidden weapons. Then he removed his sporran, and boots. A man was weakened with no boots. He even took the pin holding his plaid in place, not willing to risk what a prick from that pin could do.

Satisfied he'd thoroughly disarmed the cur, he gathered all of his own personal items and shoved everything into a satchel. Alan was still out cold on the floor, and probably would be for at least another hour. Gregor locked the door behind him, pleased to see the stable lad had returned.

"What's your name?" he asked.

"Peter."

"Dinna let anyone in, Peter, and most certainly dinna let the man out."

Peter nodded. "On my honor, my laird."

Gregor roused Samuel, giving him an overview of his night, leaving out the part that he'd wanted to get over his feelings for Kirstin in the arms of another. That was a moot point now. He'd learned it was impossible. Leaving his personal items, and those he'd gathered off of Alan, in Samuel's chamber, they returned to the main gate. Gregor tasked Owen, though he was not under his command, to man the gate until they returned, and to apprehend the prisoner should he escape. And should his friends come looking for him, they were to be arrested in the name of treason.

By the time they'd made it back to town, the other three mercenaries were gone.

"Damn," Gregor growled.

"Sir?" 'Twas Molly. She slinked forward, a bruise darkening her cheek.

"What happened?" Gregor demanded, guilt already riddling his gut before she even spoke.

"They hit me. Stole my coin."

Gregor knew who. "The bastard's friends?"

She nodded. "The one was plowed, but the other two, weren't as drunk as ye might think. When they saw me come in without him, they tugged me out back to search for him. They saw a few droplets of blood on the ground. Thought I'd harmed him. I said the blood was mine, spilled by their friend, and that he was probably sleeping it off, as I'd told Mr. Whisky."

"I'm sorry, lass, that they hurt ye. I never wanted that."

"'Tis all right, my laird. Ye paid me well, and I've been hurt worse before."

That didn't sit well with Gregor. He wanted to speak to the proprietor of the establishment. "Is Mr. Whisky the owner of the tavern?"

"Aye."

But before he did speak to the man, he had to finish questioning Molly, afore her employer silenced her. "Do ye think the men believed ye?"

"Aye." She touched her cheek.

"Ye did well, lass."

"Where did they go?" Samuel asked.

Molly shrugged. "After they attacked me, Mr. Whisky threw them out."

"Where's Mr. Whisky now?"

"Right here." The burly man Gregor had seen behind the bar earlier pushed forward. "What are ye doing back, troublemaker?"

"I'm no troublemaker. I've come to apprehend the three men who assaulted your wench."

Mr. Whisky grunted. "Ain't nothing she's never had afore," he grumbled. "No use in making an arrest."

"They are wanted for other reasons as well," Gregor said. "If ye dinna want to share where they went, then 'haps, ye'd like us to take ye instead?"

The tavern owner held up his hands, stepping back and shaking his head. "Nay, nay, nay. They be resting up in the town stables."

Gregor turned to leave, when Molly pressed her hand to his sleeve. "Sir... My coin?"

"I'll get it back for ye," he promised. It was the least he could. Hell, he felt incredibly guilty about the bruises and humiliation she endured. Wished he'd not gotten her involved. But, it was the only way to get the man out back to question him without his friends being the wiser. 'Twas a matter of the country's defense.

They left the tavern, and Samuel nudged Gregor in the ribs. "Have a nice evening with Molly?"

Gregor scowled. "'Twas not like that."

"What was it like then, my laird? All due respect, of course."

Gregor punched Samuel in the arm, hard. "She helped me to get that jackhole alone. Probably why she was targeted by his friends." *The bastards*.

"She's a pretty lass," Fingall said.

"And looking for a man to be kind to her," Gregor said. "Unfortunately, I dinna have the leisure to be that man." Leisure had nothing to do with it, but his men didn't need to know that.

"I can be kind," Collin said with a snicker, earning him a push from Fingall.

"Enough talk of tail, let us get these arseholes," Gregor said when the stable came into view.

A darkened wood building, rose up against the night sky. The doors were slightly ajar. Snores of men and snorts of horses echoed out into the night.

"Light a torch, Collin," Gregor ordered. "Sounds like a hundred men camping out inside. We'll not find 'em until dawn if we canna see."

Fingall pushed the barn doors open while Collin held up the torch. Gregor searched the sea of dark faces until he found the three maggots curled up beside one another. There was only one problem. The mercenaries were likely to put up quite a fight once roused, which might bring a dozen others to their cause. Gregor and his men could take on a dozen on their own, but not several dozen.

"We have to get them out quietly," Gregor said.

Samuel held up the rope they'd brought and Fingall

grabbed it, then he and Gregor tied them up while Colin held the light. The men roused, only after gags had been shoved into their mouths. All the noise they made was muted, and barely stirred anyone around them, beyond a snort and a grumble.

Gregor grinned, chucking one of them on the chin. "Morning, sunshine. Ye're coming with us."

Their thrashing and calls for justice were barely noticeable above the sounds of snoring and farting the rest of the brutes inside the stable were making. Gregor's grin grew. An easy extraction.

They carried the three men out, tossed them over the extra horses they'd brought then quickly disappeared from the village—mission accomplished.

Now if only Gregor knew the name of the mercenary who witnessed Alan murdering the MacLellan man. But he'd find out soon enough.

Though the night started with him going to the tavern for one reason, it had ended up being a blessing in disguise. Aye, he'd not been able to complete his earlier task, and he wasn't sure he ever would. Kirstin was engraved in his mind forever. No one could ever replace her, and he had to stop searching.

With four prisoners to question and a plot to take down Wallace's allies afoot, he would be plenty busy. Too busy to think about Kirstin. To yearn for her and for what might have been. Aye, too distracted he'd be now, dealing with traitors and matters of national security.

That was a blessing. Someone up above was looking out for him.

"What *were* ye doing at the tavern anyway?" Samuel asked.

Gregor frowned. "I needed a drink."

Samuel grunted, knowing when to leave well enough alone.

12

Kirstin feigned a stomachache, missing matins at midnight, and lauds at dawn. She felt incredibly guilty about it, but she'd had no choice. Her stomach *had* pained her, but it was not from illness. It was from nerves. From memory.

She was weak. She admitted that. A flaw she needed to work on. But she couldn't rouse herself to face the world—and Gregor. After the apple basket, she was certain he'd be waiting for her, even though she'd warned him not to do any such thing. The man was stubborn.

As stubborn as she.

Plus, she'd been up half the night fighting off the dreams of her past, and yearning for something she likely didn't deserve.

But now that the sun had risen, if she didn't show her face, she'd begin to raise more than mere concern. Concern she didn't deserve, for she was only hiding from Gregor, from her feelings. And she didn't need the attention.

Being in his arms again had been wonderful, if brief. To sink against his warmth, breathe in his familiar scent. She felt safe, cared for, cherished. All the things she shouldn't want from him—but desperately did.

Kirstin shoved away her covers, her toes touching the cold wooden floor as she rose, stretching out the kinks of travel. Donna had left for prayers, enjoying being a part of Melrose in the interim, which left Kirstin by herself, and alone with her thoughts.

Which may not have necessarily been a good thing.

She shuffled to the wash basin, going through the motions of her morning ablutions, and mustering up the strength she needed for the day. She had to meet with the abbess at some point, sooner rather than later so she could continue on her journey back home to Nèamh.

Halfway through washing her face there was a knock at the door. Kirstin wiped the water from her cheeks, and still barefoot, tugged on her robe, and answered the door.

"Gregor!" she gasped, seeing him standing in the corridor, shoulders wide and blocking all else from view.

He'd shaved his face, leaving only a trace of darkened hair on his square jaw, and around his firm mouth. He smelled clean, divine, and she was brought back to the first time he'd lifted her from that boat, smelling of leather and pine. His gaze traveled the length of her settling on her bare toes, which she curled against the cold of the floor and the heat of his perusal.

Every time she saw him, her body reacted, remembering, wanting. A thousand thoughts ran through her mind, none of them comprehensible, most of them wicked.

Their worlds didn't mesh, no matter how much she might wish they did.

"Ye canna be here," she said, then poked her head out looking both ways to be certain no one had seen him enter.

"There is no one here, and no one saw me coming. Everyone is at their prayers." He grinned. "Well, except us, and perhaps a few of the men on the other side of the abbey."

"That doesn't matter. Ye have to go."

Gregor shook his head slowly. "I canna."

Kirstin narrowed her eyes, trying to give him a stern look even if her insides were melting away at her resistance. "Ye must."

"Nay. I have questions."

She squared her shoulders. "I have no answers."

"Aye, ye do."

He stepped closer and she spread her arms, hands gripping either side of the doorframe to stop his entry.

"Not like this, Gregor. I'm barely dressed."

"I noticed. Do ye not recall I've seen ye—"

"Hush!" She'd not get rid of him so easily, obviously. She grabbed hold of his shirt and tugged him inside, shutting the door before anyone were to see him lurking.

Saints, but the man took up so much space, owning the room, overwhelming her with his presence and all that he stood for. Laughter, teasing, happiness, pleasure.

Leaning against the wood, she crossed her arms to hide the fact that her nipples were pebbling something fierce, and to protect herself from her memories and desires.

"Ye canna do this. If Mother Superior were to find out ye were here she'd toss ye out of the abbey and have me wearing a hair shirt for a month."

Gregor frowned, eyes roving over her body. "But your skin..."

"Aye, 'tis a penance, and one I would welcome."

He walked around the sparse room, unfolding his long body in one of the rickety chairs. Kirstin allowed herself a moment to admire his long muscular legs, the flatness of his belly, and the taut muscles beneath his snug shirt.

A beat later, she tore her gaze away, finding a spot on the

wall above his head. "There is no need to get comfortable." Her tone was prim and prissy.

Gregor chuckled. "Ye've not changed all that much. Still the same fire within ye."

Kirstin frowned, the spot on the wall forgotten as she stared at him. "I'm not that lass anymore."

He sat forward, his gaze burning into hers. "Where did she go?"

Her throat swelled, and she found it hard to swallow, hard to breathe. She didn't want to tell him and he couldn't make her. Silence reigned between them for several moments before Gregor drew in a weary breath. Through every precious second she fought within herself. Fought the urge to spill everything she'd kept hidden inside. To grab him by the shoulders and demand to know why he'd torment her so now by saying he'd not leave her be after he'd pushed her away so many years ago. What did it mean? What was his purpose? She was so confused.

"I dinna want to beg ye, lass. If ye dinna want to open up to me, I can understand that. I did ye wrong, telling ye to leave. 'Twas my fault, and I was an arse to make ye think I didna know it. But they were just words, spoken by a lad who'd imbibed in too much and was afraid of what was happening in his heart. I meant naught of them. I wanted ye to stay. To make a life with me."

Was it possible for her heart to break even more? Because it felt like a thousand shards of glass were cutting deep in her chest. He hadn't meant the words? Hadn't meant for her to leave?

For the love of all that was holy, did he not realize that his *drunken* words spoken *by a lad*, had changed her life forever? Was that all he could say on it? Anger ripped through her anew.

Tears of rage pricked her eyes and she stormed toward

him, slapped him hard across the face, the flat of her palm stinging fiercely. "Get. Out."

Gregor stood, his hand touching where she'd struck him, gaze penetrating hers. "I'm sorry. I'm sorry for the pain I caused. The years lost. The torment ye must have gone through. I'm sorry, Kirstin. I canna take it back, but I can make it up to ye. If ye would but let me."

"Ye canna make up what I have lost. No one can." She spoke before she could pull the words back. Before she could bury them deep down inside where they belonged.

"I know, many years, nearly nine, but—"

He didn't understand. Because she hadn't told him. "Ye're a fool," she muttered. "And only because ye are unknowing of the truth of it."

She should tell him. Why keep it a secret? What would change by sharing the truth?

Gregor straightened, the muscle in his jaw flexing furiously. "I've suffered, too, 'haps not as much as ye, love, but I have."

That only sparked her fury more. "We had a child, Gregor. A *child*." She watched his face change, a barrage of emotions happening all at one. Surprise. Happiness. Sadness. Shock. Questioning. "Our sin created life, and that life, that precious innocent life was lost because of what we did." Her voice broke, and sadness consumed her, mirrored in his features. "I will spend the rest of my days paying penance for it, and the last thing I need is to hear ye talk of days, years and the pain of your heart. Ye know nothing of pain or loss."

She was in tears now, the hot salty water making slashes down her cheeks. He reached for her, the warmth of his palm sliding over her arm, but she pushed him away. Not wanting what he offered. Not seeking comfort.

"I didna tell ye this so ye could feel sorry for me. So ye could console me." She dragged in a ragged breath. "I have dealt with the pain of it. I had come to terms with it. Locked it away. Locked our past away. And then ye had to appear, to dredge it all up again. I dinna want to see ye, Gregor. I dinna want to know ye. I want to forget, and ye're making me relive it."

His hands faltered in mid-air, indecisive as to whether he should once more try to hold her or back away. She stared at it, that appendage hanging in mid-air, wanting him to push past her barrier and grab hold at the same time she wished him to leave.

He took a step back.

Coward.

'Twas then she realized how much she didn't want him to turn from her, how deep down, she wanted him to grab onto her, and not let her go, to force her to let him comfort her, hold her. So hard and brittle she'd become, shielding herself from feeling.

"I'm..." His voice cracked. "I'm sorry, Kay. I'm so damned sorry."

And then his boot heels were clicking across the floor and the door was opening. A rush of air swirled the bottom of her nightrail, leaving a chill that curled up her body, gooseflesh following in its wake. The door closed, leaving her alone.

Utterly alone.

As it always was.

Kirstin wrapped her arms around herself, then sank to the floor, sobs tearing through her. She covered her face with her hands, not ever having mourned as much as she did right then and there. She'd finally shared the truth with Gregor. Finally told him all he should know. All she'd kept inside.

And he'd walked away from her.

It hurt so much more than she ever thought it could.

Gregor leaned his head against the door, a burning pressure rising from his chest to behind his eyes. Tears. They were tears that he let fall.

He'd had a child. *They'd* had a child.

A child that had died, and she'd had to go through that alone.

He'd not been there. Had pushed her away.

If he hadn't pushed her away, would that child have lived? Would he be running through the fields, play-fighting with a wooden sword, riding a horse? Or was it a lass, who would have picked flowers and threaded ribbons through her hair, told him she loved him? How many children would they now have if only he hadn't been such an arse and pushed her away all those years ago. He'd let his own fear get in the way.

Just like he was doing now.

Fear of rejection.

Fear of hurting her.

Fear of the future, the past, all of it.

Standing out in the hallway he felt as though he'd died. The loss was enough to crumple his soul.

"Bastard," he murmured to himself.

This was his fault, and here he stood, coward again, unable to pull her close when she needed it most.

He recalled that night, saw the light shining in her eyes as she'd rushed into his library, wanting to share something with him. How he'd been scared of that light. How he'd wanted to run from her and the responsibility a relationship with her held. 'Haps he'd known deep down what she was going to tell him, for he knew it with a certainty now.

Kay had come to tell him she was going to have his bairn. And he'd thrust her aside.

No wonder she'd run without a word. Vanished.

And where was a lass to go who was ruined and carrying a child? No family. No coin. No home.

The church.

She'd run into the arms of God and his devotees.

And suffered the loss of their child. Without him.

Gregor turned, gripping the handle, prepared to push the door open and offer her what he should have so long ago.

But he stalled. Hearing her words ring out in his mind. She didn't want him there. She wanted him out of her life.

Should he grant her that? After all he'd put her through, was it not selfish to demand entrance back into her life?

As much as it pained him, perhaps he should do as she asked. Walk away.

Nay.

He'd not make that mistake again.

Couldn't.

If she tossed him out again, he'd go, but he wasn't going to walk away just because she'd told him once.

Gregor opened the door, and took in the sight of her crumpled in tears on the floor. His heart broke even more. In one fell swoop, he slammed the door closed and dropped beside her, pulling her into his arms, settling her trembling body on his lap. She curled against him, gripped tight to his shirt, her face buried in the crook of his neck as she sobbed. He cradled her against him, feeling the beat of their hearts meld.

"I'm so sorry," he murmured over and over again.

She pulled back, her eyes swollen and red, cheeks soaked. He wiped at the tear tracks with the pads of his thumb, with the cuff of his sleeve. Her gaze went from his eyes to his mouth, and that was all Gregor needed as an invitation. He claimed her lips, remembrance rocking him as their mouths joined, slanted, treasured.

Their kiss was hungry, but more than simply the desires of the flesh, it was familiar wanting, much needed comfort. Kirstin shifted on his lap, straddling his hips, her palms pressed to his cheeks. Her kiss grew fevered as she pressed her breasts to his chest, ground the apex of her thighs to his middle. Gregor held tight to her, wrapping his arms around her back, fusing her to him and refusing to let go.

The taste of her was just as he remembered, sweet like honey and spice, and her scent, of fresh baked sweets and cinnamon. He threaded one hand into her silky tresses, massaging the back of her head, the other around her middle. Oh, how she'd changed for the better. Softer. Suppler. Warmer. Saints, how he'd missed her. Too many years had passed. Too many words unspoken.

He was never going to let go of her again. Never going to hurt her again.

"Never," he murmured. "Mine. Always."

She sighed into his mouth, kissing him deeper, harder, and he answered her demands with a thrust of his tongue, a growl of need.

And then she was grappling with his shirt, and he was helping her, pulling it over his head and tossing it. Her warm, steady hands pressed hotly to his chest, his shoulders, then scaling down his back. Her lips burned against his shoulder, his chest. Sensation whipped through him, searing him. Binding him. Hot hands splayed on his flesh. Their movements were hurried, frantic. The need to forget, and just feel.

"Kirstin—"

But she swallowed his words with another searing kiss.

13

There was no thought in her movements, her desire. Hands raking over his body. Lips tasting.

Kirstin was simply a woman in need.

A woman in need of the one and only man she'd ever loved. The one and only person in this world who felt an ounce of her pain. Knew of it. Understood it. Didn't punish her for it.

Whatever sins she had already committed could not be undone, and this, how could it be so sinful when it felt so good and right? When nothing but Gregor's arms around her was what she needed to calm the storm of emotions that were crashing through her?

"I've missed ye. Och, how I've missed ye," he was saying, but she silenced him once more by biting his lip, slicking her tongue over his.

No talking. No more apologies. Nothing sentimental.

This was purely about pleasure. A physical connection.

Purely to forget the pain. To sink back into a place, a moment in time where they'd both been full of life, excitement, hope.

At least, that was what she was trying to tell herself. She couldn't hear his words. His sentiments. His praise. That would only make her crash hard. What she needed was to escape. To *feel*.

She tugged at the ribbons of her chemise, Gregor's fingers tangling with hers, their eyes locked, memories batting back and forth between their gazes. Him firing, her deflecting.

"I want ye," she whispered. "Make love to me, Gregor."

He tossed her chemise, the flimsy fabric landing somewhere behind him, exposing her in full view to his roving, hungry eyes. The heat of his hands and arms on her naked flesh replaced the chill draft of the room, soothed the shivers of her nerves. Her nipples pebbled, breasts felt achy and heavy with wanting.

She wanted to crush her skin to his, feel their naked bodies sliding over one another.

There was no turning back. Not when she was wrapped naked around him.

Gregor cupped her breasts, massaging the weight of them, before bending to kiss the puckered pink tips. Heated spurs of pleasure volleyed, singeing her skin, firing through her body and landing at the very center of her, then all the way through to the very ends of her nerves. Between her thighs was quickly slick, her body remembering all too well the pleasure Gregor could give her. The plunge of his thick arousal, the rocking of his hips against hers.

"Ye're still just as beautiful. Ye smell the same, like sunlight and sugar."

She thrust her chest forward, fingers twisting in his hair, begging without words for him to put his mouth on her and cease his talking, else she lose her nerve. And, oh, god, did he. Hot velvet lanced over her flesh, sparking flames as he licked then suckled her nipples.

A moan escaped her, before she clamped her lips closed.

They had to be quiet. Not draw attention to themselves, else she be strung up naked for all the church to devour. Kirstin tightened her grip on his hair, her thighs clamping his ribs, shivers running over her skin like a pack of wild animals on the hunt, looking for a place to land, her pleasure its prey.

That was what this was, animalistic, carnal. She tugged harder, pulling his head back and letting her mouth crash down on his, burning forever in her memory the taste of him. Letting him know how much she missed him. Wanted him. Needed him. Kissing him for all she was worth, because this would be the last time.

The very last time.

Gregor kissed her just as passionately, his hand sliding from her breasts down her belly and then lower, cupping the dampened curls, fingers threading through her glossy folds. She cried out, shifting on his lap, wanting more and more. Magic fired from his fingertips, sliding over her, finding that special knot of flesh that reveled in every little touch, every little stroke.

"Just as responsive. God, how I've missed this. No one could ever compare to ye, lass..."

She bit his chin, sliding her tongue down over the column of his neck. "Dinna bring God or anyone else into this. I need ye. Now."

She fumbled with the ties of his leather breeches. She'd not minded overmuch, because when he grew hard, she could see the length of him, every ridge, pressed with urgency to the leather. He didn't wear a plaid when traveling, she knew that much from their time together. He was able to strap on more weapons with the breeches, better able to ride with speed. And while that was all well and good for the warrior side of him, it wasn't boding well for him as a lover. The more she tugged, the more knots she made, and the more she wished he would return to his plaid, so there was nothing to fumble with beside his thick hard shaft.

"Och, lass," he mumbled against her breasts as he wrenched open the ties of his breeches, the length of his thick erection springing free and brushing satisfyingly against her fingertips.

His teeth sank into her shoulder, scraping with exotic pleasure over her skin. Hands on her hips, he positioned her just right.

"Call me, Kay," she demanded, wanting to be that lass from years before. She wrapped her fingers around his hard shaft and guiding him toward her slick entrance, feeling the head of his arousal breech her opening.

Gregor stilled, his eyes meeting hers, the cloud of passion dissipating quicker than mist when kissed by the sun. A drunk man growing sober upon hearing dire news.

But, what dire news?

Her stomach plummeted as the fog of passion lifted.

Slowly he shook his head and she felt the heat of their union shatter, chills replacing whatever fire had been licking at her limbs.

"Ye said yourself, ye are not Kay anymore. I want *ye.* I want *Kirstin*. I'll not call ye by a name that is not truly yours, that ye dinna believe in."

The heat of their near union evaporated, leaving her suddenly cold and exposed. She scrambled from his lap, his touch. Her bare bottom hit the wooden floor, cold, barren, hard. She grappled with her discarded chemise, covering herself. Humiliation filling her cheeks. A foot away from him, she stared unblinking, wide-eyed. Mortification, anger, weakness and regret pooled in her chest. She saw the two of them through different eyes, as though she floated from her own body, or was a stranger who walked through the door.

Her. Naked, hands bracing, chest heaving, neck red from

the scrape of his whiskers, his teeth. Lips swollen, nipples hard. Willing. Wanting.

Him. Half-dressed, shoulders rigid, a scrape mark from her nails on his back, brows furrowed, lips still wet from her tongue. Sidestepping. Shutting down.

Slowly she stood, keeping her body covered with her chemise, suddenly feeling so exposed. So ridiculous. To have thought that he would... That they could...

There was something wrong with her. Had to be.

She was wicked. Deserved punishment.

Hadn't she learned her lesson in the past? What a fool she was. An utter, ridiculous fool.

Hadn't all the punishment she'd ever received been her fault? The night her parents' castle was taken by marauders, she'd been arguing with her maid. *God punishes.* Then she'd refused to leave, sobbing, and when she finally did, her maid was killed. Her sister stolen. *God punishes.* Her savior, her cousin, he disappeared forever, when he saved her. *God punishes.* She fell in love, conceived a life that was taken from her. God would not let her go unpunished.

"Please, leave. I know not what I was thinking. I shall be flogged for certain as it is the way it should be. I am full of sin and have sinned in the house of the Lord, breaking my vows."

Gregor tucked himself back into his breeches and stood, hands imploring her. "Dinna push me away. Not now. Dinna punish yourself."

She shook her head. "I have to. I..." Kirstin swallowed down the mortification of what she'd just done, feeling no sense of relief at having been able to stop before it went even further.

"Nay, ye dinna." He stepped closer, imploring her.

Whatever hesitation she'd seen in his eyes had dissipated and she swore she wouldn't look at him because she thought she saw pity. She didn't need his pity. Didn't want it.

Stilling her quivering lips, she looked him straight in the eye. "I am many complicated things, Gregor. Dinna presume to tell me what I can and cannot feel or how I should handle myself. I know I told ye that Kay was not me, that she had died long ago, but she is still inside me, still remembers ye, and I should never have allowed her to be set free. Never have let that part of myself seduce ye. For that, I apologize."

Zounds, but her world was crumbling. She could almost hear it cracking all around her.

"Ye dinna have to apologize to me!" Gregor sounded frustrated, his hands swiping down his face as he breathed hard. "Ye never have to apologize to me for your desire. For your want of me. I've wanted ye for the past decade. I wanted ye then and I want ye still."

She trembled, backing away. "There is nothing between us. We cannot be. We should never have been."

Gregor raked his hands through his hair, frustration darkening his eyes. "That's the thing ye dinna see, that ye willna allow yourself to see. There is so much, if ye will only open your eyes, your heart."

She shook her head, hugging herself tighter, squeezing her thighs together to hide the evidence of her desire that had not yet faded. "Please. Leave me."

"Dammit, Kirstin," Gregor said, stalking forward. He gripped her arms, giving her a little shake. The warmth of his fingers seeping into her cold skin. She couldn't look at him, kept her gaze cast toward the ground. "Look at me. Really look at me."

She opened her eyes wider, staring at his beautiful face and wishing she could take him back. Wishing she could take back all the years and sorrow that separated them. Wishing that fate had given them a different path. Wishing that she'd only ever known him as Kirstin, not Kay.

"Do ye see me? I am but a man. One who's made mistakes

in his past. Dreadful mistakes that I'll never forgive myself for. But I won't be punished for them forever. Not when I'm standing here before ye, begging ye to let me make it up to ye. Begging to make it right. And ye shouldn't be punished either."

She blew out a ragged breath, her mind unable to grasp wholly onto what he was saying. She wanted to. But she couldn't.

"I'm so sorry, love," he whispered. "I know I shouldn't ask ye for your forgiveness, but I want it all the same."

He wanted what she couldn't give. She wanted what she couldn't have. So many restraints. So many obstacles. She couldn't face them. Him. Herself.

Head high, she straightened her shoulders, quit hiding herself and in her most calm and authoritative voice, she said, "I need to get dressed. My companion will be back any minute. Leave me."

Gregor pointed at her, determination clear in his dark eyes, the set of his lips. "It is not over between us."

She nodded, then shook her head. "It has to be. Forgive me for leading ye to believe in something I am unable to give."

Gregor let out a low growl. "Ye were stubborn then and ye're stubborn now. Ye haven't changed a bit." He yanked on his shirt, stuffing it into his breeches and stomped toward the door, started to open it, then stilled. "I'm not giving up on ye this time, Kay. Mark my words. I'm not pushing ye away. I know what I want, and I think deep down, ye know what ye want, too. Ye want us. This. 'Tis not so much about my forgiveness as it is about ye forgiving yourself and allowing yourself to find happiness. God is merciful. He forgives, and if ye call yourself a woman of faith, ye should know that, too. Love is kindness. Love is compassionate. Ye need to forgive yourself."

Love? Forgiveness? He spoke words she'd longed to hear. To bathe in. But he spoke them too late.

Through a haze of fresh tears she stared at him, wanting to say so many things, but there she was naked, vulnerable and in a position she told herself she'd never be again. Her throat was tight, her lips unable to form words.

His frown deepened and he shook his head, disappointment clear on his face. And then he was gone. Leaving her shivering in the center of the room, the same place she'd been not a half hour before, standing warm in his arms.

It was too late.

Too late.

Late.

And yet, if she could just hold on a little longer.

Better late than never.

14

"Bring them to me." Robert the Bruce scowled at the wall in his war office, arms crossed over his chest, his anger filling the room with tension.

The news Gregor had imparted on his rightful king was not good, and he was not surprised at his sovereign's reaction. His own mood was wicked black after his encounter with Kirstin. He feared the only way to get rid of it was to beat the truth out of the prisoners—or to start a bloody war.

Gregor nodded to Samuel who relayed a message to bring forth the prisoners. The four of them shuffled in, two looking hung-over as hell, the others looking as though they regretted ever meeting Alan. And all of them reeked, worse than a swine barn in summer.

The guards shoved them down to their knees and slowly the Bruce turned to look at them, assessing.

"Laird Buchanan tells me ye have some news," the Bruce said slowly, his boot heels echoing on the wooden floor in the silence.

Alan sneered, looking his sovereign dead in the eye. "Dinna know anybody named Buchanan."

The bastard truly had no respect, evidenced by his willingness to give up Scottish lives to the English.

"Is that so?" The Bruce tilted his head, questioning, not seeming at all disturbed by Alan's attitude.

Alan didn't waver. "Never heard of him."

The Bruce glanced at Gregor who stepped forward. "Remember me?"

Alan glowered, his lip curling up to show a missing canine. "Ye're Buchanan? Maybe I was wrong then. This bloke assaulted me in an alleyway." Alan made a side-glance to his friends. "Wasn't too pleased when I told him I preferred cunny to cock."

His friends shifted nervously, none of them laughing.

Gregor just grinned. "I see ye do remember now." He stepped forward and kicked the man right between the legs. Again. "Just needed to get reacquainted with your ballocks, mate."

Alan looked ready to spit on Gregor, but thought better of it. Maybe there was an ounce of intelligence in him after all.

"Do ye know who I am?" the Bruce asked.

"A mighty lord I am to bow before? Or, nay, mayhap ye are Jesus Christ in the flesh?" Alan's voice had taken on a sarcastic note.

All of his friends, with the exception of Eyebrow, chuckled under their breath.

"Show some respect, ye swine," Gregor growled. "He's your rightful king."

All four of them sat back on their heels at once, mouths agape, eyes wide as the moon.

"Bow your head before your sovereign," Samuel demanded.

"English prick!" Alan spat.

The guard behind Alan grabbed the hair at the back of his

head and yanked it. "Careful how ye talk to Sir Samuel. Being that he's a Sassenach and all, he's likely to murder ye in your sleep. A task we'd all applaud him in doing."

The way Alan's lips worked, but no sound came out, 'twas obvious he wanted to say something, but some part of his brain seemed to have woken, and kept his mouth firmly shut. Pity.

"No need for ye to repeat what ye've already told Buchanan," Robert the Bruce said. "I'll just be needing what ye didna tell him."

"I told him everything I know," Alan growled.

Gregor shook his head. "Not the name of your accomplice."

"I have no accomplice."

The Bruce tsked. "Ye expect me to believe that after a man who knew who ye were and saw ye kill another, that ye'd just let him walk free? Knowing he held information that could cost ye your neck, and any coin ye might gain as reward, that ye simply didna get his name? Do I look like a bloody fool?" He chuckled, the sound cold. "Now, despite your traitorous actions and your penchant for English coin, and regardless of the fact that ye hold little respect for Scotland, me, or your fellow Scots, I, believe ye must have some semblance of intelligence. Am I wrong?"

"I am no traitor."

"I'm afraid whether ye are a traitor or not is not up for discussion." The Bruce stood right in front of Alan, dipping his head low to meet his gaze. "Give me the name." Their sovereign's tone had turned deadly, and only a fool would refuse him.

Alan refused to speak, his lips tightly closed, eyes filled with resentment.

It appeared this man was a fool after all.

The Bruce nodded to the guards and Alan's head was

wrenched further back, a blade pressed to the ball at his throat.

"I will not ask again. Ye know what I want," the Bruce said.

"I canna tell ye, because the man refused to give it. He said the only thing I need know was that my secret was safe with him."

"Lies," Gregor growled.

Alan shook his head, a mistake as it only caused the blade to cut his skin—though not deep. The second time a blade had grazed his neck in less than twenty-four hours. He cried out, unable to grab his bleeding neck as his hands were pinned behind his back.

The Bruce knelt before the man, dipped his finger into the blood pooling in the hollow at his throat, and wiped it over Alan's forehead in the sign of a cross. "The cut is not deep, ye whiny little pup. Quit your fussing. Hear this, we play no games. The fate of my kingdom, of my people, hangs in the balance. We will leave no stone unturned. Ye keep trying to kick yours back into place, but I canna allow it. I canna set ye and your friends free, not without certainty as to your loyalty. If ye want to prove your loyalty, ye will not only give me the name, but ye will also pledge before me now, on pain of death. And even then, I may keep ye locked up for a time, but I'll spare ye from losing your head right now."

Alan's lips twisted, eyes shifting around as he thought about the Bruce's words. A heavy choice for a traitor, to give up what he wanted and believed in to save his own life. Most men, most decent men, were willing to die for what they believed in. Alan appeared to be the type that floated wherever the jingle of coin blew.

"Tell him, Alan," Eyebrow said. "Tell him what he wants to know. I swear to ye, my lord, I was not going to go along with Alan's plan. Not ever. Ask Buchanan, he was listening in on our conversation at the tavern. I was the one telling Alan this was all madness. I am loyal to Scotland. To ye. To my fellow countrymen."

Gregor eyed the man, gauging whether or not he was truly sincere. Aye, he'd spoken out against Alan's plans, but that didn't mean he was loyal.

"He speaks the truth," Gregor said.

"What is your name?" the Bruce asked.

"Charles, my lord."

"Let Charles go free then," the Bruce said, turning his smile on the man.

Alan sputtered, unable to find purchase in his words, or maybe it was the odd angle at which the guard had tugged his head, for only imperceptible grunts came out of his mouth.

The guards unbound Charles' wrists and yanked the man up. He was murmuring, "Thank ye, thank ye thank ye," like a chant.

The Bruce held up his hand to silence the man, and returned his attention to Alan.

"Ye see? We can show mercy. I've just freed your friend."

"Ye've set him free, but now ye'll only sneak up behind him once outside the abbey walls and slit his throat," Alan sneered.

Their sovereign tsked again. "Ye've no faith in me, Alan. That is sad thing. How can I expect a man to show me loyalty if he has no faith?" He jerked his head at the guards. "Let Charles go. Take him to the gate and give him his freedom."

"Thank ye, my lord, thank ye, thank ye. I am forever in your debt. Please, if I can be of service. Let me be of service. Let me join your ranks. I am but a mercenary. I have no overlord. I will honor ye. Do your bidding. I shall never stray to the likes of any man like Alan again."

"Aye, but ye do have a clan, now, an overlord. I've just

decided. Ye're a Buchanan," the Bruce said, his steady gaze on Gregor.

Gregor now saw where the Bruce was going with such a declaration.

"Take him to the Buchanans, then, Sir Collin, just outside the gate," Gregor said. "Have the men show him the rounds, and see that he is treated as one of us. Watch him all the same to be certain this was not all a sham." He faced Charles. "Ye understand, do ye nay? That we will have to build trust between one another, it is not a right so easily given."

Collin nodded, indicating for Charles to follow him, the other two men quivered, one had pissed himself, since the floor beneath him was wet and the stink of urine filled the air.

"I swear to ye, I dinna know his name," Alan said upon seeing Charles leave the room, hands unbound, no guards touching him. A free man essentially. "But I know what he calls himself."

"Ye dinna know his name, but ye know what he calls himself?" The Bruce stood, raising a skeptical brow. "Sounds like ye know his name."

Alan shook his head, licking his parched lips. "I dinna know his given name. He calls himself The Saint."

"The Saint?" Gregor asked. He'd heard this name fleetingly on lips before, but knew not much about him, other than he was a hired assassin. If this was the man hunting down allies of Wallace, they had a serious situation on their hands.

"Aye."

"Why?" Samuel asked.

"Because, he said he's doing the work for the good Lord above."

"What work?" the Bruce asked.

"He's... A spy. An assassin. Whatever he needs to be."

'Twas as Gregor suspected. "And do ye know who he works for?"

Alan's chin trembled. "God."

"Get them out of here," the Bruce said, disgust in his tone. "We'll get nothing useful from him today. And the other two, they are simply followers, willing to take the leavings this bastard shites out."

"My lord, I am loyal to ye, and ye alone! I was just placating Alan. I wasna going to do it," one of them said.

The second chimed in, "Me, too, my lord. Let us go. We've not done anything wrong. We want to be Buchanans. Will ye not show mercy?"

"Consorting with this devil was enough to show your true colors, lads. Ye should choose your friends better in the future," the Bruce said.

"So we have a future?" The one who'd pissed himself grappled with the hope dangling on the ends of the Bruce's words.

"For now."

"See that they are fed. No utensils. They'll have to eat with their hands, while ye watch. Then they must be restrained again." Their rightful king spoke to the guards who took the men away, leaving Alan to kneel before him alone.

"What did The Saint look like? Did he travel with anyone? What part of Scotland is he from?"

Alan again licked his lips, his eyelids twitching as he racked his brain for any information that might help the king. Gregor took out his knife and began to trim his own nails, eyes on Alan, intimidating the man.

"He is from the north, the Highlands. I could tell by his accent. He's tall, ginger-haired like me. He's got a scar on his chin, right in the center like he'd fallen on a blade. There were a few other men with him. They didna dress in plaids, but rather white robes, splattered with blood."

White robes splattered with blood. Sounded like the

stories Gregor had heard as a child of avenging angels. "I see. And do ye know where they were headed when ye parted ways?"

The man shook his head. "I didna have much contact with them. They weren't with the other mercenaries helping MacLellan. They came into town to refresh their horses and then they were on their way. North I think." He shook his head, sweat trickling down around his temples and pooling near the dip in his ear. "I dinna know."

"That's enough for today," the Bruce said.

Fingall lifted the man and tugged him out of the room, but a loud screech outside had Gregor running. 'Twas a woman. What in bloody hell?

In the hallway, Kirstin stood, hands covering her mouth, eyes wide as she stared at Alan. Nay, Fingall. She looked as though she'd seen a ghost. Her body started to tremble and she swayed. Gregor rushed toward her, holding her elbow to keep her steady. She took a few breaths and then tugged away from him.

Collin, having just returned, easily took over the job of escorting Alan back to his temporary confinement and away from the spectacle that was slowly unfolding.

"Finn?" Kirstin was saying.

Fingall just stared at her, his face ashen.

"Finn! 'Tis ye!" Kirstin charged Gregor's knight and wrapped arms around him, squeezing him so tight the man's eyes bulged. "I have been looking for ye for so long!"

Finn tentatively put his arms around Kirstin, nodding.

Gregor stood in a stupor trying to figure out what the hell had just happened. And then it dawned on him, the whole reason he met Kirstin to begin with—because she'd been looking for her cousin.

Sweet Jesus. Fingall was *Finn*?

Kirstin pulled away from her long lost cousin and stared

accusingly at Gregor. He took an instinctive step back, waiting for her wrath to blow over him like a forest fire.

"Ye've had him all this time?" Her hands flew to her hips. "And ye didna tell me?"

Gregor wanted to tell her the truth, that he hadn't even known they were the same man, but instead, he frowned, and said nothing. He crossed his arms over his chest and stared at Fingall, daring him to say something. The man stood mute. Perhaps whatever excuse he had was buried. 'Twas no wonder he had made up excuses to get away from Kirstin since the moment they'd met her on the road. It was only a matter of time before she figured out who he was.

"How could ye, Laird Buchanan?" she asked, returning to formalities. "How could ye not tell me when ye knew I was searching for him?"

Gregor ground his teeth together, still refusing to answer.

"He didna know," Fingall finally answered, his voice hoarse with unspoken emotion. "Dinna blame him."

"How can I not?"

A deep ache wound its way inside Gregor's chest. Oh, how he wanted to wrap her up in his arms and tell her not to worry, to explain everything. But he still felt the sting of her rejection. The pain of all she'd revealed to him that morning. The ache of not being able to get her out of his mind. He felt like they were bound by rope, but with oceans between them. Neither could get free, nor could they seem to find each other.

Would the memory of her, his love for her, forever haunt him?

Anger suddenly filled him, taking the place of the disappointment and sorrow he'd been fighting all day. He'd told her, he wasn't going to be punished forever. He was trying, but it seemed like she was finding fault with everything he did, said, even things he couldn't have known.

"I am verra sorry, lass. Shall I gift ye another *apple*?" His words were bitter, and he could tell they stung by the way her face fell, but he couldn't help it.

There seemed to be too much sorrow overshadowing any happiness they might have once had. Too many things he'd done wrong that she wasn't willing to forgive—things he wasn't willing to forgive himself for either.

Kirstin's gaze was locked on his, fire flaming from their blue depths. He could feel the burn on his face, all the way inside his skull.

Dammit, but he needed to get out of there. Only thing was, the tavern was the last place he wanted to be.

Fingall stared at them, confused.

But it was the Bruce who spoke up, as though he'd only just arrived at a pleasant gathering of friends, breaking the spell of tension. "Ye might just be the prettiest nun I've ever come across." Then he shook his head. "Apologies, sister, that was incredibly inappropriate of me, but I seem to have lost my sense looking at ye."

Gregor bared his teeth, only pulling back the growl in his throat when Fingall stepped forward, nudging him and whispering, "Remember he is your sovereign."

And it was true. Kirstin was beautiful. Her blue eyes sparkled, creamy flesh rosy with emotion. Lord, but he could stare at her for eternity. *Fuck*.

It hurt too damn much.

"Thank ye, my lord." Kirstin curtsied, ducking her head in a show of meekness, as she should being a daughter of the church.

Affected so perfectly, so at odds with everything Gregor knew about her, he almost believed for a second that her devotion to him in their past life was just as perfectly affected.

But he refused to believe that.

"Fingall, see that your kin is escorted back to her side of the abbey. This is no place for a nun."

"There is always room for God's servants," the Bruce said, a big smile on his face.

Gregor grunted.

Kirstin, curtsied once more, and said, "I really ought to be getting back. And, Finn, we have much to discuss along the way."

Gregor watched their retreating figures with yearning and a jealousy so ripe, he could practically smell it.

"I see ye think she's a beauty, as well," the Bruce murmured.

"Aye. But a nun."

"She wouldn't be the first to renounce her vows to the church in exchange for vows with a man."

"I wouldn't ask it," he lied. He damned well would ask, and had been trying.

The Bruce's grin widened. "I would."

Lord save him, for Gregor was *so* close to pulling his sword.

15

Kirstin was reeling.

Vision blurred. Heart pounding. Palms sweaty. She could barely walk upright, and clung to Finn's strong arm for balance. How different he was than she remembered.

As a youth, he'd been wiry, not yet grown into his full body. He'd kept his face clean shaven—well, not that he had much in the way of facial hair to shave anyway—but now he had a full beard that covered nearly all his face. His hair was longer, too. Almost like he'd been trying to hide himself from the world. And maybe he had been. As next in line to the MacNeacail lairdship until Brenna's son, Theo, was born, Finn would have been hunted down by the MacLeod's until his head was on a spit they turned over their hearth fire.

Kirstin shivered. What torment her sister had been through. Kirstin suddenly felt guilty for all the grieving she'd done on her own behalf. At least she'd not been in her sister's shoes. Brenna was always the stronger of the two, ever since they were little.

"Are ye all right?" Finn asked.

"Aye." She smiled tentatively. She *was* all right. In fact, it was high time she started believing that.

High time she pulled out of her funk and lived. Followed the path that fate seemed to be taking her down. The one Aunt Aileen had mentioned she should look out for.

They got near the covered walkway toward the guest quarters when she tugged him off the path, heading back to the orchards and a private bench she knew to be there. "What happened, Finn?"

They sat down, the marble slab of the bench cool on her heated skin.

He hesitated before answering. "'Tis a long story."

"I'm willing to wait and hear it." Kirstin wasn't going to back down. She'd not seen her cousin in fifteen years. Not heard anything about him other than speculation. She wasn't going to settle for it simply being a long story.

Again he hesitated. "I'm not certain I want to retell it."

Kirstin blew out an irritated breath. Didn't want to tell her? She'd thought him dead all this time and he didn't want to tell her? She bit her lip, trying to keep her rage to herself. One massive and emotional argument with Gregor—still fresh in her mind—was enough for a single day, and she didn't even want to think about that. It still hurt to look at Gregor. The way he'd touched her, helping her to stand when she'd spotted her cousin, she was lucky not to have fallen into his arms again. Because she wanted to. Badly.

She had to admit it, and she'd known it all along—she still loved him.

Bracing herself for more of her cousin's rejection, Kirstin said, "Finn, there are a lot of people that have been missing ye for a long time. 'Tis only fair ye tell me what happened. I thought ye dead. When I heard rumors ye were at Eilean Donan nine years ago, I came looking for ye. If not for that..." She trailed off not wanting to tell him all her secrets just yet.

"I know what happened between ye and Buchanan," he said, changing the subject.

Kirstin knew he was pulling attention away from himself, but his admission rattled her enough she couldn't concentrate. "Ye know?"

"Whisperings of the mysterious Kay cover the walls of Castle Buchanan as thick as the plaster. The woman who could have been his wife. The one he still mourns and thought for dead. Kay, a spirit or fairy who inhabited the castle for a short time. Ye're legendary."

She stared off in the distance, not realizing how much she affected an entire clan in just six months in their presence. How much Gregor had thought about her over the years. She'd heard him say it, but perhaps it took hearing it from another for the reality to sink in. "They still talk about me?"

"Aye, and Gregor does, too."

She flicked her gaze at her cousin, feeling her cheeks heat at the knowledge. "And when did ye know it was me?"

"When we saw ye on the road and he called ye Kay, but I saw 'twas ye." Finn looked away, shame in his eyes.

"Why did ye not come forward?" Kirstin was hurt. He'd known it was her for a couple days now and had not bothered to come find her.

Finn shrugged, having the decency to look guilty. "A moment of fear and weakness. It had been so long and we didna know why your party was on the road, what side ye were on."

"What other side *would* I be on?"

Again he shrugged, tugged at his beard. "There are many who are not what they seem. Many who appear to be loyal to Scotland, to the Bruce, but who would rather collect coin from the English, and betray our people."

Kirstin's stomach soured. "And ye think I am one of them? How can ye say that?"

"'Tis no small mystery that Brenna is married to my enemy. The man who wants me dead."

Kirstin shook her head. His enemy? Gabriel was fully in support of the Bruce, had fought for the man. "Nay, Finn, ye've got the wrong of it. Brenna's husband is not your enemy."

"MacLeod *is* my enemy. Has been for fifteen years."

Kirstin grabbed hold of Finn's hand. "MacLeod is dead. Over a year now. Brenna is married to a good man now—Laird MacKinnon."

Finn swiped his hand over his face. "Saints... I've been hiding for so long, I had no idea. I'm so glad she's out of that monster's hands. I tried to get her out of the castle. Rallied up enough MacNeacail's that had escaped the MacLeod's siege, but we were caught on the road. Decimated. MacLeod declared that he'd not rest until I was dead." Finn blew out a deep sigh. "Thank God. Is she happy?"

"Aye. She is now." Kirstin played with a fold on the skirt of her habit, not wanting to let her questions drop, but nervous about how to ask them all the same. "Finn, ye have to tell me, why did ye not at least send word? I would not have done anything to compromise your safety. We could have even offered ye sanctuary."

"I know it now, lass, but at the time, I was scared. Running. I was nearly murdered more times than I can count. MacLeod never stopped looking for me. At least, not those first six years. I feared that if I were to come back to the abbey, they'd only break down the doors and murder everyone inside. After I took on a new identity, changed the way I looked, and let the rumors spread of my death, then I was safe. I couldn't compromise that. I knew ye were safe. That Brenna was not dead. I..." He trailed off, his voice growing gruff. "I was weak, and then once I played into my new role, it was just easier to forget about my past, about having left ye behind."

"Leaving me behind was the right thing to do. I've been taken care of, educated. I'm safe. But... I missed ye. I blamed myself for your death all these years."

"I'm so sorry. Do ye think ye can ever forgive me?"

Forgiveness. Seemed to be the word of the day. If she could forgive her cousin for assuming a new identity and keeping his old life a secret, hiding from her, letting her believe he was dead, then perhaps there was hope that she could forgive herself. Forgive Gregor. Ask Gregor to forgive her in turn. For not staying and fighting for him when he railed at her. She'd known he was deep in his cups at the time, and if she'd given it half an ounce of thought rather than reacting, she might have waited until morning when he was sober. The fact was, she'd run. She'd been scared too, and his push had been, perhaps, just what she'd been looking for.

"I forgive ye, Finn, there is no question of that." She patted his hand and smiled brightly. "I'm just so glad to have finally found ye. That ye aren't dead. Aunt Aileen will be so pleased, and Brenna, too."

Finn shook his head.

Kirstin frowned. "Dinna shake your head at me. MacLeod is dead. Why would ye not want your kin to know ye are alive? I'm not the only one who mourned ye."

Finn turned sad eyes on her. "I fear they will not be as understanding as ye."

"Why of course they will. Why would they not?"

"Ye're a different sort, Kirstin. Ye have a big heart, always have."

A big heart. She was a different sort. She'd forgotten about that girl. The kind one. The one who easily forgave, and opened up her arms to offer sweetness to anyone in need.

Even though she prayed daily, devoted her life to God, she was not that free-loving, forgiving girl anymore. Somewhere along the road, she'd gotten lost.

Well, she'd find her again.

She nodded, unable to voice her words. She did want to be that girl again. And perhaps the place to start, after speaking with her cousin, was with Gregor.

"Ye have to tell them, Finn. Ye canna hide any longer. It doesna mean ye have to give up your identity, but your enemy is dead. Brenna has several sons, ye need not worry about anyone trying to harm ye for the MacNeacail seat. Ye are safe now."

He grinned. "As safe as I can be."

"What do ye mean by that?" Her stomach flipped at the thought of more danger.

"As I said ye can never tell who is friend or foe. We are at war, cousin. A war not just between the Scots and English, but between our own people. That man ye saw me with, he is Scots."

"And a traitor?"

"Aye. He is willing to hand over any Scot to the English for a bag of coin."

She shuddered to think what that meant at large. "But he was no one."

"Aye. Years ago, 'twas the lords and landholders close to the border, easily turned by promise of safety, coin and English castles we had to fear, now anyone can be our enemy."

"Is that why ye are here?"

"Well, the prisoner is new. Gregor found him and his cronies last night, but aye, we are here because of matters of urgency to the country and our rightful king's safety."

"Ye are doing important work."

"As are ye. Does it make ye happy?"

She wasn't quite certain what that work was, but she knew it had to matter. "Aye. Why would it not?"

Finn shrugged, his signature gesture of brushing off the importance of his words. "Because I've seen the way ye look at Buchanan. The way he looks at ye. I've heard the stories of the passionate love ye shared. Seems like the stuff of fairy tales. I'd not want to see ye give it up."

"We cannot always have everything that we want," she said.

Finn looked her straight in the eye. "And sometimes we can."

"'Tis impossible." She shook her head, growing irritated, more so with herself and the word: impossible. Besides, Finn wasn't the one she should be talking to. Gregor was.

Kirstin stood, and Finn also. He pulled her in for a hug and she squeezed him tight.

"I'm glad ye're safe," she whispered.

"And ye, too. 'Haps when ye return to Nèamh, I'll accompany ye and tell our family in person that I am still alive."

"I think that's a grand idea." She had a flash of herself riding to Nèamh, Finn was there, but so was Gregor. And she was married.

"Thank ye for your forgiveness," Finn said, pulling her back from her vision.

"Forgiveness is not a gift, Finn. Ye need not thank me for it." Kirstin left her cousin, making her way back toward the cloister, intent on finding Gregor so she could speak with him when Donna intercepted her.

"I've been looking everywhere for ye." Donna grabbed hold of her arm, urgency in her tone.

"What is it?" Kristin glanced about, suddenly on high alert for danger.

"'Tis about *that thing* ye asked me to do." Donna spoke under her breath and looked around the cloister suspiciously.

Kristin nodded. "All right, let us go back to our chamber to speak."

They hurried down the covered walkway and into their chamber, settling at the table. Kirstin poured them each a small mug of ale.

"I heard them talking today, while I was sewing shirts," Donna started, then stopped to sip her ale, seeming distracted as she began biting her nails.

"And?" Kristin urged.

"We are definitely here about coin, and many of them think 'tis in here." Donna looked around, the anxious expression on her face almost as if she expected the coin to leap out from somewhere.

"I'd have known if my bag carried any coin in it," Kirstin said with a laugh and then sipped her ale. "Any substantial amount would have been heavy."

"This is true." Donna frowned. "So, why would they think that?"

"I dinna know. I need to speak with the abbess, but she's yet to call on me. I almost feel like she's making me wait on purpose, but I canna for the life of me figure out why."

"Ye could go to her, seek an audience yourself."

Kirstin tapped her chin thinking. "That is a good idea."

"Then if she accepts it, ye can find out, or if she turns ye away, ye know she's stalling for some reason."

"Have ye heard anything about the Warriors of God? Maybe they are the ones who brought the coin."

"Not much is spoken about them, just that they are fierce, and scare many of the nuns here. To be honest, they scare me a bit, too."

Kirstin frowned. John was intense, and it was obvious he felt more than keen friendship for her. Owen, too, was an odd one. She had often found him staring at her throughout their trip. It made her feel uneasy, but not enough that she said anything to John about it.

"Me, too." Kirstin brightened, changing the subject for a moment. "Do ye remember what I told ye about my cousin?"

"The one that went missing?"

"Aye! I've found him. He's here, at the abbey."

"That is peculiar." Donna frowned.

"'Tis the verra best news. He serves Laird Buchanan."

Donna's frown retreated. "Well, that is certainly better than I thought."

Now Kristin frowned. "What did ye think?"

Donna waved away whatever it was she might have been thinking. "Nothing. Silly, really."

"Tell me."

"I just thought maybe he was here, as a lure. A kind of insurance, that when it came time for ye to hand over the coin, they'd make a trade if ye resisted."

"But I've no coin."

"Aye, so it makes no sense. Just my imagination running wild. All this travel, adventure and spying has made me into one silly girl."

But her words... they held some sort of meaning. Perhaps Finn's presence was a trap. Or maybe it wasn't. Finn had warned that one could never know who was enemy or foe. Och, but she was so confused.

"Now ye have me overthinking it," she accused with a laugh.

Donna bounced out of her chair grabbing two apples from Gregor's gift basket. "Eat one. 'Twill not do ye any harm."

They munched on their apples in companionable silence for a few moments. Each heavily thinking.

"Oh, I almost forgot. Seems they believe the abbot is here to ensure that Mother Frances gets what she needs from Mother Aileen."

Kirstin let out a frustrated groan. "How am I supposed to know what they want or need or what we can even give? Aunt Aileen gave me no instructions."

"I dinna know. 'Haps that's why she sent ye instead of coming herself, because she didna know what to do either?"

That didn't sound liked Aunt Aileen at all, but what other reason could there be? Looking at the facts it would appear Kirstin had been thrown into the wind. "How bitterly frustrating."

"Agreed."

They finished their apples, Kirstin deep in thought, trying to call forth the conversation she'd had with her aunt before leaving. And then it dawned on her, the missive.

She leapt from her perch and grabbed for the satchel beneath her cot. Inside, was the rolled scroll that her aunt had handed her. She'd said to give it to Mother Frances. The urge to slip her fingernail beneath the wax and break the seal was strong. But then they'd know she'd done so.

"What have ye got?" Donna asked.

"A clue, but not one I can explore."

"Then 'haps ye have a purpose Mother Aileen knew about after all. She'd not willingly send ye into a trap."

"I know." Kirstin blew out a frustrated sigh, shoved the missive back into her satchel and tucked it under the bed. She needed a distraction. There was so much in her life that seemed beyond her control and she didn't want to dwell on it.

"Shall we feed the apple cores to the rabbits?" Donna asked.

Kirstin pursed her lips. "Rabbits? There are none, I looked."

"The birds then?" Donna nodded. "And then ye simply must come sew shirts with me. I have about twenty more to do and the nuns in the sewing hall are absolutely dreadful."

"Aye, I will, but first I must find Greg—Laird Buchanan."

They exited their chamber, and Kirstin had to walk briskly beside Donna, who was practically skipping. Kirstin shook her head. When would the lass act more her age?

"Why?" Donna asked, as though she'd just processed what Kirstin had said. She ceased her skipping and walked more demurely through the cloister toward the entryway of the gardens and orchard beyond.

"I must thank him for taking care of my cousin. Finn looks so healthy and strong. He's doing work that is valued. I could not be more happy." Well, she would have been happier if he'd told her years ago that he was alive, but she'd offered her forgiveness and wouldn't go back on it now.

Zounds, but she was feeling lighter already.

"Finn. Fingall, aye?"

"One and the same."

"He is handsome."

Once in the orchard, Donna tossed her apple core high and Kirstin did the same. A swarm of red grouse birds landed to peck at the remains of sweet apple flesh.

Kirstin raised her brows. "But, Donna, ye are to take your vows next summer. Ye shouldn't be noticing men's looks."

"I am to say vows, aye, but who knows which I shall say—vows to the church, or vows to a husband. There is still time to decide." She lifted her shoulder playfully and wiggled her brows. "Ye had a mighty adventure once. Perhaps I want one, too."

"But ye recall mine did not end well."

"Oh, Kirstin, do ye not see? It has not ended at all."

16

"Brother, I had planned to head back to Castle Buchanan for one night before I make my way to England, else my wife have me tossed in the stocks and flogged upon my return," Samuel said. "But, since ye'll be sending the prisoners there for safe-keeping while ye search out The Saint, I will escort them, along with a guard for each."

Gregor always allowed Samuel one night with his wife before sending him on any mission, simply because in a warrior's treacherous position, there was always a chance that one night could be the last. But, the timing was impeccable considering.

They stood in Gregor's own chamber within the abbey walls, returned to him now that the prisoners were rounded up outside for departure, a map laid flat on a table before them.

"Aye." Gregor grinned, though the smile did not quite reach his eyes. "Put those three in the dungeon. The fourth, that we *freed*, he shall remain here at the abbey."

A night's worth of whisky-induced sleep had not helped to

clear the fog from his brain. He could think of little else besides Kirstin and all he'd learned. He'd not seen her since yesterday morning and he suspected she was likely doing exactly what he was—throwing herself into her work. After she'd run off with her cousin, Gregor had gathered his men and they'd ridden out to the surrounding villages, questioning to see if anyone had heard of a man named, The Saint. Many had, and they said he traveled in a pack. But no one could say where he was headed. Frustrated did not even begin to describe Gregor's current mood.

"Do ye have a message ye need relayed to our allies on my way back?"

"Warn them of The Saint. Implore them to search for him, too, so that we might contain the bastard before he abducts another Scot and sends him to Longshanks. And see that any missives at Castle Buchanan or other *gifts"—mo chreach* he hoped there weren't anymore body parts awaiting him—"be forwarded to the abbey. As long as the Bruce shelters here and uses the abbey as his base, I will, too. Have the men return to the border with ye, riding in a larger party will be safer, especially if ye happen to cross The Saint yourself. Once ye're ready to cross into England, send them back to me."

Samuel nodded, and picked up a whetstone to sharpen his dagger. "Any messages I send from England, should they be sent here?"

"Aye."

"And Catriona?"

"Let her know that she is guarded well." Gregor chuckled. "She might like having us out of her hair so she can get to work on any projects we may have dismissed."

"Such as the feminization of the Great Hall?" Samuel jested.

"And the building of the bathing room." Gregor was not

against bathing, quite the opposite, but he was more inclined to do so in a natural setting, such as a loch, than a dreary, closed in room filled with tubs. Though, he could understand a woman's want of such things. "Hmm. In fact, why dinna ye tell her that I have given my approval. If she is to be without the two of us, I suppose a gift such as that should settle her mind or keep her busy when she's not mothering your new bairn."

Samuel grinned. "My thanks, my laird."

"Where will ye head first?"

"My sources tell me that Longshanks has moved from the Tower of London to a castle in Northumbria near the Scottish border. I will meet him there, with 'urgent news.'"

"And your urgent news?"

Samuel wiggled his brows. "The Bruce helped me with this one. I am to inform the *good and pure* King Edward that another general, fiercer than Wallace and Murray put together has begun gathering forces and rallying the people of Scotland."

"And who is this gentleman?"

"We know not his name as of yet, only that *the people* are calling him The Hammer."

Gregor quirked a brow. "As in Longshanks' moniker, The Hammer of the Scots?"

"Brilliant, aye? He will see this specter as a threat, mocking him."

"Likely to rile him up."

"Indeed, and when he's riled, he is more likely to act rashly."

"And perhaps likely to initiate The Saint into coming out of hiding."

"Aye. The Saint will not be able to hide for long." Samuel set down the whetstone, running his finger along the edge. "In the meantime, I will do some poking around to find out just who the Scottish bastard was that betrayed Wallace."

"Ye're a good and loyal vassal to this realm, a realm not of your blood."

"But there ye are wrong brother, 'tis my blood now that my wife has birthed me a son."

Gregor couldn't have been prouder. His chest swelled. "Stay safe. If Longshanks were ever to find out that ye have betrayed him, that ye are playing him for a fool, he will show ye no mercy. The next basket I get, I dinna want it to contain your body parts."

Samuel put his fist to his chest. "I swear it, Gregor, I will be safe. I *am* safe."

"The king will want ye to return to Scotland to find out more about The Hammer."

"Aye, and I've every hope, he'll want me to meet with The Saint, too."

"Damned lucky that would be."

"Aye. I will be back verra soon."

Gregor let out a deep sigh. "Ye had better, else my ghost comes to find yours, because Catriona will kill me if anything happens to ye."

Samuel's position in Scotland was one of the most dangerous. He traveled close to the border with guards, but then was on his own. Riding alone was never good for any man, but more so for a spy, especially along the border.

If anything were to happen to Samuel, no one would know about it.

"Wait, Samuel." Gregor stared down at the map. "Which castle in Northumbria do ye suspect Longshanks is holed up in?"

"Likely, Berwick."

"'Tis only a day's ride from Melrose." A scary thought, that the two men rivaling for the Scottish crown could be so close to each other without even realizing it. "I will ride with ye to the border."

Samuel shook his head. "Nay, ye canna. 'Tis too dangerous. More English lurk around the border than anywhere else in Scotland. Ye'll be putting yourself at risk."

"We all have to put ourselves at risk to see this through. I've got to take my search for The Saint southward. I canna stop looking in case Longshanks has no plans for the two of ye to meet, or in case The Saint has not made contact with the bloody Sassenach king to begin with." Besides, Gregor needed to get outside the abbey walls. He needed some space to think about his next move with Kirstin.

He'd been deadly serious when he said he wasn't giving up on her.

"I'm leaving now for Buchanan lands and will return the day after tomorrow."

"Good. I'll talk with the Bruce and see if there is anything else that can be done while we are near the border."

Samuel departed leaving Gregor to stare once more at the map, but he wasn't truly seeing the landmarks, mountain passes or trails. He was seeing Kirstin, her body wrapped around his, the soft exhale of her breath on his neck, her fingers stroking his skin, the heated velvet of her slick channel.

Hell and damnation! She was the reason he couldn't think straight. The reason he had to leave the abbey to get his mind back on the tasks at hand. A country that was soon to be thrown into chaos. Hours, maybe days, if they were lucky, before news of Wallace's execution was found out.

But, despite his reason for needing a few days reprieve from her, before he left, he had to speak with her one more time. Just as Samuel had to go home to his wife, Gregor had to make certain to see the woman he wished to be his wife one last time, to tell her how he really felt, let her think about it while he was away and then work like hell to get back to her.

❦

"I DINNA THINK THE ABBEY HAS EVER BEEN ANY CLEANER than it is now," Mother Frances said to Kirstin.

Standing at her full height, she towered over her. A mountain of a woman, with none of the warmness that she felt from her own Mother Superior and aunt back at Nèamh. Finally, Kirstin had been called to Mother Superior, two very long days since her arrival. But, she felt none of the relief she thought she would. And, it had been while she was cleaning the refectory, so she'd not had time to return to her chamber to gather the missive. She was sort of hoping that Mother Frances would tell her what it was all about, rather than reading the scroll and keeping Kirstin further in the dark.

"'Tis a talent I possess." A talent that took on a whole new level of aggressiveness when she was worked up over something. In this case, not having been able to find Gregor to speak with him regarding Finn, and *them*. He'd been out on a mission, of which no one would give her any details, including when he'd return.

Mother Frances smiled, though it was brittle. "Well, we do all have our talents."

"Ye wished to see me? It sounded urgent, not necessarily about cleaning?" Kirstin fidgeted as she stood in front of Mother Frances, wondering for a moment if the woman had spies around the abbey that had seen or heard Gregor in her chamber yesterday.

"Ye are correct. I did not call ye here to discuss cleaning methods, though I am certain your skill would be useful here." Mother Frances cleared her throat. "Ye were sent here as an emissary from your abbey, and now it is time for ye to work."

Kirstin waited.

"We require funds. As do most of the abbeys and monasteries. We need funds to protect our walls, your fellow sisters and brothers in Christ."

Kirstin shook her head. "I dinna see how I can help. I am unaware of the status of our funds at Nèamh."

"Did Prioress Aileen give ye something for me?"

"Aye. A missive." Kirstin made no move to retrieve it.

Mother Frances raised a brow. "Can I have it?"

Darn! She'd not be telling her what the funds were needed for. Bowing her head as she was trained to do, Kirstin said, "I shall go directly to retrieve it."

"See that ye do."

Kirstin rushed from the abbess's receiving room, heading to her chamber. Too exhausted from travel, and entirely too wrapped up in matters no nun of good standing should ever be swathed in, the missive had completely slipped her mind. Mother Frances, if she didn't already, most likely thought Kirstin a waste of a good nun's habit.

Her chamber was dark with the shutters closed, but she knew where her satchel was beneath the bed. She bent to retrieve it, settling it on the mattress and slipping her hand into the pocket where Aunt Aileen's sealed missive should have been.

But it was empty.

Kirstin felt around the rest of the bag.

Nothing.

Panic made her heart flip-flop in her chest like a fish out of water. She turned the satchel over, shaking it, expecting the missive to drop out onto the bed, but again, there was nothing.

Had it somehow fallen out when she'd shoved it back under the bed?

Kirstin dropped to her knees, squinting into the darkened recess under the bed. A few dust motes, nothing more. No missive. Kirstin sat back on her heels. She'd just seen the missive the day before. Showed it to Donna. It was here. But now it was gone. She couldn't fathom...

Had someone taken it? Donna?

Why would someone take it? What could the missive have possibly contained?

"Are ye looking for something?"

Kirstin whirled at the sound of a male voice.

"Sir Owen," she said, pressing her hand to her heart. She stood. "Ye scared me. Where is Sir John?"

Owen shrugged, his eyes roving over her in a way that made her feel very uncomfortable.

"Can I help ye with something?"

"I wonder," Sir Owen said, but then added nothing more.

Kirstin raised a brow, alarm bells starting to toll. "If there is nothing I can help ye with, then I suggest ye head back to your duties. Ye shouldn't be in here."

A queer expression covered his features, making Kirstin feel uneasy. His gaze followed the line of her body. "Well, as a matter of fact, there is something ye can help me with."

She tried for a withering glower, but it fell short of her intent, as her nerves were buzzing around like a swarm of bees on freshly bloomed lavender. "Let us discuss it as we walk, then. I am needed by the Prioress."

But instead of backing up, Owen entered her chamber. "I think not."

Saints! Her stomach flipped, lodging in her throat. Kirstin bolted forward, intent on scurrying around him and out of her chamber, but he slammed the door shut, barring her way out.

"No need to leave quite yet."

Panicked, she once more tried to gain the upper hand, fists on her hips, she glowered. "This is highly inappropriate. I am a daughter of the church."

"And I am a son. 'Tis why this is so perfect." He merely shrugged, nonchalant, chilling. Not at all concerned for their positions. This had gone too far.

Kirstin shook her head vehemently. "I insist."

Owen struck out, his big paw connecting with her chest and pushing her backwards toward the bed.

"Where is Scorrybreac Castle?" he demanded.

"Scorrybreac?" The question caught her off guard and she faltered in her steps, stumbling backward, catching herself just before she fell to the mattress.

"Aye. Where is it?"

"The Isle of Skye." Mind reeling, she regained her balance and darted around him, only to be grabbed as she passed and flung around so that her back pressed into his chest.

"Have ye been there before?"

Why in heaven's name was he asking about her childhood home? She'd not been back there since she was twelve, since she'd fled. Since that awful moment where she'd watched her maid be run through by the monster who stole her sister. Thank God, Brenna had survived. Her sister Brenna and her family resided at Scorrybreac now, her son its laird and her husband acting as guardian. Was this about them? Were they in danger? Kirstin's heart pounded with fear. Something was wrong. Self-preservation told her to lie.

"Nay. Never. I could not even describe it to ye."

"Ye lie," he whispered menacingly.

Kirstin worked to keep her voice vacant, and shook her head, feeling her headdress shift. "Lying is a sin. Just as assaulting a nun is."

Owen laughed, the sound scraping along her nerves. "But we both know ye are not pure, *Kay*."

Saints preserve her! He had seen Gregor come into her chamber. Perhaps heard their soft moans and whispers. He knew, and now he was going to use that against her. But still, what did Scorrybreac have to do with it?

She tried to straighten away from him, but he kept her pinned. "Let me go, and I will swear this never happened. Ye can still escape with your life."

He nuzzled her neck, making her skin crawl. "Oh, I intend to escape. But, ye're coming with me."

A knock at the door had them both jolting.

"Let me go," she whispered frantically. "Please. I willna tell. I promise."

The man grunted, and she felt cold metal—the edge of a blade—touch her neck where his mouth had just been.

"Sister Kirstin?" Gregor was on the other side of the door.

Owen tightened his grip around her, the force of his arm pinching painfully against her ribs. "Dinna say a word, or I'll slit your throat right here and now."

To prove his point, he pricked her skin just enough to sting and for her to feel the warm sticky trickle of blood slide down her neck.

17

"Owen," she croaked.

Kirstin held onto his arm wrapped around her neck, in an effort to ease the pain, as he slowly cut off her breath. Spots started to dance before her eyes, and her tongue felt funny. Fuzzy.

Nay, she couldn't pass out. Couldn't let him do this to her! She tried to concentrate on yanking his arm. There was a wet spot on his shirtsleeve, her blood. She pinched him hard, and he growled, though he did loosen his grip, but not enough.

"'Tis Laird Buchanan on the other side of the door," she managed to say. "Ye recall the man. Stubborn as your leader, Sir John. He will not go away. He will open the door, and when he sees ye holding me like this, he will run ye through without question."

Speaking took great effort and she found herself panting for breath.

"Not afore I cut your pretty neck from ear to ear," he rasped menacingly, removing his arm and using the tip of his fingernail to scrape exactly the route. His breath smelled rotten, and she imagined all manner of things crawling around inside his mouth. Death, decay.

She squeezed her eyes shut, and though she didn't think she deserved much mercy from the heavens whom she'd shunned when she accepted Gregor's touch, when she had sinful thoughts, and because most importantly, she wanted this man harmed—badly—she prayed anyway. Prayed that Owen would let her go without hurting her. Prayed that Owen would let her answer the door. Prayed that Gregor would see through her trying to push him away and somehow figure out a way to save her without either of them getting killed. Or at the very least, that Gregor left, and if she was able to save his life and not her own, so be it.

"Let me answer the door. Let me get rid of him. None of us need die today." She licked her lips, frantic. "Even if he does go away, he'll likely lurk around all day waiting for me to return. Ye'll not be able to leave this chamber without him seeing ye."

Owen resumed squeezing the life out of her, lifting her up so that she stood on her tiptoes making spots behind her eyes return. "What's to make me believe that ye willna try to escape, or warn him of your plight?"

Kirstin gagged, choked, tried to drag in air. Owen laughed, the sound scraping along her nerves sending shivers of fear rolling over her. He loosened enough for her to drag in a deep breath, though the angle he kept his arm, she was still on her tiptoes, and concentrating hard on not falling.

Her mind raced for answers, trying desperately to find something that would appease this madman. "Ye can stand behind the door. Ye can—" She shook her head, fear making her voice disappear altogether, and making it a huge effort to force the air past her throat to form sounds. *God, give me the strength, please...* "Ye can hold a blade to my ribs. I dinna want to die. I will get rid of him."

She prayed this worked. Prayed that Gregor would simply leave, that he wouldn't insist on rushing in, as he always did, and that Owen didn't grow fearful enough to simply dispatch her.

Dragging in another blessed breath, she attempted another bribe. "If ye promise not to hurt him, I can help ye."

"What can ye help me with?" A hint of intrigue entered his tone.

"Whatever it is ye seek. Scorrybreac. Just, please, I beg ye, dinna kill Buchanan, dinna kill me." She hated to sound so desperate, hated showing any weakness to a man intent on ill deeds.

"Ye care for the man, or simply his cock?" And then she felt the hardness of his erection probing at her rear.

Swallowing a gag, and shifting her hips forward, away from his body, she replied, "'Tis vulgar the way ye speak to me. Ye must recall I am a daughter of the church."

His blade pressed a little harder against her skin. "How d'ye think Mother Frances or the abbess at your place on Skye would feel about the way ye fornicated with Buchanan not two days past? 'Haps they will think it just if I toss ye on that cot and take what ye've been giving away already. Your proclamation of being a daughter of the church is blasphemy considering your wicked actions."

"We did not fornicate." But it was no use arguing. And besides, if he'd been standing outside when she'd been in Gregor's arms, then he heard them, and they'd been so close to joining. The truth was, they'd had every intention of doing just that, so what use was there in denying the truth?

Gregor rapped once more on the door. "Please. Answer the door," he called.

She imagined Owen ripping open the door, catching Gregor unawares and thrusting his blade through his middle.

She couldn't allow that to happen. If there was anything she could do to save him, she would.

"Please, Sir Owen, let me get rid of him." Her voice sounded stronger now.

Owen let out an annoyed huff. "All right, but ye make one mistake, and ye both will die."

Kirstin nodded and Owen backed toward the door, still holding her tight around the neck. Then he slowly let go. She sucked in air, trying to regain her balance and vision. She swiped at the blood on her neck, seeing it crimson on her fingertips. The small cut stung, but at least it wasn't deep enough to need stitching. She hoped Gregor wouldn't spot it, then her ruse would be done. She pulled on the collar of her habit, hoping to hide the cut and any markings left from Owen's grip on her neck.

She jumped when Owen poked her in the ribs with the tip of his dagger. He motioned with his head for her to answer the door where Gregor knocked persistently. With trembling fingers she touched one hand to the wooden panel, the other to the iron handle. She drew in a ragged breath, sent up another prayer, cleared her face of emotion—especially fear—and prepared to answer.

"SISTER KIRSTIN?" GREGOR CALLED AGAIN.

He could hear her inside. The sound of her slippers scuffling. Why wouldn't she answer? He knew it wasn't her companion, as the young lass had pointed in the direction of the chamber when he'd asked about Kirstin. He'd made it clear it was him, which could only mean one thing: she was hoping he'd go away.

Damned if he would! He was leaving for god only knew how long, a week, a month, and he wasn't going without telling her how madly in love he was with her. Then he'd beg her to think about marrying him, to spend the rest of her life with him, just as it should have been nine years ago.

Gregor knocked again. "I must speak with ye. Please open the door."

A beat later the door opened a crack and a fearful looking Kirstin peered out. Her face was pale, eyes watery. She looked unwell. But as soon as her eyes met his, her gaze turned vacant, her features washing of any emotion.

His blood chilled. This was so unlike her.

"Are ye all right?" he asked, frowning, concern making him reach for her.

She backed away, and he withdrew his hand. Patience. He needed to have patience with her. That was the only way to win her over. It wouldn't happen overnight, he knew that. And he was willing to work for as long as it took to bring her back to him.

She nodded emphatically. "Aye, I just tripped, 'tis all." She flashed a weary smile. "A little stunned."

He searched her eyes. "Are ye certain? Ye look... unwell. Apologies, but there is no kinder way to say it."

Another flicker of a smile before her face went blank, again. "I am fine. I promise."

Gregor swallowed, 'twas now or never. "I need to speak with ye."

She shook her head, eyes imploring. "Now is not a good time."

"Now is the best time," he insisted. He held up the bundle of flowers he'd gathered on the heath surrounding the abbey. An abundance of colors: yellow, red, purple, orange. "I picked these for ye. I remember that ye love wild flowers. The ones free to grow and blow in the wind as ye wanted to be."

A small smile turned the corners of her lips, but was fleeting enough that he wondered if it was a figment of his imagination. She didn't reach for the flowers. Didn't move her hand from the edge of the doorframe or from behind the door. Still as marble. But not as cold. There was something wrong, he could feel it. More so than a simple fall.

"I..." She chewed her trembling lip. "I appreciate the gesture, but... I am dealing with something right now. Please go away."

What in bloody hell? Nay, he wasn't going away. "I can help. Let me help. Whatever it is."

Sadness, so profound, filled her features, and he nearly dropped the flowers in favor of tugging her into his arms. But she stiffened when he moved toward her. Eyes flicking to the blooms, she let go of the doorframe and snatched them, holding them to her chest.

"Do ye remember the first time ye gave me flowers?" When she looked at him this time, he nearly drowned in her eyes the color of bluebells.

"How could I forget?" Visions of them, carefree and happy flashed before his eyes. She'd been walking through a field, fingers trailing over the petals and he'd snuck up behind her, scared the living daylights out of her. She jumped and screamed, but when she realized it was him, they'd laughed and fallen to the ground. They made love, and afterward, she'd weaved them each a crown of flowers from the bundle he'd gathered. They bathed, gloriously naked in the sunlight, the only thing they wore, those crowns.

He'd kept his for months, and only when it finally disintegrated, did he allow his maid to convince him he should press it into parchment and tuck it away in his letter box where it remained to this day.

She jerked, grimacing, as though a stabbing pain hit her in her middle.

"Kirstin," he said. "What is it?"

She winced again. "Now, please leave me alone. I am having... a feminine issue."

First a fall, and now a feminine issue? He was not one to dismiss a woman and any issues she might be dealing with, but he'd been very intimate with her most feminine parts the day before, and he was certain she wasn't experiencing anything then. 'Twas something else. He was willing to bet his life on it.

"Kirstin, yesterday—"

"Yesterday is past. Today is a new day. Now please, if ye will, I'm quite busy. And ye mustn't delay me."

Her eyes implored him, and Gregor couldn't figure out if she wanted him to leave or stay. Her eyes begged him to stay. Her words told him to leave. He felt ignorant in the ways of women, especially at that moment. He was at a loss, and getting mighty tired of the games they were playing. He'd come to her chamber with a purpose and he wasn't leaving until that purpose had been met.

"If ye will not come out, and ye will not let me in, then I shall tell ye what I came to say right here."

She swallowed hard, her throat bobbing, and he took note of the scratch that seeped blood on her neck. It looked—

"Is that a blade wound?" The incredulousness came out in his tone. He reached forward and tugged at her collar before she could back away.

For certes, there was a cut, about half an inch in width, on her delicate neck. Fresh blood oozed. Immediately he was on alert. Who could have attacked her? Cut her? All around the wound was red and irritated.

She jerked again, scoffed, rolled her eyes, grabbed her collar and covered the wound. "Aye. Stupid of me. When I tripped, 'twas in the kitchen, and I was holding a knife, helping cook. I seem to have cut myself." Shaking fingers touched her wound, covered it, and then she flinched again.

"I'll be all right. Ye needn't worry over me. 'Tis merely superficial."

There again, her eyes told a different story.

"But I do worry over ye. Clumsiness or nay, ye are hurt." He touched her cheek, stroked the line of her cheekbone with the pad of his thumb.

Again, she scoffed. "What do ye think happened, my laird? Ye think some nefarious creature has snuck into the abbey and injured me? Ye'd be wrong. Deadly wrong. No one has snuck in. And the injury, 'tis my own fault."

Her words were odd. Aye, he had a moment's suspicion but what he was saying to her had more to do with his heart and his need to protect her. "Ye canna push me away."

"I can, and I must. Your advances are not welcome. Right now."

She looked over his shoulder, as if expecting someone to be watching them, then shoved his wild bouquet back against his chest.

"I told ye I wasn't going to let ye go this time," Gregor said. "And I meant it. I love ye, lass. I'm sorry it took me so long to say it, but I do. With all of my heart. I want ye to be mine. I want to tell ye every moment of every day for the rest of our lives how much I love ye."

Kirstin let out a deep sigh, the force of which disturbed the ties of his shirt, and might as well have torn into his chest.

"'Tis an argument we'll have for the rest of our days I'm afraid, until one of us tires of it, or *dies*. Gregor, I am not *free* to be yours."

She didn't say she loved him back. But even still, she did not reject him wholeheartedly. And he could see the love and sadness in her expression, had felt it when he'd held her in his arms. He wasn't going to give up.

A glimmer of hope sparked. Perhaps the biggest obstacle

of all was her stubbornness along with the habit she wore. "And if ye were free?"

"If I were free, I would"—she paused, swallowing once more, fear skating over the recesses of her eyes. "If I were free, right now, I would go with ye, Gregor." She flinched. "But, as I said. I am not. If ye know what is good for ye, then ye'd heed my words."

Gregor shook his head in confusion, his heart soaring at her words one moment and then plummeting the next. "I dinna understand ye. If ye want to be with me, then let us talk with your abbess. Let us at least try. We failed once already. Let us not live by our past transgressions, but move forward. Forgive each other."

"Oh, Gregor," she sighed, tears in her eyes. "I have forgiven ye, and I beg ye to forgive me, too. For everything."

"Lass, I could never stay angry with ye. The moment I found out ye were alive—"

Kirstin flinched, tears spilling down her cheeks. "When will ye listen? Truly *listen*? Listen to *everything* I have said?"

And then she stumbled backward and the door slammed in his face.

18

Kirstin sat on the edge of her cot watching intently as Owen paced back and forth muttering to himself. Clearly, he'd not thought out his plan, or it wasn't going the way he'd envisioned.

Dressed in dark, leather breeches, a white tunic and a leather vest adorned with iron studs in the shape of a cross on his chest and back, he didn't look Scottish except for the rabbit and plaid sporran at his hip. His ginger hair was pulled back in a plait secured with a piece of plaid, and his beard looked unruly, unkempt. Clearly the man spent more time plotting than he did praying or taking care of his personal hygiene.

His boots scuffed along the floor as he walked, the sound slowly driving her mad.

It was nearing noon, and there was at least six or seven hours until sundown, which would be the easiest time to escape—using the cover of darkness as his aid. Unless of course, he recalled that Mass was at noon before their mid-day meal. Which... she prayed he'd recall, being that he was a member of the church.

When he started to murmur to himself, and slapped his hand against the wall, Kirstin lost all faith in being able to appeal to him in some way. *Anyway*. The man had clearly lost his mind.

She chewed the inside of her cheek. Her neck stung where he'd pricked her and so did her shin where he'd shoved her into the mattress after slamming the door in Gregor's face.

He'd not yet raped her, so she supposed she should be thankful for small favors. The fear of him doing so had been real however. She'd fallen forward onto the mattress, vulnerable. And while he'd fleetingly touched her rear, he'd only shoved her down and returned to pacing.

Too scared to move, or to call attention to herself, she'd lain very still for nearly thirty minutes, eyes darting to the door anytime she heard a noise, hoping Donna would not return, else the poor lass become a casualty.

Dear Lord, how was she going to get out of this one?

The bells rang, loud and clear and suddenly Owen ceased his pacing, grabbed her by the elbow and yanked her up. Her skin stung where he gripped her. She looked straight into his eyes, trying to see his intent before his actions, as she jerked away from him, only to find his grip tightening.

"Dinna pull away from me. Ye willna like what I do to ye should ye fight. We will leave now, while everyone is at Mass." His voice was urgent, eyes wide and frantic.

Kirstin nodded, and rushed, "Ye think the guards at the gate, or Gregor's men will simply let ye walk out of the abbey with me in tow? Ye've not thought this through. Ye need more time to plan."

Owen cracked a vile smile, and shook his head as though she were too stupid for words. "We aren't going out the front. Do ye think me an idiot?"

She didn't answer, for he wouldn't like to hear her affirm just that.

And what did he mean, not going out the front? That wasn't good.

He dragged her toward the door.

"Will ye not let me gather a few of my things? 'Tis a long journey back to Skye."

He yanked her close, his angry face coming within inches of hers. "Nay, else they realize ye've gone missing and go looking for ye. As long as your things are here they will believe ye are somewhere within the walls. At least for a short time."

"And when they see ye've gone missing?"

"We'll be well away by the time they figure it out." He shook her slightly. "Dinna bank your prayers on anyone coming to your aid."

The bells continued to toll for noon Mass. Kirstin's chamber was so far from the cloister that she couldn't hear the footsteps as the nuns made their way to the chapel, but she could imagine them. Saw their heads bowed, shuffling single file, hands on their rosary beads as they prayed. So many people, just a few dozen yards away, and not one of them realizing she was in danger. No one would come looking for her until after the full hour of Mass.

After Mass, when Donna realized that Kirstin wasn't in the chapel (since she'd instructed her to sit separately in order to glean more information from gossipmongers), she'd come back to their chamber, but that gave Owen an hour to sneak her out. There was also the fact that even if Donna didn't see her at Mass, likely she'd assume that Kirstin was with Finn or Gregor or had another stomachache.

There had to be some way to let Donna know she was in danger. How could she leave a message, something, that showed she needed help?

She spied the basket of apples from Gregor. They'd eaten nearly half the offering, but still the fruit shined in its perfection—for she'd arranged the apples just so, while Donna teased her.

An idea, however ridiculous it might have been, sprung to mind.

She jerked harder. "Wait! I'm hungry. Can I at least have an apple to take with me?"

Owen glared at her, so she tried for sweet and innocent.

"Please, it's only an apple."

"Fine. Grab one for me, too." He let go of her and strode toward the window.

Kirstin nodded and rubbed at her sore elbow. As soon as his back was turned, she launched her hand out, grabbing haphazardly at the apples, dropping several onto the floor, but keeping the basket in place.

"Oh, for the love of St. Peter! Pick those up!" Owen said, whipping around from where he stood peering out the window.

Kirstin murmured nonsense in a submitting tone, and grabbed for the apples on the floor, but she let one roll under the table, and another land just near the brazier, hoping that Owen wouldn't see them. One glance at not one but two apples on the floor in their chamber and Donna, knowing how much any sort of mess bothered Kirstin, would immediately sense something was wrong. She left two apples in the basket.

Giving a sidelong glance at Owen to make certain he wasn't paying attention, she grabbed the remaining two and held one out to him. He stuffed it in his sporran, distracted more with what was happening outside the tiny window.

"Ye're not to eat it until we're outside the walls," he barked.

Kirstin nodded. Managing to slip another apple from the

basket into a compartment sewn to the side of her habit, right alongside her Bible. Now there was only one apple in the basket. Certain to draw Donna's attention since the lass had a penchant for fruit.

"Now." Owen grabbed her by the elbow. "Try anything, and I will not hesitate to slit your throat."

Kirstin nodded, agreeing. "I'll be silent."

Owen put his hand to the door handle, then paused. "Ye open it. Look out. Be certain there is no one there." He poked her sore ribs with his dagger to show he meant what he said.

Already, her ribs had to be covered in tiny bruises from the amount of jabs he'd given her when she'd been speaking to Gregor. Oh, her heart, how she'd wanted to leap into his arms and beg him to run.

"Did ye hear me?" Owen growled.

Kirstin nodded, opening the door with the point of his dagger still stabbing into her ribs. The covered walkway was all clear and she could hear those at Mass singing hymns. The service had begun, which meant that nearly everyone was inside the chapel. She didn't hear, nor did she see, anyone outside the door.

"'Tis clear," she said.

Still holding his dagger to her ribs, he yanked her through the door and shut it behind them. She shifted her apple into her other hand so she could get to the one she'd hidden in her habit.

"Be silent," he warned.

Kirstin nodded, and as he started to drag her, she took the apple from her skirt and gently dropped it, feigning a cough when it lightly thudded on the walkway.

Owen, so distracted with his cause, didn't seem to notice her dropping the fruit, but he did squeeze her elbow painfully.

"I said be silent, wench."

"I'm sorry," Kirstin whispered.

He only glowered, then tugged her down the covered walk in the opposite direction of the cloister. Where was he taking her? She'd never been down this way before, but obviously he'd researched the layout of the abbey before he'd come to steal her missive and abduct her. Or he'd just spent the last two days skulking around enough that he'd figured it out.

They reached the end and rounded the corner. This part of the walkway edged the wall of the abbey like an alleyway. She could see green shrubs at the end, so they had to be near the gardens.

Owen walked in long, purposeful strides, dragging her along behind him. His legs were quite a bit longer than hers, so she had to half-run, half-walk to keep up with him. She prayed she wouldn't break her neck by tripping on the hem of her skirt.

The way he was bouncing her arm around she was desperately afraid of losing the apple. Already her fingers were trembling at the pain he caused by how tight he held onto her.

"Please," she whispered. "Ye dinna have to hold me. I willna try to escape."

"Shut up," he hissed.

Kirstin did as she was bade, afraid of causing a scene and getting herself gutted. They paused at the end of the corridor and Owen glanced around the garden. Then he was shuffling her through the orchard.

"There is a postern gate," he muttered. "No one is watching."

Oh, please let there be a guard at the postern gate. "How do ye know?"

Again that nasty grin. "Because, I am supposed to be watching."

Devious. That was how he'd planned on getting her out,

by taking charge of their means of escape, with no one the wiser to his plans.

Well, she would leave another clue, even if it cost her the only meal she'd possibly have for awhile. As soon as they reached the gate, Kirstin dropped her apple. Owen glared at her, and as expected did not allow her to pick it up. He yanked a key from inside his sporran and then unlocked the gate. The hinges creaked as he opened it, and he peered out, smiling when he saw no one.

"We're as good as gone." And then he was tugging her through the gate and across an open heath toward the wood beyond.

She tripped, nearly breaking her ankle, and he didn't stop, merely dragged her along until she could get her footing back. She scrambled to remain upright, the muscles of her calves crying out in exertion, her arm wrenching from being hauled like a sack of grain, and her neck sore from where he'd squeezed her earlier.

They breeched the trees, the mid-day sunlight suddenly shuttered by the trees. He dragged her a few dozen yards through the brush until they came up to a horse tethered to a tree, fully saddled and two packed bags strapped near its flanks.

"Ye prepared this." She was surprised, and her voice showed it. He might have been pacing trying to figure out something, but how to escape with her hadn't been one of them. What was it he was thinking about?

"Aye."

Kirstin dug in her heels when he tried to pull her forward. She had to stall. Every chance she got. "When?"

"I've been doing a lot of listening the past few days, while I was hiding out."

"Hiding out?" That made no sense.

"Aye." He didn't expand on what he was saying, instead dragged her forward.

She kept her heels dug into the ground, hoping to disturb the earth enough that if anyone ever made it out this far they would see where she'd been taken. "What do ye mean? Tell me, please. I want to understand."

"Shut up." He yanked her arms behind her back, pain searing in her shoulders. "Are ye going to make me tie ye up? Gag ye? Because I would love nothing more than to make certain ye couldn't speak again."

Kirstin clamped her mouth shut and shook her head.

"Ask me another question and I'll bind and gag ye."

Kirstin swallowed hard, her eyes wide as she fought off tears. Didn't want him to see how much he scared her, affected her. That was what he wanted, wasn't it? What all predators wanted? To sense their prey's fear?

Even if it killed her, she would force herself to be calm. She'd left clues for Donna, for Gregor. They'd find her. They would. They had to.

Owen tossed her up onto the horse, her belly hitting the saddle hard, and she let out an, "Oomph," as she hit the saddle hard, and all the air left her body. She tried to draw in a breath, gagging on the pain in her belly.

He climbed up behind her, and slapped her bottom. She squeezed her eyes closed, and willed herself to be numb to everything that was happening. She needed to save her energy.

At first, they walked slow enough that she was no longer in pain, she could deal with it being uncomfortable, but as soon as they hit open ground, and he urged the horse into a run, every lope had her ribs and belly slamming against the saddle, and the thick, hard pommel. Within a quarter hour, she was dry-heaving and grateful she'd not eaten even a tiny bite of the apple. At one point the pommel hit her so hard in the ribs, she cried out, tears free-flowing. It was very possible she'd just broken a rib, and thankfully, her mind decided it was a good time to shut down and she passed into unconsciousness.

When she woke, they were in an abandoned hovel. At least that's what it appeared to be. 'Twas dark, but it was a small and smelled of mold. She noticed a hint of rotting vegetables and herbs still lingering in the air. If she had to guess, whoever had lived here before had been gone six months at least. It took her eyes a moment to adjust, but once they did, she could only make out various shapes. A hearth. A window. A door. Around the edges of the door, she could see that it was still light outside, but shut up tight, it was hard to see anything at all wherever it was they were. There was no fire, and no candles, only a few cracks of light around the entrance. She needed to find out where they were. *Fast*.

Owen's shadow moved in the small slivers of light. He was across the room from her, but she couldn't be sure what he was doing. Then she heard the telltale sound of teeth biting into a crunchy apple, a slurp as he tried to save the juice that free-flowed.

"Ye're awake," he stated, still chewing.

For a moment the sickening sweet scent of his apple mingled with the musty smell of the hovel. Would she ever be able to eat an apple again without thinking of him? Of her plight?

She didn't answer him. Pain shot through her body. Ribs. Neck. Arms. Belly. Legs.

For a brief moment she wondered if he'd used her as a sparring dummy while she slept. He must have tossed her on the floor because that's where she was now, curled up on her side. She could deal with the pain and hunger, that she was sure of, but she wasn't sure she could survive whatever plans he had for her. She didn't know what they were, but the way he treated her so unpleasantly, thus far, she had no reason to believe that he meant to keep her alive. But, she'd make herself useful, indispensable, well, she'd try to at least, she'd try, until they reached their destination.

He wanted something at Scorrybreac. But what? What could her family's small castle and holding possibly give him? Even as evil as they were, she could understand the MacLeod's desire for power as the motivation behind seizing her castle when she was a girl, but one man? With no ties to anyone but the church? Well, more like Satan... It made no sense.

All she had to do was make it that far. He had no idea that her sister lived there. And she intended to keep it that way. She just had to cooperate with him a little while longer, and he'd deliver her right to her sister without even realizing it.

"Eat." He tossed something at her, and it landed near her head with a thud.

Numbly, she reached for whatever it was, grabbing hold of a crusty oatcake. She brought it to her lips. The scent was unappetizing, but she had to eat to keep up her strength, because she was definitely going to ask him to let her ride upright come the morning or whenever they left.

The oatcake was bland, no flavor, and dry. It stuck to the roof of her mouth, and only the odd sucking noises she was making to get it off seemed to make her wretched captor take note.

Something else landed near her head, thicker, heavier. "Drink."

She grabbed hold of the waterskin, pulling the cork. The stench of liquor was overwhelming. It might not quench her thirst but it would certainly numb her brain.

As she predicted, the whiskey burned its way down her throat and into her belly where it quickly warmed, and sent deadening tingles throughout her body. She sighed and drank some more, and then some more.

As much as she wanted to finish her oatcake, or even save some of it for later, she knew that leaving a clue was better than leaving nothing at all. She broke off a piece and slid it silently behind her since Owen couldn't see her well enough to know.

She tossed back the waterskin, her body now sufficiently warm and tingly, her brain slowing down her fervent thoughts. She needed to remain calm. To heal. To rest. To gather her strength.

"Sleep," Owen ordered.

The man was only resorting to one-word orders and while she would normally want to argue with his ogre behavior, right now, she didn't care. She was glad not to be in pain, and if she was going to get a few hours rest as a reprieve from his torment then she would thank her lucky stars.

Kirstin curled up beneath the blanket, ignoring the stench, and closed her eyes tight. But instead of sleep, her thoughts raced and she couldn't seem to relax enough to slumber. Her eyes kept popping open and she imagined Owen looming above her, stinking of drink and demanding she submit to him. Every time she opened her eyes, the light behind the door faded a little more. He made no sounds. Appeared to be in slumber himself.

But still she could not make herself sleep. Where was Gregor? Donna? Had they found out she was missing yet?

All she could think about was whether or not she was bringing danger right to her family's door. Would Brenna forgive her for leading an enemy to her sanctuary? Lord knows they'd been through enough. Owen was obviously unstable and wouldn't hesitate to hurt someone to get what he wanted.

Well, she couldn't let that happen. Wouldn't let him hurt

her family. When the gates were opened, and they were through, she'd warn Brenna and Gabriel that Owen was their enemy. To beware. She'd jump from the horse, risk breaking her leg and run.

They'd help her, and take *him* down.

She hoped.

She prayed.

Nay, she had to be confident or else Owen would win, and no matter what, he could not win.

Never.

19

Outside the abbey walls, sitting amongst his men on wooden logs, and sharpening his sword with a whetstone, Gregor brooded. The rhythmic movement and sound was hypnotizing. While he worked until his blade no longer held any nicks, and was sharp enough to slice through armor, he replayed the conversation he'd had with Kirstin over and over in his mind.

She'd been acting so strange. Shaky. Fearful.

Sadness crept over him. She was different than he remembered. Not her usual self. The Kay he knew had been happy, joyful, full of life and thirsty for excitement and adventure. This one was sad most of the time, barely smiled. There should have been lines at the corners of her eyes and mouth showing how much she smiled, but there were none. How long had it been since she was truly happy? He knew he was part to blame for her lack of joy, and he wholeheartedly felt responsible for bringing that happiness back into her life. Was determined to. But the way she'd acted the hour before... It was... unusual.

When she'd sobbed against him, when they'd nearly made love, those had been real, gut-wrenching emotions.

The conversation they'd just had was bizarre and left him feeling completely confused. 'Twas as though she *wanted* him to see that something was off, and piece together some clue. But even that sounded like he was reaching.

And what could she have possibly wanted? He ran through her words, again.

Listen to everything...

If he were to believe that she'd wanted him to read between her spoken words, there seemed to be some sort of cryptic message hidden within.

I am not free...

And then the most disconcerting of all, she'd brought up a nefarious creature sneaking into the walls—

Gregor dropped the whetstone and jumped to his feet, sword-hilt gripped tight in his fist. His men stopped what they were doing to stare up at him curiously.

There was no reason for her to have brought up someone sneaking in. A nefarious creature. It made no sense. He'd not even been thinking along those terms, he'd simply been concerned for her sudden clumsiness that caused her to fall on a knife. And who wouldn't be?

Kay wasn't clumsy.

He'd thought maybe she wasn't getting enough sleep, or food to eat, or that she was simply overwhelmed, but the idea of someone sneaking into the abbey to do her harm had not crossed his mind until she said it.

And maybe that was the reason *for* her saying it.

Now he couldn't get it out of his mind.

Dammit, he should have picked up on that sooner!

"Collin, have ye seen anyone odd coming in or out of the castle?"

The warrior shook his head. "A merchant delivery the day

afore last, but we checked his wagon and he came right back out."

"No other messengers?"

"Nay, my laird. Just us and the Warriors of God." Under his breath Collin muttered, "Stinking warriors think they are above everyone else, might as well be wearing white robes and calling themselves disciples."

White robes.

The Saint!

Was it possible the bastard assassin had already infiltrated the abbey right under their noses? Was that who Kirstin was afraid of? Did the bastard cut her neck?

"Where is Sir John?" Gregor demanded.

"Last I heard he was speaking with the abbot."

Gregor reluctantly tucked his sword back into his scabbard, leaving it with his men outside the walls as they'd been asked to do. Thank goodness his dagger was clean and sharp, because the way the hair on the back of his neck was prickling, he had a fair idea that there was trouble amiss, and he might have need to use it.

He sprinted toward the gate, calling for it to be opened.

Once inside, he ran through the cloister and back to Kirstin's room. Donna was standing in the middle turning in a circle, an odd expression on her face. When she spotted Gregor, she jumped.

"Where is Kirstin?" he asked.

"She's gone. I have looked everywhere, and I've asked many. No one has seen her. She has simply vanished. And taken most of the apples. I think."

Gregor's heart skipped a beat and he was brought back to nearly a decade before where the same thing had happened—minus the apples. Well, dammit, he was not going to let her simply vanish, especially since he was certain this time around, she was in trouble. "Have ye any idea where she could have gone? Or if there was someone who might have wanted to take her somewhere?"

Donna shook her head, her hands coming to her face. "I fear something is wrong."

"Why? What do ye know?" He resisted the urge to shake the information from her.

She pointed to an apple by the brazier and another under the table. "When I came back to find out if she was feeling better, I found an apple tossed by the door. 'Twas odd, because the apples should have been in the basket. But ye see there is only one. It was like she was trying to leave a message. Kirstin, no matter how sick, would never leave things out of place. I watched her organize the apples myself so that they were just so."

Another cryptic message, like the one she'd been trying to share with him when he'd come.

Had her assailant been in the room the whole time? Gregor ran his hand over his face, finding it hard not to gouge his own skin. Kristin's wincing. The sudden jerking. Whoever it was, had been there, hurting her, right before his own damned eyes! Bloody hell, he was a fool.

"She's in trouble," Gregor stated, a fierce frown on his face as he stared at the apples on the floor.

"Aye." Donna's voice shook. "But what kind of trouble?"

"I think someone has taken her."

"But why? The only man who'd want to do that is dead."

Gregor looked up sharply. "What? Who?"

"The old Laird MacLeod. He abducted her sister fifteen years ago, and planned to take Kirstin, too, but her cousin took her to Nèamh Abbey where she was safe."

"Her cousin—Fingall?"

"Aye."

That explained some things. Fingall, must have been on the run which was why he'd kept so quiet over the years about his past. He'd shown his loyalty time and again and had worked damned hard to prove himself an asset to Gregor and the men. But still, Gregor had known both Fingall and Kirstin for a decade, and neither of them had mentioned their violent past.

"Was there anything of value that Kirstin carried with her here to Melrose?"

Donna shrugged, still looking perplexed at the spilled apples. "Naught but a missive for Mother Frances."

"When did she give Mother Frances the missive? Do ye know what it contained?"

Donna shook her head, bending to pick up one piece of fruit. "She's not yet given it to her, and I dinna know. It was sealed with wax. Kirstin showed me where she kept it in her satchel."

"Let me see."

Donna returned the apple to the basket then pivoted toward one of the cots. She tugged the satchel from beneath the bed, but when she opened it, the bag was empty. "'Tis gone," she whispered.

Gregor had an idea that whatever was in that missive contained information that was important enough to get Kirstin abducted. If they were dealing with The Saint, then it had to be more enticing than a king's ransom for men who associated with the Bruce—including the Bruce himself. For certainly, if The Saint had been inside the abbey, he could have attempted to abduct the Bruce himself.

Dammit! He had to make sure his sovereign was not also missing.

"I need ye to find, Fingall," Gregor said. "I'm going to locate the Bruce."

Donna nodded emphatically. "What should I tell him?"

"Tell him to meet me with the men outside."

"Aye, my laird." Donna sounded so lost. He truly felt sorry

for her. Kirstin had been her companion, her friend, and probably a mentor, too. The poor lass must be terrified.

Gregor patted her awkwardly on the shoulder. "I'll find her."

"Ye will?" She looked so hopeful, as hopeful as he felt inside.

"Aye. Ye have my word."

Donna's lower lip trembled, and she picked up the other apple, putting it in the basket.

"Donna," Gregor gave her a piercing stare. "For your safety, and that of Kirstin's, not a word of this to anyone, even Fingall. Simply tell him to come outside."

"Aye, my laird. I promise." She crossed herself. "Do ye think Kirstin is all right? I could not bear it if something happened to her. She is so kind and sweet and... and..." Donna started to blubber.

There wasn't time for more consoling. As much as he didn't want to, Gregor had to be stern with the young nun. "Pull yourself together. Kirstin needs ye to be strong."

She pressed her lips flat and straightened, nodding. "All right. I will be strong for her."

"Go now. Find Fingall."

Gregor did not wait to see her go; instead, he took off at a jog toward the Bruce's war office. He entered without knocking to find Sir John with him. Rage immediately flooded his veins and it took every ounce of his control not to charge the man.

"Ye bloody bastard, get away from my king," Gregor shouted. He pulled out his dagger, holding it parallel to the floor, ready to attack should John make any sudden or wrong moves.

"Buchanan, stand down," the Bruce was saying at the same time John said, "I fear I am correct."

"What in bloody hell does that mean?" Gregor asked Sir John.

"My vassal, Sir Owen, is missing. His position at the postern gate was empty, save for a single, pristine, apple. There is evidence of a scuffle."

Gregor saw red, and he ground his teeth. *An apple*! Kirstin had been dragged through the postern gate with no one the wiser! "Ye traitor," Gregor growled, lunging forward.

He grabbed John by the front of his leather-studded hauberk and jammed the dagger close to his neck.

John shook his head. "'Tis not I, I swear it on the graves of my forebears. I am loyal to the Bruce, to Scotland, even to ye, Laird Buchanan. If I am found to be not then I'd gladly hand ye my own blade to run me through."

His words were spoken with such conviction, truth filling his eyes, that it was hard not believe him. Gregor narrowed his eyes studying John, and then let go, taking a step back. The man sank to his knees, hand over his heart as he glanced up at the Bruce.

"I swear to ye, my liege, I am ever at your service. As I am avowed to the church to protect its people, its relics and its places of worship, I am also avowed to my rightful King of Scotland, Robert the Bruce."

Bruce nodded, then glanced at Gregor. "Do ye believe him?"

Gregor turned back to John, seeing the man's position of supplication. The earnestness in his gaze. There appeared to be no falsities in his stance, his demeanor. But there was also the possibility that he dropped to his knees in order to save his own life. However, that seemed entirely out of character for the man, who'd been more than willing to pick a fight with Gregor. Though Gregor had only known him a few days, he'd proven to be a confident, arrogant man, and quite capable as a warrior, too. Gregor blew out a displeased breath. "I do. I'm sorry for having put my dagger to your throat."

The Bruce, satisfied, held out his hand to the man. "Sir John, rise. Tell Buchanan what ye have told me."

John rose to his full height and faced Gregor. "Sir Owen came to me some weeks ago. He traveled alone and was an ordained Warrior of God, had papers to prove it. He said he'd been sent to join my squadron just before we set out for Melrose."

Gregor took in all the information, then asked, "Could he have known in advance that ye were headed to Melrose?"

"'Tis possible." John shrugged. "I suppose many could have known. Our Bishop had received a missive from Mother Aileen at Nèamh the week prior requesting our escort for two of her nuns."

Gregor grunted. "What else?"

"He got along well with all of my men, but there were things I've been suspicious of, such as when we were traveling. He did not warn one of my men about a rabbit hole in the ground, though one of the others saw Owen's horse nearly fall into it before. That warrior, Alec, spoke to me about it privately, concerned about what he'd seen. As a result, my warrior, Bain, was injured, a broken leg, and we had to leave him in the care of others at a nearby village. Then, there was a matter at an inn we stayed at with Sister Kirstin and Sister Donna. Owen insisted we were no longer welcome and we had to leave in the middle of the night. We never got a straight answer about why, but I did see a large English garrison had arrived, and was glad for the warning. Now that I think back on it, I wonder if that garrison had been coming for him."

If he was The Saint as Gregor suspected, then there was every possibility that assumption was correct.

John continued, "He has been acting odd since we arrived

here, skulking around, moody, missing Mass and Lauds and Vespers. And now—he is gone."

"And so is Sister Kirstin," Gregor added.

"What?" Both men asked in unison, surprise registering on their faces.

"Do ye know any reason why he would take her?" Gregor asked.

John pressed his lips together, a knowing expression flashing over his face. "Aye."

"What is it?"

"Greater than any king's ransom is the treasure of Nèamh Abbey."

What in bloody hell? "Treasure of Nèamh Abbey?"

John scowled, shaking his head in disappointment. "'Tis foretold within the church that the abbey protects a treasure large enough to fund an entire country, a thousand wars, for hundreds of years. That if ever it came to needing that coin, the abbey is to be summoned."

"How could they have amassed such an amount?" Gregor asked.

John shrugged. "'Tis most likely an exaggeration, but it is not the abbey's coin, rather the church's. 'Tis safer on the Isle of Skye than on the mainland."

"And ye think Sir Owen has gotten wind of it?"

"Aye. I'm certain he knows the reason we were sent to protect the Sisters."

"Kirstin carried the treasure?"

"Nay. I'm not certain what she carried, but I believe it was instructions for Mother Frances on how to obtain it. Melrose is in danger from the English. Mother Frances summoned help and coin to pay for the Warriors of God to come and protect this sacred place."

"If ye knew this, if Mother Frances knew this, why wasn't Kirstin better guarded? Your man simply picked her up and left with her. No one the wiser," Gregor asked accusingly.

"Including ye."

A bolt of potent fury went through Gregor's veins, so visible to all within the room, that the Bruce put a staying hand on Gregor's fighting arm. For he spoke the truth. The blasted traitor had been with Kirstin in her chamber the whole time and he'd never noticed.

"There is no use in arguing who is at fault," the Bruce said.

Gregor agreed, though he didn't voice it. Mostly, he was angry at himself for not having picked up on all the clues that Kirstin laid out before him. If he had, she wouldn't be in trouble now.

"I believe," Gregor confessed, "Sir Owen is The Saint."

The Bruce and John both blanched.

"The assassin?" the Bruce asked. "Right here within our walls?"

"Aye." Thank God the bastard had not acted on any desire to kill the Bruce.

Sir John dropped to his knees. "Forgive me, my liege. I brought the greatest assassin Scotland has seen of late right into your safe-hold. He could have killed ye."

"But he didna." The Bruce remained stoic, though his color had paled.

"Nay, he found a treasure of greater value," Gregor said.

"We need to find Sister Kirstin and Sir Owen afore the man hurts her and takes the church's treasure," the Bruce said. "Stand up. We've no more time for your beseeching."

John did as he was bade. "They would be headed for the Isle of Skye."

"Then we must organize a search party and go there. Now." Gregor was ready to rip Owen limb from limb.

"Aye. My men will help," John was saying.

Gregor shook his head. "How can I be sure to trust them?"

"They have been with me for years. I trust them implicitly with my life, and our greatest treasure," John rushed.

Gregor retreated from the room, growling, "I will gather my men."

Outside Melrose's walls, his men looked antsy, their eyes shifting toward him as he stormed out.

"What's happened?" Fingall asked. "Donna would not say, but I could tell something was wrong."

There was no use withholding information from his men. Succinctly, he gave them the details. "We had a traitor among us. He has abducted Sister Kirstin and is headed for the Isle of Skye. He is considered to be very dangerous. We think he is The Saint."

The men packed up their camp, armed themselves and mounted their horses, the Warriors of God with them. Several nuns brought out provisions, which they tucked into their saddlebags. The men rode, with Gregor in the lead, around the back of the abbey, following the disturbances in the grass by the postern gate, across the heath and into the woods. Thank the heavens Gregor had learned how to track at an early age. Those skills were going to be put to the test now. In the many Scots/English battles, and clan skirmishes he'd been in, knowing how to track had saved his and his men's lives a hundred times over. And now Kirstin's life hung in the balance. He couldn't fail her.

They followed the path of hoof divots and branches cut by a blade for several miles before they came to a trickling burn. They charged through the woods at a pace that scared the deer, squirrels, rabbits and even the birds. The divots ended there, none to the left or to the right, but led straight into the water.

"He crossed here," Gregor said.

They allowed their horses a moment to sip the water, and then they too waded into the churning depths. The tide was coming in, making the burn deeper, the water more unpredictable. About a dozen yards wide, they'd not far to wade before coming out on the other side. All of them made it across without issue. Gregor studied the ground, and determined that the tracks continued on to the west. The man was headed in the direction of Skye for certain, but taking a hidden, back trail in order to remain unseen. So far, he'd not tried to hide at all where he was headed, and that made Gregor nervous. Either Owen didn't think they'd find him—or he didn't care. They could all be riding straight into a trap.

Ignoring the water that dripped from them, and the setting sun which meant nightfall would soon be upon them, they urged their horses into a gallop, and headed west, the entire time, Gregor praying that Kirstin was all right, and planning the many ways in which he was going to kill Owen once he got his hands on him.

20

"Wake up." Kirstin's blankets she'd huddled in throughout the night were jerked away and taking with it all the warmth she'd had.

There were no streaks of light around the edges of the door. 'Twas still night, or just before dawn, perhaps. She was still so exhausted it was hard to tell whether she'd slept for an hour or more. And she very well could have slept for twelve.

Kirstin scrambled to stand on wavering legs before Owen saw fit to drag her up. "Where are we going? 'Tis dark still."

Owen made a sound of disgust, his large form vaguely obscured by the lack of light moving away from her. "Do ye think I dinna know that? The dark happens to be the reason we are leaving."

She tried to stretch out the soreness in her muscles, but it did no good, and seeming to not move quickly enough for his liking, Owen yanked on her arm. "Gather those blankets, wench."

Kirstin knelt, having to yank on her arm to get out of his grip in order to gather the blankets. She fumbled with them in the dark, managing to roll them neatly despite his tapping foot and the lack of light.

"Come on," he grumbled.

She followed him through the door to where his horse was tied, already saddled. He took the blankets and tied them to the back of the saddle. The temperature had dropped considerably over the night, and even though it wasn't freezing, the chill still prickled her skin without a blanket for protection.

Just as she'd promised herself the day before, she was going to insist on not riding like a sack of grain. Her ribs still ached from being tossed over the saddle.

Trying for meek and humble, which she hoped would please her captor, or at the very least make him see things her way, she said, "Please, can I ride sitting up, in front or behind ye? I promise to cooperate."

Owen grunted. "Why should I care for your comfort?"

Kirstin straightened. Meek didn't seem to be his style. Well, she was ready to go to battle on this one. She didn't care if it ended up getting her beat by the man for it, she wasn't going to back down. "Because I'm certain ye want me to help ye once we arrive on Skye, and if I'm to ride for two weeks like a sack of goods across your saddle, I'll be of no help to ye."

Owen glowered at her, the moonlight flashing on his gnashing teeth. She braced herself for his fist, but it didn't come. "I've no time to argue with ye about it. If ye're to ride astride, then ye'll be bound."

"Fine." She had to give in somewhere, she knew. At least being bound wasn't as bad as getting her ribs pummeled for hours until she passed out of consciousness. She stuck out her arms. "Here. Do it."

Owen grumbled some more under his breath. "I'll be the one giving orders."

He did tie her however, then helped her up onto the

saddle—touching her rear most inappropriately. Kirstin gritted her teeth, but didn't say anything, afraid that if she did he would only change his mind about letting her sit that way.

But he didn't immediately get on the horse behind her. Instead, he walked back into the croft, and she saw a flash of light, and then flames. He was lighting a fire. Why would he be doing that? Had he decided to make them a meal before they left? Kirstin frowned, her belly rumbling at the thought of a hot meal. With her hands bound the way they were, if the horse decided to buck or run, she'd have no way of protecting herself. Just when she was about to call out, to offer assistance with the meal, he emerged from the croft.

A small fire burned within the small house, and another in his hand. A torch. He tossed it up onto the room of the croft, flames igniting. All at once she realized he wasn't making a meal, but something far worse.

The grin on his face as he strolled back to the horse was by far the scariest she'd seen yet.

"Why?" she asked, hope fleeting of anyone finding the half-eaten oatcake she'd left burning up in flames.

"So no one knows we were here."

"But they will know *someone* was here."

"Not us." He untied his horse from the post. "Could have been the family who lives here now, run away from a blaze."

"But the croft was abandoned."

He ignored her, seeming to like the sound of his own voice. "Not that anyone who's looking for us will know that the family does not exist, or at least not the last six months."

Kirstin's hopes fell. How would Gregor find her if there were no clues? No evidence of her being there?

Owen climbed up behind her, his thighs surrounding hers and his groin pressed to her backside.

She should have insisted on sitting behind.

"No need for ye to worry about the little breadcrumbs

ye've been leaving, wench. By the time your lover catches up, ye'll be of no use to me anymore, and he'll never find ye."

And then he was kicking his horse hard, riding at a dangerous speed for both the dark and the woods, leaving her mind still reeling.

He planned to kill her.

To bury her where no one would ever find her bones.

When her entire body started to tremble, she worked hard to keep him from noticing but he laughed menacingly, and then she was whipped in the face. All thought gone but for the sting on her forehead.

Sitting upright in front of him, she was the first to catch any low-hanging branches. They lashed against her, even as she held her bound hands up to ward off the blows. Holding her hands up, her sleeves fell to her elbows, and the branches cut into the flesh on her forearms, caught in her hood, and tugged her hair free, ripping some of it out. Fresh tears tracked heatedly over her cheeks. It would appear that no matter what place he positioned her in, she was to be tormented.

They rode at that pace until the sun started to rise, and then Owen veered through the trees to the right, stopping short where a well-trodden road cut through the heath. They'd be out in the open if he took it. Behind her, he grunted, appeared to be assessing the situation.

Lord, she prayed he would take the open road, if only to give her torn up arms a reprieve.

Her skin was bloodied, bruised, and pain ripped up and down her arms. Her forehead, too, was crusted with blood from the very first slap of a branch.

Owen grunted and kicked his horse forward onto the open road, an even faster pace than in the woods. The risk of riding the road was great, but also a blessing if he were trying to hide their tracks. So many hoof divots and wagon wheel tracks marked the road, no one would realize just what direction they'd taken—if they'd taken the road at all.

"Tell me why ye're doing this?" she asked, grabbing hold of the pommel in front of her pelvis to keep from flying over the horse's withers as they flew forward.

"Because, ye're going to take me to Scorrybreac."

She had to get more out of him than that. If she were going to die for his cause, shouldn't she at least know why? "Aye, but what is at Scorrybreac that tempts ye?"

A low laugh, and then she felt his hips press forward, the hardness of his erection against her backside. Whatever it was at Scorrybreac that he wanted, it made him lustful. Did he want Brenna? Brenna's daughter? Kirstin shuddered at the thought. She'd not lead him there if those were his reasons.

"I am not tempted, wench. I am driven."

At least he was talking, even if not giving away too much yet. Didn't an outlaw always like to share their plans with someone? Well, she was going to be that someone. "What drives ye?" she asked, growing stronger in her conviction to keep her family safe.

"Treasure."

"Treasure?" She frowned at the road.

"Aye, the treasure of Scorrybreac. Worth a thousand time's a king's ransom."

Kirstin frowned, her face draining. There was no treasure. She'd grown up there, her sister had lived there with her husband and children for the past year at least. If there was a treasure, certainly they would have shared that with her wouldn't they? But, she didn't want to say all that to Owen. He couldn't know that she had any connection to the castle.

"I've never heard of a treasure." She tried for reflective, but was afraid it fell very short and came out more like quarrelsome.

"That's because your mother superior is a selfish bitch

who wants to keep it all for herself. Claims it's to help the church fund their protection. They all want to keep it up under lock and key. Well, I'm not going to let them. I'm going to take it."

Goodness! He'd just confessed to a whole lot more than she'd ever expected, and still she wanted to know more. Had to figure out what his motivation was, his plans, else she feared she'd not be able to escape him. "What will ye do with it?"

"None of your damned business." He pinched her thigh hard, perhaps a punishment for even asking.

Placating him, she said, "I know it isn't, I was simply curious." She licked her lips, threaded her fingers tightly together around the pommel. "Its just that, ye're obviously a verra cunning fellow, else ye'd not have been able to so perfectly plan our escape."

He grunted.

"And I was hoping ye had already made more plans."

"Hoping, were ye?"

"Well... I'd be lying if I didna say I wished to be set free or saved, but isn't that the truth of every captive?"

Another grunt.

"I just wanted to know if ye had the rest of your plans as well laid out."

"I do."

He obviously didn't want to share them, which was fine—for the moment. At least she had gotten started somewhere. She knew he was looking for a treasure. A vast one if he truly thought it was worth a thousand king's ransoms.

But where could it be?

Kirstin mentally went from room to room in the castle. It had been fifteen years since she'd been there, but she could not think of anything worth that much money. Even her grandfather's claymore which had hung above the hearth, its hilt crusted in jewels, could not be worth that much, and it had probably been taken from the castle by MacLeod during their siege anyway.

Thinking out loud, she asked, "Why would the church want to keep their greatest treasure at Scorrybreac? Why not hold it themselves?"

"Ye dinna understand." He spoke as though she were a complete imbecile, which in this instance, she certainly felt like one. "Keeping it away from the church ensures its safety."

"They must have great faith in the lairds of Scorrybreac."

"Or they are paid well."

This time *she* grunted.

"Tell me of Scorrybreac."

Instantly she was on alert. "I dinna know much about it."

"Tell me what little ye know."

"There is not much to tell. I know 'tis a smaller clan, once ruled by the MacLeods."

"Once?"

"Aye."

"And who rules there now?"

"I believe it has fallen back into the lines of the MacNeacail clan."

"What do ye know of their laird? Is he a religious man? Do they visit your abbey?"

"I know not. They've not come to our abbey," she lied. How could she tell him that Laird MacNeacail was a fifteen year old lad, and his guardian the Laird of MacKinnon? That would be her knowing too much, and letting too much be known by him.

"Interesting."

"Why is that interesting?" she pressed, her heart racing.

His hand splayed over her chest, fingers pressing against her breasts. She bit the inside of her cheek to keep from making any noise.

"I can feel your heart beating fast. Ye are either lying to me, or ye aren't telling me something. Which is it?"

Kirstin drew in a shallow breath, trying to calm herself, her body, but her fear, her nerves, they seemed to have a mind of their own, and were not communicating with the rest of her. "I swear, I'm telling ye all I know."

Owen chuckled menacingly, and yanked his horse off the road and around a giant boulder. He leapt down and grabbed her off the horse, dragging her on the ground, then lifting her up to pin her back against the boulder, and his body pressed along the length of hers.

"Ye think I'm stupid?" he growled.

Now that it was light she could see the way his dark eyes held a measure of the devil. Staring into them made her afraid for her soul.

She shook her head, fearful of what he would do in order to show just how powerful he was.

He grabbed her forearm, squeezing and every cut from the branches screamed out in agony. He ground his erection against her hip. The man had been aroused since the day before. She feared it was only a matter of time before he took his lust to the next level.

She had to placate him, to calm him down.

Pinning herself against the rock, trying to sink into its depths and away from him, she looked him in the eye, the rising sun making pink and orange slashes across the sky behind his head.

"I swear to ye, I know naught of the religious dealings of the laird of Scorrybreac. What I do know, is that they are pious, and they make their tithe to the abbey monthly."

"Do they offer your abbey protection should it be asked?"

She nodded. "Most of the surrounding clans do."

"Why is it, ye were sent on behalf of your abbey to

instruct Mother Frances in regards to funding and ye know nothing of the treasure?"

"I dinna know. I was sent with the missive. The one ye've read, that I have not. Ye know better than I."

His face came close, only an inch away as he hissed, "Dinna sass me."

Kirstin clamped her lips closed, afraid of the threats that were likely to come out of her mouth if he didn't get his stinking body away from her.

She pressed her hands back against the rock, feeling the coolness of the rough structure sink into her skin.

"I'm going to get that treasure, and ye're going to help me. Else, I kill every one ye care about. I will massacre Nèamh if I have to."

She nodded, wanting desperately to shout out that he didn't know anything about the people she cared about, but instead, she kept those words safely corralled on the tip of her tongue.

He rammed his body against her, startling her more than she already was. "Swear it on the life of your lover."

"I swear on the life of my lover, that I shall help ye find the treasure."

"On pain of death," he urged.

"On pain of death," she whispered.

And then he smashed his mouth against hers, teeth crunching against her own in a bruising, vile kiss. His body rubbed over her and she fought the urge to gag. Was certain now would be when he raped her.

But, he yanked just as quickly away, dragging her back to the horse, and when she happened to glance back at the spot where he'd held her, she saw the clue she'd left behind—the blood from her arms smeared against the boulder.

21

"Bloody fucking hell," Gregor shouted to the dawn wind, to no one.

They'd been on The Saint's trail for nearly two days, and every time he thought they were close, the blasted man slipped right between his fingers. Again and again.

They'd stopped the night before, resting only because they had to for the horses' sakes, else Gregor would have forgone sleep until he was certain Kirstin was safe and The Saint had been caught—and executed. Catching The Saint would send a powerful message to any of the other men who thought that taking a king's ransom for the English was a good idea. Revenge for Kirstin. For William Wallace.

Owen's trail had been intermittent with rash traces that he'd either not cared about leaving behind, or hadn't realized he was. Hasty. And thank god for them, because they had helped Gregor and his men get closer.

But those bits of evidence... They tore at his heart each time.

Clumps of long, raven hair. Bits of gray wool fabric that

resembled Kirstin's habit. And god help him, droplets of blood, had been found smeared on branches.

'Twas almost as if Sir Owen had intended to lead them straight to his whereabouts all along. His movements were reckless, and while they all had their suspicions that he was in fact The Saint, Gregor was also starting to have doubts simply because of how clumsy he was being in his escape.

Gregor stalked the perimeter of their small camp, the scent of smoke wafted around them like pre-dawn mist.

"There's a fire. A big one," he muttered.

There were two other men on guard duty with him, and they both came to tell him just the same thing as he said it. The men were starting to rouse and ready their horses.

"Pack up. We need to see what's going on." Even if it was simply helping a crofter contain their fire, they needed to, but this smelled of Sir Owen.

A distraction to keep them from pursuing him. Well, Gregor was not going to be distracted from his goal.

The men roused, saddled their horses and soon they were off toward the scent of smoke. As they grew closer, they could feel the heat of the blaze, and see the orange glow consuming an entire croft. Luckily, it had yet to spread to the surrounding trees.

"Make sure no one is inside!" Gregor ordered.

But the closer they got the more serious, and massive, he realized the fire was. Even if someone had been inside, there was no way they could get to them now. The roof shuddered, a loud echoing creak sounding, before it collapsed into the building sending a rush of heat and sparks outward.

"Back up!" he shouted to his men.

They did as instructed.

"We have to find a way to settle the flames." They had a duty, even if their mission was delayed an hour, to settle the flames before it spread throughout the forest causing further damage.

The men pulled bucket after bucket from a nearby well and flung them onto the collapsed house. With the roof caving in, at least the fire was more contained.

The hairs on their arms singed with the heat, and they breathed in the heavy smoke, not letting it bother them in their haste to get the fire under control.

Wetting the perimeter of the croft, they were able to keep the flames from spreading outward, and the dozens of buckets they tossed onto the center of it seemed to quell the flames enough that they were no longer worried it would spread or rage out of control.

"Ye keep going ahead to Loch Alsh, where ye'll have to cross to get to Skye. We'll make certain there are no bodies in the burned out croft," Sir John suggested, as he threw another bucket onto the flames.

Gregor shook his head, tossing water. "Nay. We'll both make certain."

John swiped sweat and soot on his brow. "Ye dinna fully trust me."

"I trust no one, but my own men." Gregor sprinted back to the well.

Sir John followed. "I can understand that."

Gregor nodded, not even bothering to say that it was too bad Sir John didn't have the luxury of trust with his men given *his* retainer was the one who'd kidnapped Kirstin, and could possibly be the most sought after assassin in Scotland.

"Keep coming with the buckets!" Gregor ordered the men. He tossed on the water, then passed his bucket off. He went to find a long, thick, dry, stick he could use to poke at the rubble to ascertain if anyone had been inside.

Sir John, seeing him, did the same. "We'll work together," Sir John said. "And soon ye will come to trust me."

"Likewise," Gregor mumbled.

Smoothing off tiny branches and leaves from a thick branch, Gregor used it to sift at the parts of the fire that had been contained. Embers smoldered, but so far he didn't see anything close to resembling a body.

John did the same as the men continued to dump water. Maybe four hours passed. The men coughed from inhaling the smoke, and so did Gregor, his lungs tight. Still, they couldn't stop until he was certain.

"I dinna think anyone was inside," he said at last.

"Neither do I," John added. "Safe to move on?"

"Aye."

They each issued orders to their men, and then Gregor checked the ground around the croft for clues in case it was Owen who'd been here.

"If 'twas Owen, why would he set the fire?" Gregor asked John. "Does it mean anything to ye?"

John shook his head. "Simply a distraction I'm guessing. Look how long we spent to contain it. Bought himself nearly half a day."

"True. I had thought that myself." Gregor glanced toward the ground. "And we've mucked up the ground so much, if it was him, there is no evidence of which direction he's gone."

"We know he's headed to Skye. Let us continue in that direction, and we will pick up his trail again soon. He cannot get there too quickly. "'Tis at least a two week journey to Nèamh, he's got a woman with him, and we've only been going two days, faster than he'll be traveling with Sister Kirstin."

"Think ye he'll follow the route ye took on the way to Melrose?"

"Guessing so, or at least stick close to it as he has been."

Gregor hated guessing. Hated not knowing exactly what

Owen's next move would be. But he had to settle for that. They needed to keep moving. The fact that the fire had been raging when they arrived meant that if it was Owen who'd set it, they were hot on his tail. He couldn't have been here too much before them, maybe an hour. Their horse would tire more easily as they had only one with two riders.

They'd be upon him before they got to Loch Alsh, before they were able to cross over to Skye, of that Gregor was certain.

However, there was one thing about certainties, they weren't really always assured. And that was the case with catching up to Owen and Kirstin. The man seemed to simply have vanished, as if he'd gained powers from the flames, and while he most likely got a half day's ride ahead of them, it could be more or less.

The men mounted up and continued in the direction of Skye, coming to an open road. Gregor jumped down, examining the hoof prints. The roads were so filled with divots and wagon wheel tracks that it was hard to tell which direction he'd gone, if it was truly even his horse taking part in some of the markings.

Then he spotted a few droplets of blood. "This way!"

They came across hoof prints veering off the path, and a cursory check revealed a boulder beside the road with blood smeared on it. Even though there was no telling that it was Kirstin's blood or that of an animal, Gregor just knew it was hers. What awful, heinous things was Sir Owen doing to her. Each passing hour brought Gregor's temper closer and closer to being completely out of control. But he had to keep himself in check, else he make a mistake. A mistake that could cost Kirstin her life.

Two more days went by without a single sighting, and Gregor was starting to lose his mind. They were at the base of the Cairngorms Mountains, treacherous to travel alone. Thank the saints it wasn't winter, else Owen would have been leading Kirstin straight into a death trap. Hungry animals, the possibility of an avalanche, a snowstorm that could bury them, just one slip on ice sending them tumbling over the side.

"Think he went up or around?" John asked.

"Up would be stealthier, if that was what he was going for. Seems sometimes he is and sometimes he isn't."

"Aye. But with a woman, think he'd risk it?"

Aye, Gregor did think Owen was willing to risk Kirstin's life. "When ye came to Melrose, did ye go up or around?"

"Around."

"Then he went up. He's stuck mostly to your route so far, with a few times veering off. Once here, he's going to try to lose us for good. He'd not go the same way."

"I agree," Sir John said.

That decided, they restocked their provisions in the local village, asking if anyone had seen a woman and a man, both of the church, traveling through. No one had. But oddly, the day before, there had been several things stolen in the night from various crofts and shops. Nothing truly valuable, just a few provisions: food, whisky, a whetstone, a bow and a set of arrows, a lantern, some candles.

Gregor and John exchanged glances. Had to be Owen. He'd not come into the town to shop before going up into the mountains, but he'd certainly come in to steal.

They finished gathering their supplies and paid the merchant an extra coin for the information he'd shared.

If that had only been the day before, than Owen was only a day ahead of them.

They were that much closer.

Even if it felt so far.

They'd not heard or seen anything the day before, so this

bit of news was welcome, as Gregor was starting to worry if they'd lost them altogether.

Not wasting another moment of time, they picked their way as fast as they were willing up the mountains, not wanting to hurt any of their mounts because they had no replacements. Perhaps fifteen miles north of the village, the sun was beginning to set, there was a sound. A muffled cry perhaps, that seemed to echo from all directions.

Gregor stiffened. Listened.

Silence.

"Could have been an animal. A wild-thing catching a rabbit maybe," Collin offered.

"Aye," John agreed.

"Or it could have been Kirstin and the bastard is hurting her," Gregor growled. "Again."

Mo chreach he was going to make the bastard suffer.

Fingall shook his head. "He'd not take her all this way if he wanted to... hurt her."

Gregor looked at Fingall, wondering if the man had lost his sense. "Dinna be naïve. He can hurt her in many ways and still keep her alive. Ye saw the blood on the branches, on the boulder. She *is* hurt."

Fingall blanched and looked away. "I only meant, he'd not kill her."

"Look, I know she is your cousin, that ye care about her. And so do I. I dinna want to think about her as being hurt by this bastard, but we have to be prepared that when we finally find them, that Kirstin may well need the attention of a healer, and she will certainly need your prayers." Gregor felt like his head was ready to explode. Even just thinking about her being harmed sent him into a mad rage. Sweat beaded on his brow, trickled down his spine. He stilled the sudden shake of his fists.

"I say we make camp for the night here," John said. "If it

was indeed her, then they may be making camp, too, and we might be able to scout them out on foot after dark."

Gregor agreed. "I'm going to be on the first mission."

"So am I," Fingall said.

Gregor shook his head. "Nay, ye go on the second, so at least one of us is there should she be found."

The men set up camp, and Gregor gathered five to scout with him. "No horses. No fire. Use your eyes, ears and sense of smell to ferret out anything unusual. Bring your weapons in case ye need to fight off nature, or The Saint. If ye find them, protect Sister Kirstin with your life."

"Aye, my laird," all the men echoed.

THEY MOVED OUT, THEIR FOOTFALLS SILENT ON THE GRASSY summer forest floor. Gregor must have walked at least two miles in every direction before his time was up, but he'd not found anything. Not heard anything. Couldn't smell anything. Not even the smallest hint of a campfire. Didn't even see the faintest glow of a candlestick.

Once more The Saint had vanished with the love of Gregor's life.

Begrudgingly, he made his way back to camp, punching a tree as he arrived. The bark cut into his skin, and it released only a minor amount of his anger.

Fingall approached. "We'll find her, my laird."

"Swear to me, Fingall. Swear to me that ye'll protect her."

"I swear to protect her with my life this day and all days forward, just as I always have."

Gregor lay on the bare ground, a plaid rolled up behind his head. He'd not slept in two days. And though his mind raced with every possibility, his body was exhausted. His knuckles throbbed. But if he didn't sleep now, likely he'd be off his game in the morning, and he couldn't risk it. He closed his eyes and let himself sink into a dead sleep.

A sleep that was not dreamless...

They were at Castle Buchanan. Outside, the rain pelted with fury against the castle walls. But inside could have been a sweet, summer day. Two dozen candles burned in their chamber. Kirstin was dancing around, legs kicking up to touch her knees, singing him a song she'd learned in the village of a lost lover.

"She came to him in the morning, dressed in fairy white. A song she sang, of love and glory amongst warrior's might..."

Gregor reached for her. "Come here, my love, I will show ye my warrior's might."

Her head tilted back and she laughed, picking up the hem of her breezy chemise and sashayed forward. She grabbed up a bunch of grapes and sat on his lap, feeding him a globe of succulent fruit. Her body was warm, supple and fit so perfectly against him.

"Ye need not show me your warrior's might." She kissed his brow, his nose, his lips, sharing in the juice of the grape. "For I have seen it many times."

Turning serious, he said, "I will protect ye always."

She popped a grape into her mouth. "I know ye will."

Gregor kissed her deeply, tasting sweetness, hoping to show her with his lips just how much he loved her. He stood up, lifting her in his arms and twirling her about. He kicked up the same jig she'd been doing, bouncing around while she squealed in his embrace.

"My god, ye are beautiful," he whispered.

She touched his cheek, gazing with such affection into his eyes that his heart lurched behind his ribs. "So are ye."

He loved her so damned much. If only he could find the courage to say the words. To tell her...

Gregor bolted upright, momentarily unaware of his surroundings and then the world came crashing back down around him.

Kirstin was still in the clutches of a madman.

22

For the past three days, Owen had become more and more irate, grumbling and murmuring and treating her roughly. At night, he'd taken to tying her to a tree and gagging her when they made camp, and then he would leave for hours on end, only to return with more curses spilling from his vile mouth.

Whatever sense of the Lord he'd had in him before had dissipated greatly, leaving nothing but a demon obsessed.

When she tried to ask him what had turned his mood, if only to get him to speak, perhaps to calm his fury, he only gnashed his teeth. And she had one good idea of what—or whom—it might be.

Gregor had to be on their tail. And he had to have many men with him, else Owen would have tried to take him out of the equation.

Luckily, she was right between her two saviors. If she could reach even one of them before Owen decided it was time to kill her. She hoped she could delay him or escape before that time came. Hope that soon she would be saved—either by her people at Scorrybreac, or by Gregor.

Gregor had to have found out where they were headed. To Skye, but most likely, he only knew to search for her at Nèamh, and not Scorrybreac.

Owen charged her, stabbing his dagger into the tree above her head, glowering down at her. Would this be the moment he put his threats into action? Spilled her blood. But then he backed away.

With all her might she called out to Gregor with her mind. Praying that some miracle of Fate would allow him to hear her.

He was close. She could sense it in her heart, not only in the increasing bad temper of her captor.

Once more they left their makeshift camp before dawn, traveling at high speeds. They rode through the day, racing toward the shallowest, southern part of Loch Ness and making their way across on horseback rather than securing passage on the ferry.

Owen wanted no one to see them. To remember them.

When they needed provisions, he tied her up, disappeared and returned with a satchel full. Never too much, but never too little.

He gave her enough food to keep the edge of hunger just at bay, but not enough for her to regain her strength completely. She was grateful that on one of his raids, he did bring her an ointment for her arms, and clean linens. She refused his help in administering the ointment, and instead cleaned her arms with whisky, though it burned and he balked at seeing his drink wasted. She didn't care how he felt about it. There was no way she was going to allow herself to lose an arm because the fool had not allowed her to properly care for herself. The cuts and scrapes had scabbed and were healing well enough. They itched something fierce whenever she tried to fall asleep, which only told her they were well on their way to being healed completely.

The sun was high in the sky, and she guessed the time to be around noon or a little after. They'd ridden up yet another rise, and Owen had stopped to let his horse rest a moment and give her a chance to relieve herself. She guessed they might have been traveling a week or so.

"See there?" he asked, pointing in the distance beyond the tops of the fir trees.

"The castle?" Looming up below and surrounded by water was Eilean Donan Castle. Her square tower jutted into the clouds.

So many memories she had of that place. So many lovely memories.

"Aye." Owen did not say more, instead ripped a piece of jerky from his satchel and began to chew on it as she imagined a wildcat would tear into the flesh of a rabbit.

"What about it?" she goaded, trying to get a sense of his thoughts.

They'd not talked much over the last few days, as every time she opened her mouth, he usually either stuffed a gag inside, or smacked her. For the sake of survival, she'd kept quiet, wanting to keep healing in the places she'd already been injured and to gather her strength. She was fairly certain now that the pain had dulled considerably that she'd only bruised her rib on the pommel and not broken one.

"Loch Alsh is just beyond the castle. And Skye, a boat ride away."

Perhaps this was her chance. The time she should try to escape, even if it killed her. Once they made it to Skye, and he was on his way to Scorrybreac, he'd likely dispose of her as he'd threatened.

"How will ye get a boat without being seen?" she asked. "Ye didna want to ride the ferry at Loch Ness. Are we going to ride as far south as we can to ford across?" Was there even such a point?

"I'm going to steal a boat," he boasted, grabbing another piece of jerky and not offering her one.

There wouldn't be a boat big enough to steal that his horse could fit on. "And your mount?"

"I will tether him to our boat and he can swim across."

Kirstin swallowed down her fear. If the horse could swim no longer... If he grew tired... And he was tethered to the boat and he started to sink, they'd sink, too. This was a death trap. In her mind it was settled. She had to escape. Soon. While he was getting the boat.

"We'll rest here until dark, and then I will steal a boat. We will go, when no one can see us."

Owen started to undress, and Kirstin's heart thudded loudly, and she was afraid he could smell her fear. Was now going to be the time that he raped her? That he made good on the hundred threats he'd shouted at her since he'd first abducted her?

She averted her eyes, not willing to look at his naked body. But he didn't come near her. Instead he pulled on other clothes. A linen shirt, a plaid, a belt. He was dressing like a Highlander, and not like a Warrior of God. He must have stolen the clothes.

He opened up his satchel and then tossed a worn gown her way, the fabric falling at her feet.

"Change," he ordered.

She jutted her chin forward. "Untie me."

Owen narrowed his eyes as he trudged forward. "Try to escape and I'll gut ye."

She believed him. He was crazed enough the past few days that he might simply do it before they even crossed. How many times could he have killed her? Three dozen at least. She'd offered him little to no information regarding Scorrybreac. Why would he keep her alive?

With the *sgian dubh* from his sock, Owen sawed at the rope around her wrists.

When the cord gave way, she rubbed at her sore skin.

"Turn around, please," she asked.

"Nay."

He would watch her. Fine. She wasn't going to look at him. Kirstin stood quickly. She'd rush through this, not give him a chance to savor whatever it was he was looking for. She turned her back, then realized with her back turned she couldn't see anything he was doing. He could pounce on her. Zounds, but if she spun back around he might take it as an invitation—and she was *certainly not* going to invite him to do anything. She couldn't wait to be rid of this man.

Back to him it is.

Keeping her ears keen to his every movement, she worked at the ties of her habit, and divested it as quickly as she could, keeping her chemise in place. Then she bent, picked up the other gown and yanked it over her head, yanking it over her hips. It was a little snug in nearly all areas, tight around her shoulders, the bandages on her forearms, her breasts, waist and hips. It was probably a good inch too short. But it would have to do.

Dressed, she turned back around, her face void of emotion, gaze toward his feet.

"Take off your hood."

She unpinned the hood from her hair and then tugged out the ribbon holding her hair in a plait and combed through her locks with her fingers, until she felt she'd sufficiently gotten rid of the tangles. She re-plaited it and tied the ribbon at the end.

"I can see why Gregor and John are infatuated with ye." Owen's voice had taken on a husky tone.

Kirstin ignored him.

"Ye are a vision." He stepped closer, lowered his head, and

she was afraid he'd repeat that bruising kiss he'd given her days before against the boulder.

"I am a nun. To violate me is to violate God's daughter," she spoke to the air beside him.

Owen grunted, and grabbed hold of her elbows, pinching. "I am God's soldier. If I think it necessary to feel the lushness of your body around my cock, then I will see it done. Besides, we both know ye aren't pure. Moreover, God might will me to meet out your punishment."

She swallowed hard, refusing to say another word. But if he tried to rape her, she would not be meek. She'd scratch his eyes out, manage to steal his dagger and stab him to death. And then she'd beg forgiveness for her sins. She'd gotten good at that.

Owen shoved her down, and she fell to her knees, catching herself with her hands before her head hit the ground. He dropped behind her, pressed his erection against her buttocks, but did not grapple with her skirts. Even still she clawed her way forward and away from him. He let her go, chuckling in that evil, vile way he had.

"Ye see? If I wanted to, I could have ye," he said.

She wondered if that was all he wanted, the threat of raping her hanging over her head.

He grabbed her discarded habit and hood and added it the pile of his own clothes.

"Dig."

She rolled over onto her bottom, staring up at him. "What?"

"Dig a fucking hole."

Kirstin swallowed, grateful that instead of being raped, she was just digging. But, oh, heavens, why was she digging? Was he making her dig her own grave? Dressing her in common clothes so when her body was discovered no one would be the wiser as to who she was?

Kirstin shook her head.

Owen backhanded her so hard, she fell to the side, lip stinging, blood metallic on her tongue.

"Dig."

She grabbed a stick and jabbed it into the earth. Repeatedly. Pretending it was his face, his chest, his groin. She mentally killed him over and over again.

She used her hands to scoop the loosened earth, watching him out of the corner of her eye. Wanting to rush him and jab the stick for real into his flesh.

She dug for what felt like hours until finally he told her that was enough.

He dumped their clothes in the hole.

"Cover it up," he ordered, then turned his back poking around in the satchel again.

So it was not her grave. Relief rushed through her, making her hands shake more than they had already.

This was her chance to leave another clue, she grabbed for her hood, planning on tossing it behind a tree, when the man whirled back around.

"Dinna even think of leaving one of your damned breadcrumbs. The bastards have been on our arses for days. And it's all your fault." The last words, he bent and screamed into her face.

Kirstin reeled back from his anger. The man was going mad. She had to escape before they reached their destination. Because the more she thought on it, the more she realized, he had no use for her. Especially if he'd made her change into normal clothes. Dressed as a nun, she could have gotten them entry into Scorrybreac as two church missionaries. Dressed as common folk, there was no reason for the gates to be opened to them.

She finished burying the clothes, stuffing a sharpened rock up her sleeve that she'd found, and then sat in silence, watching him pace and mutter to himself until the sun came down.

As it started to set, he pulled out the familiar length of rope and tied her tightly to the tree, then stuffed the rag into her mouth.

"Dinna make a sound. I'll return after I have the boat." He slunk into the woods, the sounds of his footsteps echoing in time with her heartbeat and soaring hope.

Well, she didn't plan to be there when he returned.

She would cut through this rope and make a run toward Eilean Donan, hoping that someone in the village would take pity on her, remember her, and keep her safe.

Kirstin worked to get the sharp stone from her sleeve and when she finally had it, she closed her eyes and murmured prayers as she gently sawed at the rope, nearly dropping the stone thrice. One tendril of the rope sprung free and she blew out a breath, giving her stiff fingers only a moment to recoup, then she sawed again until the next twine snapped, and then the next. She worked tirelessly, intent on getting loose and at long last, the final bit of her bindings snapped free.

"Thank the saints," she muttered, pressing her hands together and looking up at the darkened sky, willing the blood to return to her appendages. "I will pray more later. But right now, I must escape."

She started to run and then thought better of it. The horse. She'd get away, toward help, faster if she had a horse.

Kirstin untied the horse from the tree and mounted, the stirrups too long for her feet to reach, but she didn't have time to fix them. She leaned forward, stroked the horse's mane and clutching her thighs to his middle, she gave him a kick and begged him to, "Go."

The animal listened with a slight and pleasant nicker, and then stepped slowly forward.

"Quicker, please," she begged.

The horse seemed content to walk slower than she could crawl.

Owen had descended the ridge to the right, well she wasn't going to go the same direction. With a mighty kick Kirstin got the mount moving. She descended to the left, going slow, and leaning low so as not to get caught on a branch she couldn't see in the dark. She wished she had a weapon. Because if he found her—free and riding his horse—he'd likely kill her then and there.

Metal scraped against her knee. She reached down and touched the cool hilt of a sword that he'd tucked beneath the saddle.

"Thank ye, God!" She might be a sinner, but it appeared someone was on her side.

23

They were closer than ever before, Gregor could feel it. Like the air vibrated, pushing him toward Kirstin.

Cresting the ridge that overlooked Eilean Donan, majestic as it rose moonlit from the loch, Gregor was taken back to his more carefree days. How naïve he'd been back then.

"Look," Fingall said.

Where the fir trees were not so tightly clustered together, the night sky shone down on the ground. A spot before a tree that looked like a scuffle, and—

"Looks like something was buried here," Gregor said. He dismounted and bent to the ground, pushing dirt away from the odd mound on the ground until his fingers brushed fabric. He tugged it from the earth, his heart sinking.

A nun's hood.

He jerked his hand away, terrified for a moment he was about to find Kirstin's body. Fingall knelt opposite him, helping to dig, but all they found were her hood, her habit, with blood-stained arms (only her arms, nothing more!), and Owen's clothes.

"Why would he make them change clothes?" Gregor wondered aloud, his mind still reeling to see that perhaps she was only injured on her arms. Thinking back to what they'd found on the trail that made sense. She'd been using her arms to block the branches as they whipped against her. Shaking his head, he said, "To blend in?"

"Aye," John offered. "By now he must know we're following and he doesn't want to be recognized for his affiliation with the church."

Gregor touched the disturbed spot on the ground, finding rope in what he at first thought was a stick.

"She was tied up." He pulled the frayed ends toward his face. "Either she somehow escaped. Looks ragged, like she cut it with something. Mayhap she got hold of a dagger. Or, he's already absconded with her." Gregor stood straight, imagining Kirstin running through the woods in the dark, a madman chasing after her.

"They'll not be far," Collin said. "Horse dung is still fresh over here."

"A man's sized footprints lead this way."

"Over here are hoof prints."

In his gut, Gregor believed she'd escaped. He prayed it wasn't wishful thinking. "Follow the hoof prints. We need to get to her before Owen does."

"Mount up! We're going to split into four groups going in each direction. If ye find her, go to the castle, tell them ye are with me and they will give ye sanctuary. I'm a friend of Torsten Mackenzie, brother to Laird Cathal Mackenzie. Beware of the laird, he's not always as friendly. Their father was a good man. If ye find him—find and gag him. Dinna let him escape."

The men split up, Fingall and Collin with Gregor, and

they headed west down the ridge, taking it slow so they could listen for any unusual sounds. There was the caw of an occasional night bird of prey. Insects singing, and then every so often what sounded like an animal crashing through the trees.

"Think ye that's her or him?" Fingall asked.

"I dinna know, but we'd do best to follow it," Gregor said.

Over fallen trees, between boulders, down the ridge they went, following the sounds of the intermittent crashing. Whoever it was, was also headed down the ridge, which ruled out an animal that would likely stick to its territory.

Without making a sound, Gregor signaled his men to speed up as stealthily as they could. He wanted to catch whomever it was making all that racket before they hit the bottom of the ridge and rode over the moor toward the castle or escaped over the loch, or to the village, even. They couldn't lose them. *Her*.

Gregor caught sight of a blurred shadow riding on horseback through the woods. Ducking in and out. Weaving around trees. Completely wild. Out of control even.

The Saint would not be so reckless would he? The man had worked hard to hide any traces of them, though not hard enough at times, but this rider was erratic.

The figure was small, too small to be Owen. Was it Kirstin? Looked to be a female.

He watched her list to the left and then the right of the horse. If she kept up at that pace, she'd get themselves killed.

"Kirstin!" Gregor called out, in hopes that he had the right of it, and kicked his horse into a faster pace. "Kay! Stop! Slow down!"

It was too hard to see much beyond the shadow of her form, but it looked like she turned around—and then went faster!

The sight of three warriors chasing after her was probably terrifying given what she'd been through in the last week.

"Kay! Its Gregor!"

"And Fingall!"

"And Collin!"

All of them were riding frantically toward her, Gregor cursing under his breath. Why wouldn't she stop? She'd break her neck at this pace.

"Stop!" Gregor shouted again.

He heard a female cry, saw her body wobbling on top of the horse, like she was grappling with the reins, but couldn't quite get ahold of them.

"Dammit! The horse is out of control," Gregor growled. He had to save her.

Leaning over his mount's withers, he coaxed him to go faster, leaping over fallen branches and roots jutting from the ground.

He was nearly upon her, just a few more feet and he could grab hold of the reins.

"Slow down," he shouted.

But she ignored him, and then something whizzed past his head, slicing against his ear and slamming into a tree. An arrow?

Kirstin turned around to see him, fear all over her shadowed features. "He's going to kill us. Keep running!"

The Saint. He'd found her crashing through the forest, just as Gregor had. His relief at finding her alive, blended with his fury at her plight and his need to murder Owen.

And the bloody bastard had arrows.

"Nay, love, he will not." Gregor reached forward and grabbed hold of her horse's reins, pulling both their mounts to a jerking stop.

Fingall and Collin joined him as another arrow whizzed past, slamming into the trunk of yet another tree.

"He's not got verra good aim," Fingall muttered.

"'Tis dark and we were moving targets," Gregor said.

"And now we're sitting ducks," Kirstin said, her entire body trembling and making her horse skitter on his feet.

"Nay, we're not." Gregor passed her reins to Fingall. "Protect her with your life. Collin, come with me."

Kirstin protested, but Gregor silenced her with a brush of his lips on hers. "I'll come back. I promise."

They charged through the woods, shouting out for Owen to show his face and fight like a man. But no matter where they went, they couldn't seem to locate him, and the arrows had stopped. Which made him fearful for Kirstin all over again. Gregor doubled back and found her and Fingall safely where he'd left them.

"Where is Owen?" Kirstin asked.

"He's disappeared."

She started to sob. "He will come for me again. He's after a treasure ten times a king's ransom."

"I won't let him harm ye," Gregor said. Tugging her against his chest, letting her tears wet his shirt. He stroked her back, hoping to comfort her. "I promise."

Just then another arrow whipped past, lodging in Fingall's right shoulder. He cried out, at the same time as Kirstin. The momentum of the arrow, shoved Fingall backward, and he started to lose his seat, but righted himself before he fell from his mount.

Gregor yanked out his sword, turning his horse in a circle. "Blast it, Owen! Show your face ye coward!"

The bloody bastard's laughter sounded from somewhere in the trees and Gregor had a fleeting moment where he believed the man was truly possessed by the devil.

"Shields!" Gregor shouted, and his two men, even the bleeding Fingall raised their shields, protecting Kirstin from any incoming arrows.

"Come out and fight me like a man!" Gregor demanded. "Let us settle this here and now!"

A thud behind him, and a shuffling in the leaves upon the ground. Gregor whirled to see Sir Owen's shadow present itself.

"Quite entertaining watching ye all run around like a bunch of naked ninnies searching for their underclothes." Owen laughed.

"Lay down your weapons," Gregor demanded.

"Och, now that doesn't seem fair, does it? Ye promised me a fight, and a fight is what I've come for."

"Ye'll not be winning this fight."

Owen shrugged. "We shall see."

Gregor jumped from his horse and Collin scooted his mount forward to take Gregor's place beside Kirstin, keeping her safe.

"Gregor, please! Dinna do this," Kirstin begged.

As much as he wanted to give her what she asked, he simply couldn't. Not this time. Owen had gone too far and was too much of a threat to all of them, including their rightful king.

"Swords," Gregor said.

"Works for me." Owen tossed his bow and arrow to the side, his sword glinting in the moonlight.

Gregor was not going to let him leave this land alive.

They circled one another a moment, each assessing the other's stance, build, energy level. The rush of battle flowed vigorously through Gregor's veins. He was ready to pounce. To pummel the jackhole to the ground.

Gregor bared his teeth, daring Owen to make the first move. He might be an assassin, accustomed to slinking into the shadows and killing people when they were not expecting it, but Gregor was a tried warrior. A man of action. A leader. A trainer. And while Owen might match him in size, this bastard had no chance.

Owen lunged, predictably, forward, his sword thrust out

as though he expected Gregor to open his arms wide and allow the blade to sink home.

Gregor dodged left, catching his blade against Owen's, he swirled his edge around Owen's enough to throw the man slightly off his balance.

"Ye'll have to do better than that if ye expect to best me," Gregor said.

Owen growled, twisted in the air with a little leap and brought his sword down. Again Gregor simply deflected the blow and then shot out his own sword slicing into the back of Owen's opposite hand. He didn't want to cut his sword hand yet, that would only end the fight too early and Gregor wanted the man to suffer. A lot.

Owen was starting to sweat. All that slinking around, and possibly a few fights with his victims hadn't trained him enough to fight a war-laird. Gregor had fought beside William Wallace himself, and had learned much about fighting the English way from Samuel. He was well prepared. Sir John was probably disgusted at Sir Owen's display, having accepted him onto his squadron of warriors.

"Ye bloody bastard! I'm going to shred ye and then sew ye up until ye resemble the fox that ye are," Owen growled parrying again. He was coming forward quickly, swinging to the left, to the right. Reckless and angry.

"A fox, eh?" Gregor chuckled, blocking each blow easily. "I'm a might bit bigger than a fox."

"Not by the time I'm done hacking ye to bits," Owen threatened, running at him again.

Gregor ducked slicing across both of Owen's shins before rolling backward and leaping to his feet as his opponent dropped to his knees. It wasn't a blow that would cripple him, but it would hurt like bloody fire. Owen quickly figured out he wasn't lame and leapt back up to his feet, angrier than a cornered boar.

"If ye've had quite enough, I'd like my turn," Sir John called out.

"Aye, and then me," Fingall said.

Gregor laughed. Owen faltered in his steps, and Gregor flipped his sword to his left hand, reached back and punched Owen in the jaw with his right.

The man faltered, stepping backward, shouting obscenities. As much as Gregor wanted to finish him off, 'haps he did owe it to John to fight a man who betrayed him and threatened his own reputation in Scotland.

Regrettably, Gregor backed away. But then he heard Kirstin's whimper, and he knew he'd done the right thing, he needed to comfort her.

"He's all yours, John."

John leapt from his horse, the clanging of swords echoing in the night.

Gregor lifted Kirstin from her horse, holding her in his arms, tight. He whispered into her hair, kissing her face, telling her how much he'd worried over her, how much he loved her. She trembled in his arms, clutched to him.

"My laird," Collin called.

Gregor turned to see that John had forgone his sword, had leapt on Owen, and proceeded to give him a beating that rivaled any Gregor had seen before, to the point that, Collin was actually trying to pull John off Owen's still body.

"I'll be right back," he whispered to Kirstin, settling her back onto her horse.

"He's gone man," Gregor said, rushing to John.

"I could beat him into dust," John growled, pummeling Sir Owen's bloody face.

"Aye, but ye need not. Let the wolves claim his body now."

Sir John relented, backing away. He spat on Owen's dead body.

Certain Owen wouldn't again attack, they all mounted

their horses, but Gregor couldn't go forward until he had Kirstin in his arms. She readily came to him, clinging, her arms around his neck, her face pressed to his shoulder.

"Gregor," she murmured. "Thank ye."

"Ye need not thank me, lass, there was no other choice but to save ye. I could not bear for ye to disappear from my life for a second time. I love ye, with all my heart and soul. I want ye to know that, to believe it. I am yours."

"Aye, I know it, and I love ye, too. So verra much."

And then he kissed her with all the urgency, fear and relief he felt inside. His tongue plundering her willing mouth, and her eager tongue lashing him back. They clung to each other, the world disappearing, savoring every single breath, every beat of their hearts.

Until Fingall cleared his throat. "My laird... If ye dinna mind, I'd like to seek a healer at the castle for this arrow wound?"

Gregor chuckled against Kirstin's mouth, rubbing his nose against hers. "Aye, I suppose that's a request I can honor," he teased. "We'll shelter there, and have a healer look at Kirstin, too." Then to Kirstin, he whispered, "and I'm not letting ye out of my sight."

"Nay, I'm not letting *ye* out of *my* sight, Gregor Buchanan. Ye're mine, whether ye like it or not."

"There is but one problem..." He murmured.

"Nay, there is no problem that cannot be easily solved. I am yours and ye are mine."

"God, I never thought I'd hear ye say it."

24

Cathal Mackenzie was not at home and the way his brother, Torsten, shifted his eyes away, Gregor had an idea that the man was raiding again. He'd done that a lot when they were younger, but his father had always been able to keep him reined in. Not so, now that their father had gone on to his great reward and Cathal was the new laird.

"Ye can stay as long as ye need to recover," Torsten said. "I've already ordered the healer roused for your man. He's lucky, another few inches and that arrow could have pierced his lung."

"Aye."

"I remember ye," Torsten said, glancing at Kirstin. "Ye look just as happy as ye did all those years ago."

Gregor grunted.

"Ye need a healer, too," he said.

Kirstin nodded. "If she has a salve, I'd be most grateful."

"Come with me," Torsten's frail looking wife said, holding out her hand. Her belly was round with child, but her skin was gray and her lips white. "I'll take ye to the room that ye'll share with your husband."

Not one person spoke up to let the lady know that Gregor and she were not married, even Fingall, though he did shift his eyes to Gregor's warning in their depths.

"Are ye certain? Are ye all right?" Kirstin asked the woman.

Gregor leaned close and whispered to Fingall, "She'll be my wife afore the week is out."

Keeping a keen eye on his woman, Gregor watched them talk as they walked away.

The woman smiled to Kirstin. "The bairn has been keeping me up at all hours of the night."

"Ye have another child?"

She shook her head and patted her large middle. "Nay, this one. I'll have the servants prepare ye a bath while ye wait for the healer, and have a gown that might suit ye better delivered."

Kirstin turned to Gregor before she followed the slow-walking lady up the spiral stairs to a chamber. He winked at her, itching to chase after her to be certain she was all right. But he knew she would be. And he had to tell Torsten what had happened.

Gregor filled Torsten in on all that had occurred—Wallace's execution, the threat to the crown, The Saint, and the possible outlaws that would be rising given the reward for allies of Wallace. Gregor asked after Cathal, ascertaining whether the Bruce could count on Mackenzie support . Torsten nodded though he looked disappointed. Seemed Cathal didn't care too much for politics as long as he was getting in plenty of whoring, raiding and drinking. Torsten would have made a better laird. In his absence, Cathal was lucky to have a brother responsible enough to take care of their clan.

After speaking with Torsten, Gregor made his way upstairs to find Kirstin. She'd finished her bath and the healer, having already fixed up Fingall, was already there setting out her supplies.

Gregor sat with Kirstin, holding her hands as the healer rubbed a fresh, herbal salve onto her wounds and then rewrapped them.

"Your wounds looked to have mostly healed, lass. Ye'll be just fine," the healer said.

"Thank ye. And my cousin?"

"He will heal nicely. Gave him a tincture to help him sleep. The arrow didn't go in too far, and shouldn't impair his mobility too much."

Gregor paid the healer and once she was gone, he poured Kirstin and himself a cup of wine, and sat beside her at the table.

"To us," he said.

"To us." She smiled at him, though the edges of her eyes were still filled with worry.

"My love, this time I want to do right by ye." He knelt to the floor in front of her, took her hands in his. "I know there is much between us, much sadness and sorrow, and I will be eternally sorry for all of it, but do ye think ye could ever forgive me?"

"I already have," she said, stroking her thumbs over his. "Can ye forgive me? For running away? For pushing ye away? For tricking ye into thinking I didna want ye?"

"Och, lass, ye need not ask for forgiveness for I never once begrudged ye." He brought her fingertips to his lips. "I should have said this to ye years ago. Should have told ye how much I loved ye. How much I couldn't live without ye. How happy ye make me. But I'm saying it now. I want to spend the rest of my life at your side, and it would be the greatest honor in the world to call myself your husband."

Tears sprung to her eyes and for a moment, he worried that he'd said the wrong thing, asked too much of her but then she pressed her hands to his cheeks and kissed him sweetly on the lips.

"Aye."

His eyes widened. Had he heard her correctly? "Aye?"

"Aye!" She kissed him again, more lingering this time. And when she pulled away, there was such a glow about her eyes and cheeks, and a flushed happy smile on her face that Gregor could not help his answering grin. "When Mother Superior, my Aunt Aileen, sent me to Melrose. She said there was a path I had to follow. I didn't know what she meant at the time, but I think she'd received a message of some sort, from an angel, or maybe she prayed I'd find ye."

For a moment, his happiness faltered. "Are ye all right with leaving the church behind, because I'd never want to force ye—"

Kirstin laughed and playfully tugged his ear. "Gregor, I love ye. I always have. I never forgot ye, and even if I felt ye'd abandoned me, I couldn't ever stop loving ye, despite how much I wanted to. This is the right path for me. Ye are what I want, what I need." She slipped from her chair, kneeling in front of him, and wrapped her arms around his neck. "The man I desire. Make love to me. It has been far too long."

Gregor slipped one hand around her waist, caressing the line of her back, the subtle feel of the knobs of her spine. His other hand he tucked against her cheek. God, how he loved her. He gazed into her eyes, admiring the blues and grays, the way her pupil's dilated.

"I love ye so much," he whispered, his chest swelling.

He brushed his lips against hers, breathing in her sweet scent, tasting cinnamon and wine on her tongue.

"I love ye, too." Kirstin's hand came up to touch his, stroking the back and then down his arm. She gripped onto his upper arm, squeezing, before moving up his shoulder to massage the knots of muscles there, then to his hair. She tugged at the leather thong holding his hair back, discarding it, and threading her hand into the hair at his nape. Kissing him deeper. "I missed ye so much. I dinna know how I even survived so long without ye."

Gregor slid his hands around her hips, to cup her behind, and then he stood, her legs wrapped around his waist and he carried her to the massive four-post oak bed that had been provided to them. He gently sat her down on the edge of the mattress, lips sliding over her chin to her ear.

"I'm not sure I did survive. A part of me died, and ye've wakened me from death," he whispered, biting her earlobe, fingers skimming over the collar of her dress.

Her skin was so soft and warm.

"We need to get ye out of this gown," he murmured. "I want to see all of ye. I want to touch and kiss every inch."

Kirstin grinned, and tugged at the ties at the side of her gown, loosening it enough that he was able to gently slide it off of her arms, revealing the thin chemise beneath, all the way to her hips.

"Lift up," he whispered.

She leaned back on her hands, her feet braced on the wooden base of the bed and lifted her hips as he slipped the gown down her legs, over her feet and then tossed it over a chair. Beneath the thin chemise, he could see the dusky pink of her nipples—taut against the fabric.

"Ye, too," she said, reaching forward, pulling the brooch free at his shirt. Then she tugged at the ties of his shirt until it was unlaced, exposing the skin over his heart. "Take off your shirt."

Gregor yanked it over his head, her gaze on his center, the place where his plaid was lifted by his engorged cock. Damn it had been so long since he'd actually been able to sink inside her. He wasn't certain he'd be able to last as long as he wanted, as long as she deserved. Well, he was going to make certain to satisfy her over and over again. He dropped to his knees, hands circling her ankles.

"I've missed ye," he murmured, winking at her.

Kirstin licked her lips. "I've missed ye more."

He slid his hands up over her calves dipping into the indentation behind her knees, sliding halfway up her inner thighs. He edged forward, reaching up and winding his hand into her hair, pulling her down for a searing kiss, tasting, licking, loving, until she was panting. He scraped his teeth along the column of her neck, over her collarbone, and then over the gauzy fabric of her chemise to her taut nipple. He flicked his tongue over the puckered tip, fluttered around until she moaned softly, arched her back and begged for more. The sounds she'd made. He'd dreamed of hearing them again over the years. It was all so overwhelming, he could have wept, but instead, he kissed her hard, claiming her, loving her.

"I want ye," she crooned. "Now, please."

Gregor could never hold back with her, he always wanted Kirstin to have whatever it was she desired. But he also liked to tease her. Tempt her. With his teeth, he untied her chemise, the lace-ties going near to her waist. He nuzzled the fabric open until both of her beautiful breasts were exposed, then he buried his head between her breasts, kissing and licking the skin from one breast to another, and finally suckling on her nipples, paying each equal homage. She tugged at his hair, moaning softly, panting.

He wanted more. All of her. To taste her very core.

Gregor glided his mouth lower, over her abdomen, over her hipbone and her thigh where he'd bunched the hem of her chemise. He glanced up at her catching the look of anticipation in her eye. He grinned. A knowing, teasing grin.

They'd been down this road many times, and he knew just how much she liked it when he put his mouth on her. He skimmed his teeth up over her inner thigh, feeling her legs tremble, and her breath quicken.

"Och, lass, I love the scent of ye," he said, reaching the apex of her thighs and breathing in deep.

Kirstin whimpered, her hand in his hair tightening. Gregor chuckled right over her mound, nuzzling the soft flesh just over the soft curls, below her navel, teasing her folds with his hot breath. But he wasn't simply teasing her, he was also tormenting himself. He had to taste her.

Splaying his hands on her inner thighs and opening them wider, he dove in to kiss her hot, slick folds. Kirstin cried out, collapsing onto the bed.

He tucked her legs up higher, then used his thumbs to separate the folds, exposing her silky pink flesh to his eyes and his tongue.

"Sweet like honey," he murmured over her tiny nub of pleasure.

He licked from her center up and over the taut bead, drinking in her essence and groaning. Kirstin writhed beneath him as he kissed her, licked, sucked. He was relentless in his pursuit of her pleasure. Until he felt her thighs tighten around his head, her body shuddering against his mouth. A fresh rush of desire slickened over his tongue. And her cries of pleasure, of release, made him shake.

He kissed her hot sex until her trembling subsided, and then he stood up, gripped her thighs and tugged her toward him. A swift flick of his belt and his plaid dropped, his cock pressing against her glistening sex.

"This is even better than I remembered," he said.

"No memory can compare to the true thing," she crooned, tucking her legs around his hips, she pushed up to sitting, scooting herself closer, hands on his hips, and then boldly reaching back to grip his arse. "Take me."

"Oh, aye, now, and forever." He palmed his cock, notched it at her entrance and thrust home.

Both of them cried out as he sank deep, the feel of her heated muscles wrapping around his turgid flesh. Gregor fell forward, bracing his weight on his arms, and kissed her, hard. Demanding. Carnal. Claiming.

She was his.

And he was hers.

He withdrew his tongue and shaft at the same time, making love to her with his body as his kiss mimicked the movements. Blast, but he couldn't get enough of her. She felt so damn good. And the way she was moving beneath him. How could he have ever hoped to get over her? Kirstin was inside him, just like he was inside her. No one could replace her, not now, not ever.

Their cries echoed in the room. The bed scraped against the floor with the force of their heated lovemaking. He could feel himself getting close, but he didn't want it to end. Then Kirstin was pushing him, and he was rolling over onto his back, her climbing on top of him, her fingers scraping over his chest, her eyes glittering with wicked intent and tempting passion. She ground herself against him, riding him fast and hard.

Gregor held tight to her hips, feeling totally out of control as she claimed him just as he'd claimed her and then her mouth was falling open and a moan that skated up and down his spine fell from her lips.

"Saints, love, ye are so beautiful," he whispered as she climaxed.

But it wasn't over yet. He flipped her back onto her back, bracing himself on one elbow, his other hand skimming over her thigh, squeezing tight. He wanted her to climax again. Gregor drove deep, swiveling his hips, withdrawing, and repeating. Slow, then fast. Hard, then soft, until she was crying out again. He bent down, sucked her lower lip into his mouth, swallowing her moans of release, absorbing the shudders of her body, and letting himself go completely.

A rush of pleasure, so complete, so perfect, so damned satisfying, ripped through him, and he pounded into her, letting his body break apart inside her.

They stayed connected for a long time after that, both of them still breathing hard, their bodies slick with sweat, legs and arms still entangled and trembling.

"That was amazing," Kirstin breathed out.

"Mind-blowing, love." Gregor rolled to the side, tugging the covers up over them, and pulling her taut to him. "Do ye realize we've made it back to the place where we first met? Where I first fell in love with ye?"

Kirstin giggled, and turned over to embrace him, her eyes connecting with his. "Sometimes to find your way back, ye have to start all over again. I love ye so much, Gregor, and this time, I'm not going to run away again."

"Och, my heart, my love. 'Tis a promise, I will never let go."

And then he made love to her all over again, slow, and sweet, and filled with promise.

EPILOGUE

Late December, 1305
Two days before Hogmanay (New Year's)

"This washroom is simply magnificent," Kirstin said to her husband as he walked into the steamy room.

She'd been luxuriating in the large copper tub for the better part of an hour. Her sister-by-marriage, Catriona, had the entire room decked out in all the bathing finery a lady could want. Scented soaps, candles, bathing oils and the softest linen towels. There was a massive copper tub, commissioned just for this room that could easily hold two people—which Kirstin and Gregor had enjoyed more than once since returning to Castle Buchanan. There was always a large iron kettle warming on the hearth, along with several heating stones, so if a bath was required, one did not have to wait long for warm water.

Kirstin felt like a queen as she soaked.

"Ye look like a goddess," Gregor said, stepping behind her to wash her hair. "A tempting, sensual goddess."

Catriona's husband, Samuel, had financed the entire project as a gift to her for struggling through the birth of their firstborn son, but she'd said Kirstin, being the mistress of the house, could use the special bathing chamber whenever she liked (but Kirstin always asked, just to be certain).

"Won't ye join me?" Kirstin asked, bending her head back to catch Gregor's eye, a wicked smile curving her lips.

He returned her grin. "I'd love to, but... Our guests have arrived a day early."

"Already?" Since their wedding ceremony had been quiet, and the clans had not yet gathered for a feast to celebrate, nor had they had a chance to throw a celebration for the birth of Catriona and Samuel's son since Samuel had been away on a mission, Gregor had agreed to Kirstin's suggestion that they throw a multi-clan Hogmanay festival.

Och, but the planning had nearly done her in—hence why she'd chosen this precise moment to sink into Catriona's tub with a host of herbs and oils scenting the water to calm her.

She'd not yet gotten used to being the lady of the castle, as she'd never been trained in anything other than the care and keeping of an abbey—and even with that, most of the duties had fallen to her aunt. Catriona had been such a gem in helping her to learn the needs of the castle, and she was grateful for it. She was even more excited to have a lovely friend at home to spend the day with when Gregor was off training the men or running an errand for the king. Besides, Catriona had needed the distraction while Samuel was away —and now he'd thankfully returned, safe and sound.

There were still men trying to abduct allies of Wallace, and the country was sadly divided, though not in half, in regards to where the English stood. She was proud of her husband for being a part of the *right* side, and soon she hoped their rightful king could be crowned.

"The castle is filled with the scent of your apple cakes," he mused.

"My apple cakes..." She'd completely forgotten that she'd been preparing them before she got into the tub. Saints, but her brain had been in a fog, but not simply because of all the planning. There was another, more special reason. One in which she wanted to announce that evening since she was certain about it now, and that her husband would be ecstatic to hear. "Och, but I'm suddenly famished."

Gregor laughed. "Ye've hardly eaten all day. Seems every time I look at ye, ye're darting this way or that. Ye'll run yourself ragged if ye keep it up. Come, let me help ye from the tub, and then I'll escort ye downstairs to meet our guest, and ye sit down, and I'll do whatever it is that needs to be done."

Kirstin laughed, and waved away his offer. "I am so pleased to do this, believe me, husband. I am beyond thrilled!"

Gregor leaned close, finished rinsing her hair and whispered into her ear, "Just as long as ye are awake to celebrate the new year with me in private tonight."

Kirstin turned around in the tub, her wet hands on his bare knees and she pinched his thighs, teasing. "Ye know I will be."

Gregor kissed her hard on the mouth, one that left them both wanting, but then he reluctantly grabbed hold of a soft linen towel and held it out to her. She stood, climbing from the water into the shivery air and let him dry her. He paused at her belly, which was no longer as flat as it once had been. She chewed her lip as he flattened his palm to the small knot.

"What's this?" he asked, his eyes brightening as he locked his gaze on hers.

She'd managed to keep her body hidden the last month by seducing him in the dark, or making frantic love to him with her chemise on in the light.

"Too many apple cakes," she said with a wink.

Gregor raised a brow, but didn't press her, only continued to dry, his hands managing to find their way back to her belly repeatedly. "Are ye certain?" he asked.

Kirstin laughed, deciding to put him out of his misery instead of waiting until she could announce it tonight.

"What do ye think has happened?" she asked. "Too much venison and herbed butter?"

"Och, ye tease me!" he growled, nipping her shoulder as he stood behind her to dry her hair.

"I do." Kristin whirled in his arms, placing her hands on his shoulders. She couldn't hold it in any longer, else she burst from excitement. "I believe I am with child."

"With child..." Gregor's expression went from excitement to fear and back again. "How far along?"

"At least three months now." When she'd first missed her monthly, she'd been terrified. After all, she'd nearly broken when she'd lost their first babe, but over the last two months, she'd grown more joyful, more hopeful. She was going to do everything she could to keep this bairn.

He blew out a deep sigh, and wavered on his feet. Kirstin guided him back to the stool he'd occupied while washing her hair, laughing softly.

"Are ye all right?" she asked. "Should I get ye a dram of whisky?"

Gregor laughed, but it was more of a nervous sound. "I am... Last time..."

Kirstin pressed two fingers to his lips, and looked him right in the eye. "I, too, am fearful, but this time, we will have each other. We will love this child, help it to grow, and provide it with a loving home. Whatever happens, we will be together this time."

Gregor nodded. "Aye, we will." His hands pressed to her

belly and he leaned forward to kiss her there. “I love ye so much,” he said.

Kirstin moved to straddle him. “I love ye, too.”

And despite their guests waiting downstairs, they made use of that stool and Kirstin’s nakedness, with frenzied, passionate, celebratory lovemaking.

A MERE HOUR LATER, WHEN THEY FINALLY EMERGED FROM the upper chambers and entered into the great hall, more than one set of guests had arrived, in fact, it appeared they were nearly all there!

Before the hearth sat very stoically, Gregor’s giant wolfhounds, three of them, and between two was her newest pet—a comely white and black lamb named Skye, a wedding gift from her husband. Skye was pretty certain she was a dog, too, and she did her best to sit tight between them, nipping at the skirts of the serving lasses as they walked past.

The tables had been pressed to the walls, allowing room for dancing before the grand feast. Servants weaved in an out of the crowd with cups of wine, and trays of tiny treats such as mushrooms stuffed with venison sausage, and eel baked in tiny sweet rolls, and cubes of cheese. Och, but her mouth was watering!

Aunt Aileen, Donna, her sister Brenna, her husband Gabriel and all of their children, rushed to embrace her, a large group filled with her loved ones. ’Twas a precious gift she’d cherish for a long time to come.

“Ye’re glowing,” Brenna said, flicking her gaze to Gregor. “I am so glad ye are happy, sister.”

“More than I could have ever dreamed, or anyone could possibly know,” Kirstin answered.

They embraced, and then Brenna looked down at Kirstin's belly. "More than anyone else knows, too," Brenna whispered.

Kirstin couldn't help the joyful laugh that escaped her. "Aye! And I've just told Gregor."

"That explains the twinkle in his eyes, though from the flush of your cheeks, I had thought it was for another reason." Brenna winked wickedly.

"Well..." Kirstin drawled with a lift to her smile. "There is that, too."

Brenna laughed and hugged her tight again, while her husband Gabriel patted Gregor on the back, him and Samuel dragging the other gathered men toward the hearth where an old, bottle of Big Abe's whisky had been uncorked.

"There are so many people!" Kirstin said with a clap of her hands.

"Aye," Catriona said. "Let me introduce ye to my sisters-by-marriage."

Two beautiful, golden-haired ladies crossed the Great Hall. "Arbella, Aliah, let me introduce ye to Lady Kirstin Buchanan, my delightful sister-by-marriage and your host."

The two ladies dipped into curtsies.

Kirstin reached forward, and hugged them both. "Let us not be so formal, we are practically family! Call me Kay."

For she'd finally embraced who she was truly meant to be —and Kay and Kirstin were one and the same. Kay saved for those close to her.

"Arbella's husband is Magnus, the Earl of Sutherland, right over there beside Samuel, and on the other side of Samuel is Sir Blane Sutherland, Aliah's husband."

Kirstin studied the men, and smiled at her two new sisters. "They are verra handsome."

"And so is your Gregor," Arbella said, in a silky English accent. "When is your bairn due?"

Kirstin gasped, glancing down her belly. "How did ye know?"

Arbella laughed, her eyes twinkling. "I've had half a dozen bairns myself. I can tell."

"Congratulations," Aliah said, pressing her hand to her own womb.

"She's not announced it yet, but my sister has not been able to stop touching her own belly for quite a few weeks," Arbella teased.

Aliah gasped and elbowed her sister, though gently.

"I think I am due sometime after May Day," Kirstin said.

"Me, too!" Aliah chimed in.

"Me, too," Catriona said, clapping her hands.

All three glanced from Arbella to Brenna and back again, expectantly, both of whom held up their hands in surrender, laughing.

"Not me," Brenna said.

"And not me, either," Arbella giggled.

Across the hall, Kirstin spied Donna, making eyes at Finn who'd been drinking whisky with the men. He excused himself, and sauntered toward her.

"It appears, that perhaps, Donna also has a different path." Aunt Aileen appeared beside Kirstin and Brenna, a knowing smile on her face.

"'Twould appear that our Mother Superior loves to play matchmaker," Brenna teased.

Aunt Aileen laughed. "I do love a good *histoire d'amour*."

"And ye've gotten to be a part of many love stories, haven't ye?" Kirstin said.

"The verra best," Aunt Aileen said.

Just then the minstrels began to play a lively tune. The first to the center of the floor were the many children, but then, Kirstin spied her handsome husband sauntering toward her, and she felt herself come alive with excitement. Every time she looked at him, her belly fluttered with wonder, and she was so pleased to have had a second chance at loving him.

"My lady, may I have this dance?" He held out his hand to her, bowing over it.

"Why, of course."

The other men followed suit, asking their wives to dance —and even Finn asked Donna, who surreptitiously gained permission from Aunt Aileen, since dancing with a man was forbidden to her. They all formed a line, bowed and curtsied, then proceeded to kick up their heels, and swing around to the music.

"I have never been so happy in my life as I am with ye," Kirstin said to Gregor as he whirled her.

"And every blessed day gets better and better." He leaned in to nuzzle her neck.

Kirstin blew out a contented sigh. "Aye, I cannot wait to see what the future holds."

"I know what it holds," Gregor said, a wiggle of his brows. "After this feast, I'm going to whisk ye upstairs to our chamber, and I'm going to..." He leaned in close and whispered all the naughty, sinful, delicious things he was going to do with her body, until her face heated and her skin tingled. "But for now, we dance."

And then he was lifting her into the air, whirling her in a circle, and shouting to all who would listen that he'd married the most beautiful, loving, giving, wondrous creature in all of Scotland.

ABOUT THE AUTHOR

Eliza Knight is an award-winning and *USA Today* bestselling indie author of over fifty sizzling historical romance and erotic romance. Under the name E. Knight, she pens rip-your-heart-out historical fiction. While not reading, writing or researching for her latest book, she chases after her three children. In her spare time (if there is such a thing...) she likes daydreaming, wine-tasting, traveling, hiking, staring at the stars, watching movies, shopping and visiting with family and friends. She lives atop a small mountain with her own knight in shining armor, three princesses and two very naughty puppies. Visit Eliza at http://www.elizaknight.comor her historical blog History Undressed: www.historyundressed.com. Sign up for her newsletter to get news about books, events, contests and sneak peaks! http://eepurl.com/CSFFD

facebook.com/elizaknightfiction
twitter.com/elizaknight
instagram.com/elizaknightfiction
bookbub.com/authors/eliza-knight
goodreads.com/elizaknight
pinterest.com/authoreknight

EXCERPT FROM THE HIGHLANDER'S GIFT

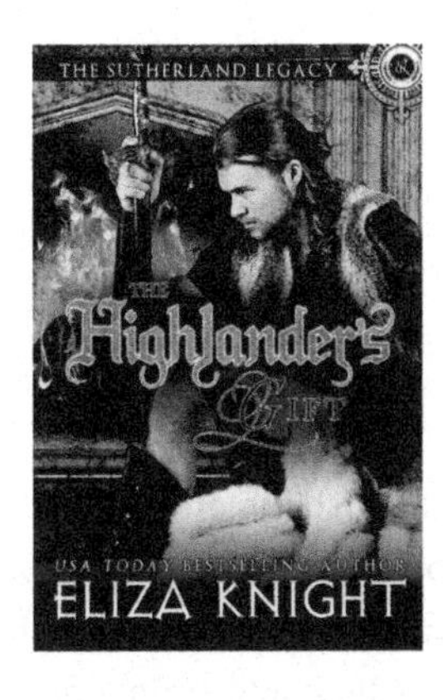

An injured Warrior...

Betrothed to a princess until she declares his battle wound has incapacitated him as a man, Sir Niall Oliphant is glad to step aside and let the spoiled royal marry his brother. He's more than content to fade into the background with his injuries and remain a bachelor forever, until he meets the Earl of Sutherland's daughter, a lass more beautiful than any other, a lass who makes him want to stand up and fight again.

A lady who won't let him fail...

As daughter of one of the most powerful earls and Highland chieftains in Scotland, Bella Sutherland can marry anyone she wants—but she doesn't want a husband. When she spies an injured warrior at the Yule festival who has been shunned by the Bruce's own daughter, she decides a husband in name only might be her best solution.

They both think they're agreeing to a marriage of convenience, but love and fate has other plans...

CHAPTER ONE

Dupplin Castle
Scottish Highlands
Winter, 1318

Sir Niall Oliphant had lost something.

Not a trinket, or a boot. Not a pair of hose, or even his favorite mug. Nothing as trivial as that. In fact, he wished it *was* so minuscule that he could simply replace it. What'd he'd lost was devastating, and yet it felt entirely selfish given some of those closest to him had lost their lives.

He was still here, living and breathing. He was still walking around on his own two feet. Still handsome in the face. Still able to speak coherently, even if he didn't want to.

But he couldn't replace what he'd lost.

What he'd lost would irrevocably change his life, his entire future. It made him want to back into the darkest corner and let his life slip away, to forget about even having a future at all. To give everything he owned to his brother and say goodbye. He was useless now. Unworthy.

Niall cleared the cobwebs that had settled in his throat by slinging back another dram of whisky. The shutters in his darkened bedchamber were closed tight, the fire long ago grown cold. He didn't allow candles in the room, nor visitors. So when a knock sounded at his door, he ignored it, preferring to chug his spirits from the bottle rather than pouring it into a cup.

The knocking grew louder, more insistent.

"Go away," he bellowed, slamming the whisky down on the side table beside where he sat, and hearing the clay jug shatter. A shard slid into his finger, stinging as the liquor splashed over it. But he didn't care.

This pain, pain in his only index finger, he wanted to have. Wanted a reminder there was still some part of him left. Part of him that could still feel and bleed. He tried to ignore that part of him that wanted to be alive, however small it was.

The handle on the door rattled, but Niall had barred it the day before. Refusing anything but whisky. Maybe he could drink himself into an oblivion he'd never wake from. Then all of his worries would be gone forever.

"Niall, open the bloody door."

The sound of his brother's voice through the cracks had Niall's gaze widening slightly. Walter was a year younger than he was. And still whole. Walter had tried to understand Niall's struggle, but what man could who'd not been through it himself?

"I said go away, ye bloody whoreson." His words slurred, and he went to tipple more of the liquor only to recall he'd just shattered it everywhere.

Hell and damnation. The only way to get another bottle would be to open the door.

"I'll pretend I didna hear ye just call our dear mother a whore. Open the damned door, or I'll take an axe to it."

Like hell he would. Walter was the least aggressive one in their family. Sweet as a lad, he'd grown into a strong warrior, but he was also known as the heart of the Oliphant clan. The idea of him chopping down a door was actually funny. Outside, the corridor grew silent, and Niall leaned his head back against the chair, wondering how long he had until his brother returned, and if it was enough time to sneak down to the cellar and get another jug of whisky.

Needless to say, when a steady thwacking sounded at the door—reminding Niall quite a bit like the heavy side of an axe—he sat up straighter and watched in drunken fascination as the door started to splinter. Shards of wood came flying through the air as the hole grew larger and the sound of the axe beating against the surface intensified.

Walter had grown some bloody ballocks.

Incredible.

Didn't matter. What would Walter accomplish by breaking down the door? What could he hope would happen?

Niall wasn't going to leave the room or accept food.

Niall wasn't going to move on with his life.

So he sat back and waited, curious more than anything as to what Walter's plan would be once he'd gained entry.

Just as tall and broad of shoulder as Niall, Walter kicked through the remainder of the door and ducked through the ragged hole.

"That's enough." Walter looked down at Niall, his face fierce, reminding him very much of their father when they were lads.

"That's enough?" Niall asked, trying to keep his eyes wide but having a hard time. The light from the corridor gave his brother a darkened, shadowy look.

"Ye've sat in this bloody hell hole for the past three days."

Walter gestured around the room. "Ye stink of shite. Like a bloody pig has laid waste to your chamber."

"Are ye calling me a shite pig?" Niall thought about standing up, calling his brother out, but that seemed like too much effort.

"Mayhap I am. Will it make ye stand up any faster?"

Niall pursed his lips, giving the impression of actually considering it. "Nay."

"That's what I thought. But I dinna care. Get up."

Niall shook his head slowly. "I'd rather not."

"I'm not asking."

My, my. Walter's ballocks were easily ten times than Niall had expected. The man was bloody testing him to be sure.

"Last time I checked, I was the eldest," Niall said.

"Ye might have been born first, but ye lost your mind some time ago, which makes me the better fit for making decisions."

Niall hiccupped. "And what decisions would ye be making, wee brother?"

"Getting your arse up. Getting ye cleaned up. Airing out the gongheap."

"Doesna smell so bad in here." Niall gave an exaggerated sniff, refusing to admit that Walter was indeed correct. It smelled horrendous.

"I'm gagging, brother. I might die if I have to stay much longer."

"Then by all means, pull up a chair."

"Ye're an arse."

"No more so than ye."

"Not true."

Niall sighed heavily. "What do ye want? Why would ye make me leave? I've nothing to live for anymore."

"Ye've eight-thousand reasons to live, ye blind goat."

"Eight thousand?"

"A random number." Walter waved his hand and kicked at something on the floor. "Ye've the people of your clan, the warriors ye lead, your family. The woman ye're betrothed to marry. Everyone is counting on ye, and ye must come out of here and attend to your duties. Ye've mourned long enough."

"How can ye presume to tell me that I've mourned long enough? Ye know nothing." A slow boiling rage started in Niall's chest. All these men telling him how to feel. All these men thinking they knew better. A bunch of bloody ballocks!

"Aye, I've not lost what ye have, brother. Ye're right. I dinna know what 'tis like to be ye, either. But I know what 'tis like to be the one down in the hall waiting for ye to come and take care of your business. I know what 'tis like to look upon the faces of the clan as they worry about whether they'll be raided or ravaged while their leader sulks in a vat of whisky and does nothing to care for them."

Niall gritted his teeth. No one understood. And he didn't need the reminder of his constant failings.

"Then take care of it," Niall growled, jerking forward fast enough that his vision doubled. "Ye've always wanted to be first. Ye've always wanted what was mine. Go and have it. Have it all."

Walter took a step back as though Niall had hit him. "How can ye say that?" Even in the dim light, Niall could see the pain etched on his brother's features. Aye, what he'd said was a lie, but it had made him feel better all the same.

"Ye heard me. Get the fuck out." Niall moved to push himself from the chair, remembered too late how difficult that would be, and fell back into it. Instead, he let out a string of curses that had Walter shaking his head.

"Ye need to get yourself together, decide whether or not ye are going to turn your back on this clan. Do it for yourself. Dinna go down like this. Ye are still Sir Niall fucking

Oliphant. Warrior. Heir to the chiefdom of Oliphant. Hero. Leader. Brother. Soon to be husband and father."

Walter held his gaze unwaveringly. A torrent of emotion jabbed from that dark look into Niall's chest, crushing his heart.

"Get out," he said again through gritted teeth, feeling the pain of rejecting his brother acutely.

They'd always been so close. And even though he was pushing him away, he also desperately wanted to pull him closer.

He wanted to hug him tightly, to tell him not to worry, that soon enough he'd come out of the dark and be the man Walter once knew. But those were all lies, for he would never be the same again, and he couldn't see how he would ever be able to exit this room and attempt a normal life.

"Ye're not the only one who's lost a part of himself," Walter muttered as he ducked beneath the door. "I want my brother back."

"Your brother is dead."

At that, Walter paused. He turned back around, a snarl poised on his lips, and Niall waited longingly for whatever insult would come out. Any chance to engage in a fight, but then Walter's face softened. "Maybe he is."

With those soft words uttered, he disappeared, leaving behind the gaping hole and the shattered wood on the floor, a haunting mirror image to the wide-open wound Niall felt in his soul.

Niall glanced down to his left, at the sleeve that hung empty at his side, a taunting reminder of his failure in battle. Warrior. Ballocks! Not even close.

When he considered lying down on the ground and licking the whisky from the floor, he knew it was probably time to leave his chamber. But he was no good to anyone outside of his room. Perhaps he could prove that fact once and for all, then Walter would leave him be. And he knew his brother spoke the truth about smelling like a pig. He'd not bathed in days. If he was going to prove he was worthless as a leader now, he would do so smelling decent, so people took him seriously rather than believing him to be mad.

Slipping through the hole in the door, he walked noiselessly down the corridor to the stairs at the rear used by the servants, tripping only once along the way. He attempted to steal down the winding steps, a feat that nearly had him breaking his neck. In fact, he took the last dozen steps on his arse. Once he reached the entrance to the side of the bailey, he lifted the bar and shoved the door open, the cool wind a welcome blast against his heated skin. With the sun set, no one saw him creep outside and slink along the stone as he made his way to the stables and the massive water trough kept for the horses. He might as well bathe there, like the animal he was.

Trough in sight, he staggered forward and tumbled headfirst into the icy water.

Niall woke sometime later, still in the water, but turned over at least. He didn't know whether to be grateful he'd not drowned. His clothes were soaked, and his legs hung out on either side of the wooden trough. It was still dark, so at least he'd not slept through the night in the chilled water.

He leaned his head back, body covered in wrinkled gooseflesh and teeth chattering, and stared up at the sky. Stars dotted the inky-black landscape and swaths of clouds streaked across the moon, as if one of the gods had swiped his hand through it, trying to wipe it away. But the moon was steadfast. Silver and bright and ever present. Returning as it should each night, though hiding its beauty day after day until it was just a sliver that made one wonder if it would return.

What was he doing out here? Not just in the tub freezing

his idiot arse off, but here in this world? Why hadn't he been taken? Why had only part of him been stolen? Cut away...

Niall shuddered, more from the memory of that moment when his enemy's sword had cut through his armor, skin, muscle and bone. The crunching sound. The incredible pain.

He squeezed his eyes shut, forcing the memories away.

This is how he'd been for the better part of four months. Stumbling drunk and angry about the castle when he wasn't holed up in his chamber. Yelling at his brother, glowering at his father and mother, snapping at anyone who happened to cross his path. He'd become everything he hated.

There had been times he'd thought about ending it all. He always came back to the simple question that was with him now as he stared up at the large face of the moon.

"Why am I still here?" he murmured.

"Likely because ye havena pulled your arse out of the bloody trough."

Walter.

Niall's gaze slid to the side to see his brother standing there, arms crossed over his chest. "Are ye my bloody shadow? Come to tell me all my sins?"

"When will ye see I'm not the enemy? I want to help."

Niall stared back up at the moon, silently asking what he should do, begging for a sign.

Walter tugged at his arm. "Come on. Get out of the trough. Ye're not a pig as much as ye've been acting the part. Let us get ye some food."

Niall looked over at his little brother, perhaps seeing him for the first time. His throat felt tight, closing in on itself as a well of emotion overflowed from somewhere deep in his gut.

"Why do ye keep trying to help me? All I've done is berate ye for it."

"Aye. That's true, but I know ye speak from pain. Not from your heart."

"I dinna think I have a heart left."

Walter rolled his eyes and gave a swift tug, pulling him halfway from the trough. Though Niall was weak from lack of food and too much whisky, he managed to get himself the rest of the way out. He stood in the moonlight, dripping water around the near frozen ground.

"Ye have a heart. Ye have a soul. One arm. That is all ye've lost. Ye still have your manhood, aye?"

Niall shrugged. Aye, he still had his bloody cock, but what woman wanted a decrepit man heaving overtop of her with his mangled body in full view.

"I know what ye're thinking," Walter said. "And the answer is, every eligible maiden and all her friends. Not to mention the kitchen wenches, the widows in the glen, and their sisters."

"Ballocks," Niall muttered.

"Ye're still handsome. Ye're still heir to a powerful clan. Wake up, man. This is not ye. Ye canna let the loss of your arm be the destruction of your whole life. Ye're not the first man to ever be maimed in battle. Dinna be a martyr."

"Says the man with two arms."

"Ye want me to cut it off? I'll bloody do it." Walter turned in a frantic circle as if looking for the closest thing with a sharp edge.

Niall narrowed his eyes, silent, watching, waiting. When had his wee brother become such an intense force? Walter marched toward the barn, hand on the door, yanked it wide as if to continue the blockhead search. Niall couldn't help following after his brother who marched forward with purpose, disappearing inside the barn.

A flutter of worry dinged in Niall's stomach. Walter wouldn't truly go through with something so stupid, would he?

When he didn't immediately reappear, Niall's pang of

worry heightened into dread. Dammit, he just might. With all the changes Walter had made recently, there was every possibility that he'd gone mad. Well, Niall might wish to disappear, but not before he made certain his brother was all right.

With a groan, Niall lurched forward, grabbed the door and yanked it open. The stables were dark and smelled of horses, leather and hay. He could hear a few horses nickering, and the soft snores of the stable hands up on the loft fast asleep.

"Walter," he hissed. "Enough. No more games."

Still, there was silence.

He stepped farther into the barn, and the door closed behind him, blocking out all the light save for a few strips that sank between cracks in the roof.

His feet shuffled silently on the dirt floor. Where the bloody hell had his brother gone?

And why was his heart pounding so fiercely? He trudged toward the first set of stables, touching the wood of the gates. A horse nudged his hand with its soft muzzle, blowing out a soft breath that tickled his palm, and Niall's heart squeezed.

"Prince," he whispered, leaning his forehead down until he felt it connect with the warm, solidness of his warhorse. Prince nickered and blew out another breath.

Niall had not ridden in months. If not for his horse, he might be dead. But rather than be irritated Prince had done his job, he felt nothing but pride that the horse he'd trained from a colt into a mammoth had done his duty.

After Niall's arm had been severed and he was left for dead, Prince had nudged him awake, bent low and nipped at Niall's legs until he'd managed to crawl and heave himself belly first over the saddle. Prince had taken him home like that, a bleeding sack of grain.

Having thought him dead, the clan had been shocked and surprised to see him return, and that's when the true battle for his life had begun. He'd lost so much blood, succumbed to fever, and stopped breathing more than once. Hell, it was a miracle he was still alive.

Which begged the question—*why, why, why*...

"He's missed ye." Walter was beside him, and Niall jerked toward his brother, seeing his outline in the dark.

"Is that why ye brought me in here?"

"Did ye really think I'd cut off my arm?" Walter chuckled. "Ye know I like to fondle a wench and drink at the same time."

Niall snickered. "Ye're an arse."

"Aye, 'haps I am."

They were silent for a few minutes, Niall deep in thought as he stroked Prince's soft muzzle. His mind was a torment of unanswered questions. "Walter, I...I dinna know what to do."

"Take it one day at a time, brother. But do take it. No more being locked in your chamber."

Niall nodded even though his brother couldn't see him. A phantom twinge of pain rippled through the arm that was no longer there, and he stopped himself from moving to rub the spot, not wanting to humiliate himself in front of his brother. When would those pains go away? When would his body realize his arm had long since become bone in the earth?

One day at a time. That was something he might be able to do. "I'll have bad days."

"Aye. And good ones, too."

Niall nodded. He longed to saddle Prince and go for a ride but realized he wasn't even certain how to mount with only one arm to grab hold of the saddle. "I have so much to learn."

"Aye. But as I recall, ye're a fast learner."

"I'll start training again tomorrow."

"Good."

"But I willna be laird. Walter, the right to rule is yours now."

"Ye've time before ye need to make that choice. Da is yet breathing and making a ruckus."

"Aye. But I want ye to know what's coming. No matter what, I canna do that. I have to learn to pull on my bloody shirt first."

Walter slapped him on the back and squeezed his shoulder. "The lairdship is yours, with or without a shirt. Only thing I want is my brother back."

Niall drew in a long, mournful breath. "I'm not sure he's coming back. Ye'll have to learn to deal with me, the new me."

"New ye, old ye, still *ye.*"

Want to read the rest of ***The Highlander's Gift***?

Made in the USA
Middletown, DE
22 July 2024

57843486R00149